THE RED CITADEL

Michael Lynes

First published by Romaunce Books in 2023
Suite 2, Top Floor, 7 Dyer Street, Cirencester, Gloucestershire, GL7 2PF

The Red Citadel

Paperback ISBN 978-1-7391857-4-9

Cover design and content by Ray Lipscombe

Printed and bound in Great Britain
Romaunce Books™ is a registered trademark

The Red Citadel

Heretic. Spy. Murderer.
Is this Isaac Alvarez?

Michael Lynes

An Isaac Alvarez Mystery

BLOOD
LIBEL

*Can Isaac find the real killer to protect
his family and his true faith?*

BLOOD LIBEL

1495 Seville, Andalusia.

As the Inquisition closes in can Isaac protect both his family and his faith?

The Inquisition is determined to execute heretics like Isaac - those who practice Judaism in secret. Friends and family are arrested and set against each other. Isaac's best friend is accused of heresy and he is forced to choose between him and his own family. King Ferdinand offers to help him - can Isaac trust him? As the mystery unravels what secrets will Isaac uncover about himself, his friends and his family?

Can Isaac discover the real killer and disprove the 'blood libel'?

If you enjoy reading Blood Libel please leave a review: Amazon UK or Amazon US

You can download a free short story and !nd out more about the Isaac Alvarez mysteries at www. michaellynes. com.

Michael Lynes

An Isaac Alvarez Mystery

the
Heretic's
daughter

───────✦───────

*Can Isabel prevent her father from
destroying their family?*

THE HERETIC'S DAUGHTER

The second enthralling Isaac Alvarez Mystery.

Seville, 1498. As the Inquisition's grip tightens Isaac and Isabel must choose between family and faith. Will they survive the consequences?

Isaac seeks revenge on Torquemada for murdering his wife and best friend. He's not the only one who wants The Grand Inquisitor dead. The King commands Isaac to investigate. Should he save the man he hates? Fail and he loses the King's protection — the only thing keeping him alive. Feeling abandoned by her father and con"icted by his heresy, Isabel sets out to discover the truth. The trail leads to the darkest places in Seville. She's unnerved by a shocking revelation and a surprising discovery about her real feelings. Can Isabel use what she unearths to save her father and their family?

Discover what happens next:

Amazon US Amazon UK

*For my granddaughter
Lily*

'Three things are necessary for the salvation of man: to know what he ought to believe; to know what he ought to desire; and to know what he ought to do.'

St. Thomas Aquinas, *Two Precepts of Charity*, 1273

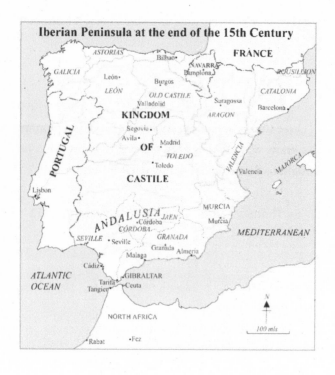

Iberian Peninsula at the end of the 15th Century

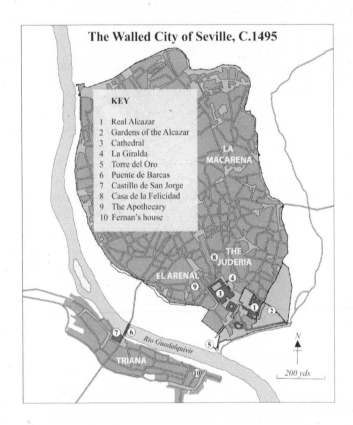

The Walled City of Seville, C.1495

KEY

1 Real Alcazar
2 Gardens of the Alcazar
3 Cathedral
4 La Giralda
5 Torre del Oro
6 Puente de Barcas
7 Castillo de San Jorge
8 Casa de la Felicidad
9 The Apothecary
10 Fernan's house

LA MACARENA

THE JUDERIA

EL ARENAL

Rio Guadalquivir

TRIANA

N

200 yds

CONTENTS

PROLOGUE

The Convent of St. Thomas Aquinas, Ávila, Spain, Midnight,
September 15th, 1498

BOOK I

Ten months later ...Seville and Granada, Andalusia, July 1499

BOOK II

Five months later ...Granada, December 1499

BOOK III

Granada, January, 1500

PROLOGUE

The Convent of St. Thomas Aquinas

Ávila, Spain,

Midnight, September 15th, 1498

ISAAC LURKED IN THE SHADOWS OUTSIDE Torquemada's bedchamber, contemplating which would be more satisfying: the smothered screams of the old bastard from beneath the pillow as his life slipped away, or the spurt of blood from his slashed throat?

It had been easy to gain access to the convent the former Grand Inquisitor had built for his retirement. Isaac had kept watch on the main gate from the seclusion of the forest, surprised it wasn't protected by the queen's guards. Was Torquemada so confident of divine protection, or was he just out of favour? No matter, it made Isaac's mission easier. Once the sun had dipped behind the hills he slipped in before the bells tolled for Vesper prayers. He'd hidden in this dark corner and waited.

A creak from the stairs. One of the sisters checking on Torquemada? His leg spasmed and Isaac suppressed a cry of pain. Ducking down, he drew his cloak around him, trying to render himself invisible. He peered through the darkness towards the top of the staircase. The moonlight shimmering across the flagstones remained undisturbed. Nobody. He stood up, felt the back of his leg, and shook the tension out of his shoulders. He exhaled and his breath formed a brief cloud. The air was cooling, it would soon be morning. He'd waited long enough. The door handle was cold. He levered it down – surprised to find it unlocked – slid inside and turned the key in the lock.

With his back to the door, he waited for his eyes to adjust to the gloom. Mounds of books and papers emerged from

3

the darkness. The air was stuffy and dry with an odd smell – deathly sweet, like incense burning over rotting flowers. The embers of a fire muttered in the hearth, throwing just enough light to see an enormous, raised fourposter bed about ten paces away. Torquemada lay on his back, shuffling and snorting. A single high-backed chair stood in front of the dying fire. A decanter and a glass sat on a low table next to it. He must have had a nightcap of Jerez sherry from his private stock. Isaac had shared a glass with him once. Before the bastard had executed his wife, Maria, and his best friend, Juan.

Isaac walked heel to toe across to the side of the bed nearest the hearth. He was halfway there when a log shifted and popped. The snorting stopped. He froze. Torquemada turned away from the fire. Isaac waited until the snoring started again before moving. Did he have the strength to pull Torquemada toward him and smother him? The Grand Inquisitor had gotten fat in retirement. Perhaps slicing his throat was easier? He reached for the dagger at his waist.

It had taken Isaac three years to be ready to end this demon's life. Yet he hesitated – still torn between the desire for vengeance and the prospect of hell. If he committed the mortal sin of murder, he might never be with Maria in heaven. But he could repent after dispatching Torquemada, couldn't he? Or was he just a coward? If he did nothing he wasn't sure he could live with himself. If he killed Maria's murderer he'd be signing his own death warrant and perhaps condemning his soul to damnation. Hell wasn't having no choice; it was having to make a choice between terrible things.

Torquemada abruptly heaved himself upright. Isaac stepped back and took a long, steadying breath, hoping it might quieten his thumping heart. Torquemada slumped back down with a snort and rolled over toward him. The firelight flickered across his hideous, sagging face that seemed to melt into the pillow. A yellow boil covered the tip of his nose. Mouth agape, his blackened tongue lolled over his bottom lip. Perhaps it was true that your face comes to reflect what's inside of you.

A muffled sound from outside the chamber. Isaac glanced at the door. The bells were announcing the Lauds' service. The convent would soon be stirring. He'd wasted too much time. Again.

He turned back and unsheathed his dagger.

Torquemada's eyes were wide open ...

BOOK I

Ten months later ...

Seville and Granada,

Andalusia

July 1499

CHAPTER
ONE

G*ranada*

AS THE MUEZZIN'S CRY ANNOUNCED ANOTHER DAWN, shafts of sunlight from behind the peaks of the Sierra Nevada crept across the face of the Alhambra – situated high on the Sabika hill – suffusing the citadel's red walls with a saffron glow. The variegated light glided down the brick ramparts of the fortress to find Granada at its base. It moved on to illuminate the city's terracotta tiled rooftops, pomegranate studded trees, and blue and white mosaic tiled fountains. It even insinuated itself into the shadowy alleyways of the labyrinthine Albaicín, creeping into the homes of the *Mudéjares* finishing their prayers, most too afraid of their Catholic masters to complete their devotions in the few remaining mosques. The sun did not discriminate though - it lit the houses of poor and rich alike. It brightened the home of the wealthy spice merchant, Abdul

Rahman, where he lived with his brother Abu Ali Sina – the last remaining apothecary in Granada.

A while later, it found its way into the furthest corner of the Albaicín, through the window of Bar Aixa where even at this early hour, in this devout city of the worshippers of Allah, men were drinking alcohol. Or at least Lorenzo Calderon was. The spice merchant and the apothecary deemed it *haram*, forbidden. But Calderon just called out for another glass of sherry from his recumbent position upon a bench in the shadows.

'Would the señor like some *mojama* to go with his liquid breakfast?' Teresa the brunette serving girl asked, hands on hips. She wore a short-sleeved yellow tunic over a green skirt. Both were tight fitting.

'No, the señor would bloody well not,' he replied, waving her away.

She stood with narrowed eyes, itching to say something. Deciding against it she stalked away, talking to herself in a low voice.

'My dear Teresa, if you had seen what I have, done what I have, been where I have, you wouldn't question my choice of morning refreshment,' he said.

She continued muttering from behind the bar as she noisily put away mugs and tankards. She returned, thumped his sherry down, spilling drops of the golden liquid that reflected sunlight as they pooled on the table.

As he sat up, he raised an eyebrow at her.

She raised one back and cocked her head.

'Thank you, my dear.' He blew her a kiss and reached for the glass with a trembling hand. He took a sip, 'Nectar,' he sighed contentedly. 'When you lose a family, your position, and your ... *status*...' exaggerating the sibilance of the last word, he fell silent. He stared at Teresa's backside as she sashayed back behind the bar. Finishing the rest of the drink in one greedy gulp he put his feet up on the bench.

'Don't get too comfortable,' Teresa called out. 'I'm expecting a big crowd by lunchtime. Their Majesties are passing on their way to the Alhambra. I'm hoping to catch sight of their youngest, the Infanta Catalina. I've heard tell she's got beautiful golden-red hair.' She pulled one of her straggly locks to her eyes and grimaced.

Calderon twisted his head towards the bar. 'Isabella and Ferdinand are coming?'

'Didn't you know?' She shook her head. 'Too busy sleeping off the sherry.'

He looked around as though dazed. He cupped his chin in his hand and narrowed his eyes. 'They've been wandering the Kingdom for seven years. Why are they returning now?'

'Her Majesty did send word to me, but I can't share it with you,' Teresa deadpanned.

Calderon glanced back at her, and she widened her eyes. 'How would I know why Their Majesties do anything?'

He grunted. 'They're not expected until the afternoon you say?'

'That's what I heard.'

'Plenty of time then.' Arranging his cloak as a makeshift

pillow, he stretched out along the bench, put his wide-brimmed hat over his face, crossed his arms and was soon snoring softly.

Isaac glanced up at the sun as he entered the now crowded Bar Aixa. It must be midday. Teresa returned his nod with a warm smile. He regularly enjoyed a snack and a glass of sherry before returning for lunch at Abdul Rahman's house. Living with the spice merchant and his brother Ali Sina had many advantages but alcohol wasn't one of them. They drank a lot of *nabidh*, and he could only drink so much of the sickly sweet, lightly fermented date juice. Besides, he was drawn to the name of the bar: "Aixa," Arabic for "alive and well." He was certainly the former.

Isaac looked around for somewhere to sit but the only place was taken by a man sprawled across a bench. Isaac gently shook his shoulder. The man turned on his side, away from the cause of the interruption. His impatience stoked by thirst, Isaac wrenched the man's shoulder, commanding him to "wake up." He sat up and reached instinctively for a weapon concealed at his waist.

'I wouldn't,' said Isaac as he pushed his cloak aside and touched the handle of his rapier.

The man wiped a hand over his face. Then he bent forward, appearing to reach for something.

Isaac took a step back and drew his sword halfway.

At the sound of metal on metal the man looked up and held

out his hat. 'It fell on the floor when you so rudely awakened me.'

Isaac sheathed his weapon.

'Who the hell are you?' the man said, jutting his jaw.

'I'm Isaac Camarino Alvarez,' he said with a small bow.

'Why in God's name did you disturb my rest?'

Isaac turned a palm upwards, swivelling his head to indicate the packed tavern.

The man grunted his acknowledgement and slid across the bench. 'Lorenzo Calderon,' he said, holding out a hand. Isaac shook it and sat down in the space Calderon had vacated.

Teresa elbowed her way through the throng and placed a glass of sherry and a plate of glistening *mojama* in front of Isaac. She acknowledged his thanks with a nod. Then she rolled her eyes at Calderon, who gave her an enquiring look in return.

'You've had enough.' She shook her head as he started to protest. 'No. You can have something to eat, and that's all.'

Calderon sighed.

'Add it to my bill,' said Isaac.

Calderon appraised him for a long moment. 'Most generous,' he finally muttered.

As they sat side by side in silence Isaac stole a sidelong glance at his new companion. Calderon appeared a little shorter than him, stouter too. Something in his bearing made Isaac think he was in his late thirties, almost a decade younger than himself. But anger seemed to have aged him. It was in the deep lines on his forehead, the tightness of his mouth and the hazel eyes tinged with malice. His own eyes were the same colour. He hoped they didn't reflect the anger he felt inside. Spite, that was the main feeling he got from Calderon. What had happened to him?

Teresa returned with another plate of the cured tuna and a basket of rye bread. They murmured their thanks.

Calderon said, 'My apologies, señor, I was sleeping off a heavy one,' as he balanced a sliver of *mojama* on a hunk of bread, eyeing it suspiciously.

'I see,' Isaac said, as though he understood, but it was many years since he'd been drunk. Not even after the death of his beloved Maria had he permitted himself such indulgence.

Calderon nibbled at the bread, winced, and rubbed his stomach. He put it back on the plate.

'Are you here to see Their Majesties?' Isaac asked.

Calderon narrowed his eyes at him. 'Why do you want to know?'

'Making conversation, that's all,' he replied, taking a sip of sherry.

'My apologies, señor.'

Isaac dipped his head in acknowledgement.

'Alcohol makes me more suspicious.'

'Why drink so much?'

'When you've lost as much as I have it's sometimes the only way to get through the day.'

Isaac considered his own losses: his best friend Juan executed by the Inquisition; his wife, Maria, murdered by the Grand Inquisitor; and his own exile by the king from Seville.

He'd never considered alcohol the answer. 'What have you lost? If you'll permit the intrusion ...'

'Don't worry señor. I should give you something in return for this fine food.' He glanced at the *mojama* and scowled. 'Even if it's only my story.' Calderon cleared his throat. 'I used to have a large mulberry estate on the outskirts of Granada, on the road to Avila. You might have seen it?' He paused and looked at Isaac expectantly.

'No, I've never ridden that road.' It was an instinctive denial; no-one must ever know of his journey to Avila the year before. And he certainly didn't want anyone finding out what had happened that night in Torquemada's bedchamber. Isaac registered the disappointment in his companions' eyes. Calderon obviously craved recognition for his former status. Having once been a trusted adviser to King Ferdinand, Isaac understood.

'Anyway,' Calderon cleared his throat, 'our trees produced some of the finest berries that were made into the silk the tailors use in the Albaicín. I farmed the land with my two sons.' His eyes softened and he was silent for a long moment.

'What happened?' Isaac asked gently.

'Those Inquisition bastards took everything,' he said banging his fist on the table. 'Claimed they had reports we were employing *conversos* who were holding secret prayer meetings on the estate. Can you believe it?' He looked at Isaac. 'Why would I give room to a bunch of Jews pretending to be Catholics?'

'Why indeed?' Isaac shook his head and shifted away from

Calderon. As a *converso* himself he found the direction of the conversation disturbing.

'They seized the farm and forced me to move my family into a stinking hole in the Albaicín. Surrounded by Moors. *"Allah hu akbar"* day and night, driving us crazy.'

Isaac resisted the impulse to say that it was more respectful to use *"Mudéjar"* than "Moor." He could have added that the main customers for Calderon's silk were his noisy neighbours in the Albaicín. But it would be pointless. It would just spiral into an argument. He saw Calderon eyeing his sherry glass, so he picked it up, drained it and sighed with exaggerated contentment.

'My wife died within a year.'

Isaac felt a twinge of guilt for his pettiness.

'My sons are with my sister in Seville.'

Isaac could empathise. His own children had remained in Seville after his exile. His eldest, Isabel, took care of his son Gabriel as well as his two wards, Juana and Martîn. They had been orphaned when their father, Juan, had been executed and his wife, Ana, had apparently taken her own life. What he couldn't agree with were the man's obnoxious views. He remained silent.

'What's your story?' Calderon asked.

'Oh ... very boring, compared to yours. Nothing of note. I must be going.'

'What's the rush? Stay and have another drink. Perhaps Teresa will relent.'

'I have an appointment.' He paused deliberately, holding

Calderon's eyes. 'With His Majesty.' He couldn't resist the lie. A small punishment for the drunkard's intolerance of Jews and *Mudéjares*.

Calderon raised his brows in surprise.

Pleased by this reaction Isaac stood and gave a small bow. He reached into the leather pouch slung around his waist and placed two silver coins on the table. He caught Teresa's eye, and she smiled at him. Pretending not to see Calderon's outstretched hand he pushed his way through the crowd towards the door.

Emerging onto the street he gave thanks that, although there were some similarities to their stories, he hadn't become a drunken bigot like Calderon. He wondered what the man was hiding. Why was he so on edge when asked whether he was waiting for a chance to see Their Majesties? Why exactly were they visiting Granada? He had a suspicion.

More importantly, how could he engineer an audience with the king to plead for an end to his exile?

CHAPTER
TWO

*S*eville

THE EARLY MORNING BREEZE blowing across the Guadalquivir River scattered wisps of brunette hair about Isabel's face. She loved to watch the sunrise from the roof terrace of Casa de la Felicidad. She wrangled her hair with a purple silk shawl and then drew it across her chest to ward off the early morning chill. Papa had given it to Mama as part of her wedding trousseau. Isabel wore it whenever she needed to feel Mama's presence. She luxuriated in its calming softness and for a few moments it was though her mother embraced her.

A chill of another sort went through her as the rising sun silhouetted Castillo de San Jorge on the far bank of the river. Mama had been murdered there four years ago in an Inquisition torture chamber at Torquemada's hands. So much had changed. Isabel was now solely responsible for the three children. Gabriel at fifteen had begun to understand his role as man of the house. He'd lost his puppy fat and acquired an elegant, graceful manner. He revelled in being taller than her. She'd noticed the admiring stares he drew from the groups of young ladies when they took an evening walk together. The twins had been so withdrawn after their parents' deaths but now thrived under her tutoring. Juana was as feisty as ever and her brother Martín still fiercely protective of her. She hoped Mama was proud as she looked down from heaven.

Their housekeeper, Catalina, looked after them in her robust, stubborn style. Catalina had married Rodrigo whose wife had died of heartbreak after the murder of their son, Fernan. The Jews were blamed for it, the so called "blood libel." Things may have turned out differently had Papa stayed out of the murder investigation. He might be here with them.

And yet so much remained the same. She was still unmarried and a governess. She would be eighteen soon. Nobody's wife, nobody's real mother. She believed – hoped? – she had the power to change that in an instant. The letter from Ali in Granada offered an opportunity. She felt a sense of lightness as optimism took hold.

Alejandro too remained unmarried. He was now senior advisor to the king, Papa's old position. An eligible, handsome, bachelor. Why hadn't anyone else captured his heart? Did he still yearn for her the way she did for him? If she told of him of her regret for spurning his marriage proposal he would come back to her. Wouldn't he? Her skin tingled with the same excitement she'd felt when accepting his proposal on this very terrace, just a year ago. And then she'd reneged. For what? She'd been angry at him for accusing her of betraying Papa. Once the tempest had passed and the truth had proven more slippery than either she or Alejandro had realised, she'd been too stubborn to speak to him. She hadn't talked to him properly since. They acknowledged each other when their paths crossed in the *calles*. They could hardly do otherwise; the lanes were so narrow. Pride was terrible. A cardinal sin.

'Señorita?'

'What is it?' She turned to face Catalina who, despite her increasing stoutness, had crept up on her, so lost was she in regret.

'A visitor. Señorita,' the housekeeper replied, clenched fists on hips. Glaring.

Isabel got the message – the tone of her reply had been unnecessarily sharp. She'd been annoyed by the interruption of her memories of Alejandro. She looped an arm through Catalina's, but she refused to budge. Isabel flashed her a smile, the housekeeper shook her head and they went down the stairs into the main house arm in arm.

'Who is it? I wasn't expecting anyone. Not this early.' Could thinking of Alejandro have conjured him? Her stomach lurched.

Catalina said, 'You can wipe that smile off your face.'

Isabel stopped halfway down. 'Who is it?'

'It's not who you hope it is. Someone you've not seen for a long time. I told him you were busy, but he said it was urgent. And I didn't like to turn away a man of the cloth.'

Isabel came to an abrupt halt at the threshold to the small chamber adjoining the main hall. A monk sat in one of the two high-backed chairs positioned in the centre of the room. The chairs were angled towards the hearth so he could not see her, but she could see his profile.

Despite not seeing him for four years, she immediately recognised the long, sallow face, the hooked nose, and brown gimlet eyes. The friar was calmly threading a string of rosary beads through his fingers, praying *sotto voce*.

A surge of white hot fury burnt through her. How dare Catalina let *him* in? Had she lost her mind? She looked around but the housekeeper had scuttled away. The moments spent casting around for Catalina allowed her rage to subside, a little. Hadn't the friar and Catalina been friends long before Isabel had been born? He'd probably played on her sentimental nature. It wouldn't be the first time he'd manipulated someone. She reminded herself that wrath was another of the cardinal sins. Taking a deep breath, she looped the shawl behind her back and over her forearms and crossed the threshold.

'How are you my child?' Friar Alonso de Hojeda, Torquemada's former deputy, said in honeyed tones as he stood. He made the sign of the cross and pocketed the rosary beads. 'You aren't pleased to see me?' he said with a slight smile.

Not for the first time she regretted that her facial expressions betrayed her genuine emotions so easily. 'Would you expect me to be? Father.' She took a position facing him but did not sit, neither did she invite him to.

'I hoped that time would have healed some of your pain, my child. As we read in Matthew, "If you forgive other people when they sin against you, your Heavenly Father will also forgive you."' He skewered her with a piercing look.

How dare he, second in command to the man who'd killed her mother, ask for forgiveness? Was he in the chamber when she died? And yet, his words and the look on his face unmoored deeper feelings in her. She didn't know whether it was conscience, piety, or guilt that pricked her more sharply. She sat and motioned for him to join her.

'Why are you here?' Yes, she admitted to herself, there was also curiosity.

'I returned from the Indies at the end of last year, at Father Tomás' request.'

She bristled at the mention of the former Grand Inquisitor.

'Imagine my desolation at discovering he had died during my return voyage.'

This was rich: expecting empathy from her. She fixed him with a dead-eyed stare and said nothing.

'I wouldn't expect you to share my feelings.'

He had some self-awareness after all. 'I didn't mean why are you in Seville, or why have you returned from exile, I meant why are you in my house?' She asked slowly and with deliberate menace, registering with pleasure the flicker of surprise that passed over his face.

'The Church sent me to the Indies to save the souls of those poor savages. I was not exiled.' He paused. 'Unlike your dear Papa.'

She clenched the rounded ends of the armrest, her knuckles whitening from the pressure. The rage was returning.

'To answer your question, I'm here to thank you.' He paused. 'Yes, you heard correctly, to thank you.'

God's blood! Look at what he was doing to her, she was cursing now. Once again he'd read her mind from the feelings that had escaped onto her face. 'For what?'

'For what you said to me that night at *La Giralda*.'

She raised her brows. She'd tried to forget the moments they'd shared at the top of the cathedral bell tower four years ago. When he'd abducted her.

'When I asked you the first time for forgiveness.' He looked away towards the hearth. 'When I sought your absolution.'

And in her youthful innocence – or was it arrogance? – she'd been flattered into giving it to him. But forgiveness had come with a condition. 'That's in the past. I'm not interested in discussing it.'

'Very well.'

'If that's all. Father?'

'There was one other matter.'

She composed a smile. *Now we get to the real reason you're here.*

'You recall Brother Andreas?'

Of course she did. Another of Torquemada's acolytes. Possessed of a beautiful singing voice, and an endearing innocence embodied by an oversized habit that swaddled him like a child. Her smile seemed to encourage Alonso.

'I know you met with him, and he told you of our story.'

She glanced through the window to the courtyard and remembered the two occasions she had sat and talked with Father Andreas there. On the first he sang mother's favourite hymn to her, Madre de Deus. She felt again the pleasure of listening to his soaring soprano. On the second he'd revealed to her the love he and Alonso shared when they were novitiates at the Monasterio de San Juan de los Reyes. Now she remembered! That was also where Catalina had first met Alonso. She'd sneered at Andreas when he'd said, "love", assuming it was carnal and sinful. He'd assured her it was a deep, fraternal bond. There was such sincerity in his voice that she'd believed him. He admitted they'd been young and foolish and taunted the master, who had his revenge by willfully misinterpreting their relationship. In almost the same way she had. But he'd done it with malice. The master sent Andreas away, and they never saw each other again. Hold on, what had Alonso just said?

'But he told me you never saw each other again. How do you know he told me about your, your ... love?'

Alonso smiled.

She was almost touched by its apparently genuine warmth.

'Because I've been meeting with him every week for the last few months. When I'm permitted.'

His voice had softened, and she found herself leaning in to hear him. 'Permitted?'

'He's a prisoner in the Castillo in Seville. Accused of murder.' He furrowed his brows. 'I thought you knew?'

She shook her head. Another disadvantage of not communicating with Alejandro: she hadn't kept up with political events. 'Murdering who?'

'Father Tomás. Her Majesty was furious after her confessor's death, so someone had to be blamed for the suspected arsenic poisoning. Andreas was an easy target.' He sighed. 'An outsider, a gentle soul.' Alonso broke eye contact with her for the first time and looked down at his hands, writhing in his lap. 'He's being kept in the most appalling conditions.' He glanced out at the courtyard. 'I've been seeking an audience with Their Majesties to get them to understand the injustice of his imprisonment. He would never do such a thing. But they will not see me.' He blew out a long breath through pursed lips. 'I petitioned Cardinal Cisneros. As the queen's confessor I thought he would have some influence. But he refused to intervene and referred me to Señor Alejandro.' He turned to look at her.

'Hm hm,' she said, not trusting herself to say anything else.

'You used to be ... close?'

She said nothing.

'He claims he's too busy in his new position as senior advisor to see me. Be that as it may, I can't let Andreas linger in that squalid cell any longer. His condition gets worse every time I see him. And the people they keep him locked up with.'

25

He shook his head. 'Vermin.'

She raised an eyebrow.

He added hastily, 'Although they are God's children too. And, of course, I pray for all their souls.' He crossed himself. 'You recall his beautiful voice?'

'It's impossible to forget.'

'The water cure injured his throat.'

Cure? Isabel shuddered. The Inquisition's torturers, or "seekers of truth", bound their victims and forced water into their lungs until they lost consciousness. The only thing it "cured" was your ability to breathe.

'Andreas can barely talk now, let alone sing.' He looked down at the floor.

Was he crying? Her heart shifted, just a little. 'What is it you think I can do?' she asked gently.

'Ah, that's where we come to some ... difficulty,' he said, brushing a palm over his eyes as he looked back up at her.

CHAPTER
THREE

G *ranada*

AS HE LEFT BAR AIXA, Isaac pushed away thoughts of Calderon. The man was not worth his time. Making his way to Abdul Rahman's compound, where he now called home an annexe at the back of the main house, he made slow progress through the crowded, rambling zigzag of alleys that formed the Albaicín. So different from his hometown where at least the *calles* gave an illusion of order. He missed Seville. Most of all he missed his children.

It was much noisier here, filled with the chatter of the veiled *Mudéjar* women in their long white robes of silk or cotton. The greeting of *"Salaam"* seemed obligatory for everyone, and the *muezzin's* call to prayer punctuated the air five times a day. He wondered how much longer Their Majesties would allow that to continue. In Seville people were more reserved, more respectful of privacy. The Albaicín was a village where everyone knew each other's business. You could stop anyone on the street and ask the whereabouts of someone and there was a good chance of being told their exact location. In Seville, you would be rewarded with a suspicious stare, even if the person knew the answer.

If Isaac wasn't fully adjusted to the sounds of his adopted city, he loved the smell of it. At mealtimes the air was suffused by the soft, spicy aroma of *ras-el-hanout* - the mixture of cumin, cinnamon, nutmeg, cardamon and ginger that Abdul Rahman had made his fortune from selling. Business was good as the *Mudéjar* loved to rub spice into their meat. At other times the scent of heavy, oaky incense curled its way into his nostrils. Nuggets of sandalwood and frankincense were set alight in burners, the smoke perfuming houses and even clothes.

Using his broad shoulders to winnow a way through a particularly narrow lane he emerged at a horseshoe doorway flanked by tall cypress trees. He rapped the iron door knocker shaped as a downturned hand. It represented the Hand of Fatima, the name of Prophet Mohammed's daughter, and was used to ward off evil. The heavy door groaned inward to reveal Khaled, Abdul Rahman's trusted retainer. He wore a long white robe, cinched at the waist by a thin leather belt.

'*As-salamu alaykum*,' Khaled said, closing the door with a small bow.

'*Wa-Alaikum-Salaam*,' Isaac replied, stepping into the courtyard to be greeted by screeching parrots flitting between the palm trees. Ahead of him was a portico of three whitewashed bays. The central one was double storey. A bear of a man wearing a red silk robe stood on its balcony reading a book.

'*Salaam*, Abdul Rahman,' Isaac called up. He let his fingertips play in the water as he walked past the burbling fountain. '*Salaam*, Isaac. Just in time for lunch,' the spice merchant called out with a huge grin, proudly revealing a set of gleaming teeth. He swore that chewing on a *miswak* stick five times a day kept them shining white. Isaac had tried it but didn't like the earthy, bitter taste. Abdul Rahman was about the same age as Isaac, but his energy and enthusiasm always made Isaac feel old.

A long trestle table was set out in the shaded walkway beneath the balcony. Abdul Rahman lumbered down the stairs and clasped him firmly by the hand. He was always amazed by the warmth of host's greeting, even after only a short absence.

'Sit, sit,' the spice merchant said, clapping his hands.

Servants appeared and began loading the table with couscous, grilled vegetables, and roasted lamb. The air became fragranced with spice. Abdul Rahman sat at the head of the table, with Isaac on his right, with his back to the fountain.

'Ali Sina not joining us?' Isaac gestured towards the plate set out opposite him.

'My brother has yet to return from the Apothecary,' Abdul Rahman replied peering up at the position of the sun. 'He'll be here soon. We can begin.' He filled his plate with lamb and couscous, muttered, '*Bismillah*' and began eating with his fingers. Isaac was no longer uncomfortable with this custom and followed suit.

Abdul Rahman beckoned a servant who filled their earthenware mugs with pomegranate juice. Isaac first drank it here with his son two years ago. Gabriel grimaced as the mug of sticky purple liquid was placed in front of him. Abdul Rahman told him how important the pomegranate was, both religiously and as the symbol of Granada. It could cleanse your heart and fill it with light, keeping you free from sin and temptation. Isaac smiled to himself recalling the spice merchant's delight as Gabriel gulped the juice down and asked for more. 'Now you are a true Grenadino!' their host had shouted.

'Where have you drifted off to?' Abdul Rahman asked.

'Memories.'

'Good ones, by the look of you.'

'Yes, good ones,' Isaac replied as he helped himself to more food. 'Delicious.'

'What have been up to this morning? Anything of interest happening at the archbishop's office?'

Isaac appreciated his good fortune in securing a position as a lawyer working for Talavera. His father's close friendship with the archbishop had helped. He was grateful to work for a principled man who the *Mudéjar* called Santo Alfaqui - the Holy Teacher.

'Only the preparations for Their Majesties' visit.'

Abdul Rahman took a gulp of pomegranate juice. 'And why are they coming?' He wiped the back of his hand over his mouth and raised an eyebrow. 'Top secret?

Isaac shrugged. 'All I know is Their Majesties are tired of wandering the Kingdom and intend to set up court in the

Alhambra for the foreseeable future.'

'I can hazard a guess.' Abdul Rahman paused. 'Cisneros accompanying them?'

'Yes.' Isaac scowled.

'Santo Alfaqui must be pleased,' Abdul Rahman said sardonically. 'First,' he rapped the table with a forefinger, 'Cisneros becomes Queen Isabella's confessor – a position Talavera coveted –and now,' another rap, 'he's being posted here.' He shook his head. 'To speed up our conversion to the "One True Faith."' He chewed his food furiously. 'Do you know how many mosques we used to have in the city?'

Before Isaac could hazard a guess Abdul Rahman said, 'More than two hundred. Now less than a tenth of them remain.' He blew out a long breath. 'Their Majesties –the queen in particular – want rid of us. Cisneros will no doubt use Inquisition tactics.' He growled. 'In the end everyone talks under torture. It doesn't mean they tell the truth.'

He tried to get a word in, but Abdul Rahman gave him no opportunity. 'He's just a cut-price Torquemada. At least Talavera tries to explain the supposed benefits of conversion in Arabic.' He rapped the table again. 'Cisneros believes explaining Catholicism to us is like 'giving pearls to pigs.' His voice grew louder.

'Indeed. Carrot versus stick.'

'Are we to be treated no better than donkeys?' he roared.

'My apologies, I didn't mean to …'

The spice merchant laughed and banged his fist on the table. 'You're too easy to tease Isaac. Stop being so serious.'

'These are serious times.'

'When are they not?'

'What are you two arguing over now?' Ali Sina asked, placing a hand on each of their shoulders.

'You crept up silently, brother,' Abdul Rahman said with a smile.

'It wasn't difficult with the racket you two were making,' the apothecary said sitting down to his brother's left, facing Isaac. He filled his plate with food. Isaac wondered where he put it all, he was so slender. He was a few years younger than his brother, but the worry etched into his face made him seem older. They told him what they'd been discussing.

There's growing unrest amongst my customers,' Ali said. Mandrake root is much in demand.'

Isaac furrowed his brow at Ali, who said, 'It's for stomachache, a sign of choleric imbalance that I believe is related to mental distress.'

Abdul Rahman said, 'I find a glass of mint tea works just as well.' He paused. 'If they're upset now wait until Cisneros starts his work. I'm sure the Royal visit is to confirm his new position as cardinal. He'll be using the stick freely before long.' He raised an eyebrow at Isaac who smiled at the joke.

'Any news of Aisha's return?' Isaac asked, trying to steer the conversation onto more pleasant matters. Abdul Rahman's wife and three children were visiting their grandmother in Fez. She'd joined the other *Mudéjar* who had fled to Morocco once Their Majesties' liberal approach to religious freedom following the *reconquista* of Granada began to disappear.

Abdul Rahman narrowed his eyes at Isaac. 'Are you missing her?' he asked with a broad grin that exposed his wolfish teeth.

Ali looked nervously back and forth between the two.

'Of course,' Isaac replied. 'Mainly because the food tastes better when she's here to oversee the kitchen.'

Abdul Rahman sat back in his chair and studied Isaac. 'You are free to eat your meals elsewhere.'

Ali Sina coughed and said softly, 'Brother.'

Isaac held Abdul Rahman's eyes for a long moment.

Then they both burst out laughing.

'For goodness' sake,' Ali said as he washed his long, delicate fingers in a small bowl.

'According to the last letter I received she'll be here within the week. If she can get passage on a ship,' Abdul Rahman said.

Isaac said, 'You'll be glad to see her and the children. It's been almost three months.'

The spice merchant was silent. He looked down. 'The children will remain with their grandmother.'

Ali gave Isaac a meaningful look. He understood. They were preparing for the situation in Granada to become dangerous and wanted the children to be safe. Aisha had converted from Catholicism to Islam to marry Abdul Rahman. Cisneros deemed her an apostate and therefore a target. Apostates represented doubt and that was a threat to 'the one True Faith.' Isaac knew the dangers of appearing to embrace another religion. This painful reality was mutually understood and they didn't need to dwell on it.

Isaac said, 'I've no time for a siesta today. I'll return to the

Alhambra and talk to Talavera about the Royal visit.'

'To seek an audience with His Majesty?'

Isaac nodded.

Ali said, 'It's only been a year since your exile, Isaac.' He pursed his lips. 'Surely it would be better to wait another before seeking your return to Seville?'

Isaac glared at the apothecary. How dare he? What did he know of being separated from his family? Then he recalled their shared tragedy: the loss of a beloved wife. His mood, and his expression, softened.

'Perhaps you're right old friend. I'm still going to try. You never know.'

CHAPTER
FOUR

*S*eville

ISABEL COVERED HER HAIR WITH A BLACK LACE mantilla and slammed the main door on Catalina's enquiries as to where she was going all by herself and when would she return. She wanted to shout back, 'Never!' but restrained herself. Catalina was right to be concerned, she shouldn't be out alone. But she didn't care.

When she found herself wanting to scream in frustration and anger, the best remedy was to leave Casa de la Felicidad. To walk at a furious pace until exhaustion was upon her. Until physical discomfort promised to overwhelm emotional pain. How dare that stupid hawk-nosed Friar come to her house and make accusations? She wished he'd acted on her suggestion and thrown himself off the top of La Giralda that night four years ago. She shuddered. What had possessed her to say that to him? If suicide was a mortal sin then encouraging it must be even worse. An unpardonable sin?

She reached into the pocket of her gown. The letter from Ali was still there. She would read it again in peace without being interrupted by Gabriel or the twins. Its contents needed careful consideration. She pushed her fingers deeper into the pocket and through the slit she'd had sewn into all her gowns to find the comforting outline of her little friend strapped to her thigh; the dagger Catalina had given her all those years ago. The handle was encrusted with small purple sapphires, the hilt finished with pretty curlicues that made it appear almost innocuous. It had been useful on more than one occasion. It had saved her from ruffians in Triana and she'd threatened Torquemada with it. The dagger made her feel safe.

She turned left down Calle Abades, heading for the river. Wagons, traders pushing barrows and fast-paced pedestrians passed her in all directions. She walked as quickly as her gown, the cobbles, and the midday heat would permit. Once she reached the dirt path that ran alongside the river she could stride with more freedom. She hoped for a cooling breeze from the Guadalquivir.

She arrived at the rear of the cathedral. The bells for Sext prayers reminded her it was lunchtime and she felt hungry. She couldn't go into a bar unaccompanied by a man. A red-capped orange juice seller stood behind his handcart in the far corner of the plaza. That would have to do. She took a sip from the earthenware mug he handed her. Good, it wasn't too sweet, she wanted to taste the bitterness. As she gulped the rest of the juice, the seller raised his brows. Who cared about propriety? She was thirsty. She was tempted to wipe the back of her hand over her mouth and smack her lips, just to see his reaction. As Gabriel once had, exactly in this place, whilst Mama had been in the Cathedral consulting Father Gutierrez about whether they should flee Seville and the clutches of the Inquisition. Perhaps that would be a better idea? Talk things over quietly with the elderly cleric? But she wasn't in the mood for measured conversation. Her thirst was assuaged but her body was still ablaze with the nervous energy generated by anger at another man of the cloth. She walked.

Arriving at the Puente de Barcas she considered braving the rickety bridge of loosely connected boats to walk the *calles* of Triana. But that was too risky, even in daylight. She and Alejandro had once nearly been killed in that bleak, impoverished neighbourhood. It would also open the door to other dark memories of a murdered child and an inconsolable mother. She scrambled down the bank onto the river pathway and turned left towards the countryside.

The river shimmered in the midday sun as though covered with shards of tin. There was no breeze and so, after a cursory look to see if anyone was around, she let her mantilla fall over her shoulders and felt a little cooler. A calmness washed over her. If she left Seville she would miss seeing the river and inhaling its salty tang. But other cities had rivers, surely not as grand as the Guadalquivir. How many could carry you to the ocean and the world beyond? A tall, masted galleon drifted by, making the final leg of its journey from the Indies to unload its cargo of sugar, silver, and gold. This was the driver of Seville's recent explosion of wealth. The reason so many of its citizens were distracted from their moral duty to study the Bible. The motivation for so many peasants to come here to seek their fortune, only to end up as vagrants. Or as fuel for the Inquisition's pyres. Her anger returned.

Isabel looked for a place to sit and read the letter again. She chose the shade of a stand of cypress trees set back from the riverbank. Her gown would get dirty but never mind. She smiled when she recalled the time she'd asked Catalina to deliberately dirty her clothes, as part of a plot to disguise herself. For an adventure with Alejandro she thought ruefully. She took out Ali's letter and read:

> *"My dearest Isabel,*
> *I realise it's been quite some time since I last wrote to you.*
> *Be not alarmed, I do not send bad news. I hope you will*
> *consider the contents to be quite the opposite ..."*

Having alerted her to the possibility of good news he digressed into great detail about his busy days at the Apothecary. She'd skipped this passage the first time but was now fascinated by his description of the people who consulted him, how he decided on the best remedy and his method of preparing it. He described some differences between the medical complaints of the residents of the two cities. Although he was too humble to say it, he was clearly making a big success of his new shop in Granada. He didn't mention Papa except in one, brief passage:

"Your Papa seems to be adapting to his new life quite well. His position with Talavera allows him to exercise his many talents, though not to the extent he might wish. I think he finds life with myself, my brother, and his wife reasonably tolerable. He seems to enjoy Aisha's food very much."

She interpreted this to mean that he found much of the work at the archbishop's palace boring. Why did he mention Abdul Rahman's wife in this way? In his previous letters there had been no mention of her, beyond the fact she was well. Perhaps she was reading too much into it. Papa liked his food and Ali was just reassuring her that he was eating well. She read on:

"When we were in Seville I was overjoyed that you expressed interest in my work. In your last letter you mentioned how restless you were now that the children no longer need you as much. I'm starting to feel my advanced years and my thoughts have turned to taking it easier. To enjoy what time I have left in Granada pursuing my religious studies and spending time with my nephews and nieces. In short, my dear, I have been considering taking on an apprentice who could eventually take over the business from me. I have no children of my own and you have become a daughter to me. Would you consider such a position?"

Her heartbeat quickened with excitement. She folded the

letter and tried waving it as a fan to cool herself. The air was so thick it was pointless. How could she leave Seville and her responsibilities here? But Ali had already thought of a solution – a three month trial and, if she decided to stay, Catalina, Rodrigo and the children could live at Abdul Rahman's compound. He had already arranged it with his brother. In the meantime, the housekeeper and her husband would take good care of the twins, and Gabriel hardly needed looking after anymore. A new life in a new city. Away from the terrible memories. Then she felt irritated with Ali. Why was he dangling something so impossible in front of her?

She pushed these thoughts away and returned to the main cause of her displeasure: Friar Alonso de Hojeda's accusations against Papa. He had the temerity to accuse him of murdering Torquemada. To her face. As if Papa was capable of such a thing. He'd killed men in self-defence and when the family was threatened. But he would never take a life in cold blood. And poison? It was preposterous. And when she asked him for evidence to support the heinous accusation he'd come up with what sounded like absolute nonsense. But something he'd said nagged away at her. It had the ring of truth about it. She needed to talk to someone. There was one person who should know and who would surely prove she was right to dismiss these allegations as lies.

CHAPTER
FIVE

 ranada

THE STIFLING HEAT OF THE EARLY AFTERNOON SUN had emptied the alleyways of the Albaicín. It made Isaac's return journey to the Alhambra quicker, though he still had to dodge around the sheep and goats taking refuge in the shadows. He reached the base of the citadel and, shading his eyes with a palm, looked up at the towering rust red walls. By the time he'd reached the top of the hill he was out of breath - a year ago he'd not have felt this tired. But Seville was a lot flatter. His shirt stuck clammily to his back as he laboured along the avenue of tall cypress trees leading to the Gate of Justice. The red-tuniced soldier saluted him through.

As Isaac made his way through the sprawling maze of the palace his footsteps echoed off the stone walls. He stumbled around numerous oddly angled rooms and hallways, he always struggled to orient himself – even after six months of working for the archbishop. He wandered past rooms accessed through hidden doors or gloomy passages. The sultans designed it to create a sense of vulnerability and surprise at every turn; only those with an intimate knowledge could navigate with confidence. The air was thick with a heady mix of scents - smoke from nearby fires and sweet wafts of *azahar,* an aroma of orange and lemon blossom that perfumed the citadel. He felt a constant sense of unease as he searched for Talavera's chambers.

Isaac reached his room and put an ear to the door that connected directly to the archbishop's. Silence. Probably enjoying a siesta. But he must speak to him about arranging an audience with the king. Isaac slumped down behind his desk and poured himself a mug of water from an earthenware jug. Gulping it down he looked around the sparsely furnished, windowless room. A far cry from his luxurious chambers in the Real Alcazar in Seville when he had been senior adviser to King Ferdinand. He would like to decorate his room with tapestries like those that adorned the rest of the Alhambra, but Talavera preferred an austere environment that reflected his asceticism.

He felt sluggish. It wasn't only the heat – he'd eaten too much lamb at lunchtime. He belched. Perhaps he needed some mandrake root. It wasn't the only discomfort he felt after the conversation with the brothers. He was still irked by Ali's questioning of his right to seek a return to Seville. And how much did Abdul Rahman sense about the strength of his real feelings for Aisha?

He picked up the only petition on his desk. In Seville it would have been one amongst many as he helped Their Majesties to bring order to the rapid expansion of trade with the Indies. He scanned through the thick sheaf of paper. It was a long-winded request for the return of lands seized by the Inquisition. So pompous and verbose he barely restrained himself from tearing it into pieces. But the archbishop wanted his advice to determine how, or even if, he should respond.

His eyelids began to close, his head dropped and then bobbed up and down on his chest. A shift in the air jerked him awake. How long had he been asleep? Talavera stood on the other side of the desk, a slight smile playing across his lips. Isaac took a moment to study him. He wore a white tunic with a brown scapular across his shoulders. His arms were folded into the long sleeves of his tunic. For a man of his age – he must be almost seventy – his upright posture was impressive. His grey beard and tonsure were perfectly groomed. An aquiline nose separated his deep blue eyes. His kind appearance disguised a sharp mind and an impatient nature.

'Have you finished reviewing the petition?'

'My apologies, Your Grace.'

Talavera said nothing.

'I won't leave before finishing it.'

'I don't want to prejudice you as to its merits,' the archbishop said, 'but the petitioner's family and mine go back a long way.'

'I understand, Your Grace. I will give it my full attention

directly.' He cleared his throat. 'There was another matter.' He gestured towards the high-backed chair in front of his desk.

The archbishop sat down, crossed his legs, and took out a string of rosary beads from his pocket. A confident pose. Was the ease with which he adopted this posture a sign he was comfortable with his conscience? He remained silent.

'It's about the king's visit.'

Talavera cocked his head to one side and held his gaze.

'I must get an audience.'

The archbishop threaded the rosary beads through his fingers.

'Can you help or not?'

Talavera widened his eyes.

Isaac had allowed himself to become irritated by the archbishop's taciturn manner. His tone had become disrespectful. 'I'm sorry, Your Grace.'

The archbishop inclined his head to acknowledge the apology. 'There is no need for me to do anything.'

Isaac took a deep, calming breath. He mustn't jeopardise this relationship. Talavera was one of his few remaining influential allies. He waited.

'It is my understanding,' Talavera paused and looked down at the rosary, 'that His Majesty intends to summon you.'

'Are you sure? Your Grace.'

'My sources at court are reliable.'

'Thank you.'

'There's no need. I did nothing.' He looked thoughtful as he continued to thread the beads. 'If the king grants your wish

44

you will return to Seville.' He sighed. 'You will be difficult to replace.'

The compliment gave him the courage to ask, 'No doubt your sources have told you about Cardinal Cisneros?'

The archbishop's benign expression darkened in an instant, as though a bank of clouds had blotted out the sun. 'What about him?'

On Torquemada's death Isabella had appointed Cisneros to be her confessor - an appointment Talavera coveted. 'Their Majesties intend to formally assign him to take charge of the conversion of the *Mudéjar* in Granada.'

'I'm aware.' Talavera's eyes were hooded.

'It will increase tension.' Isaac paused. 'And may lead to violence.'

'Obviously.'

'You have my full support.'

'I have no doubt. Except,' he hesitated, 'in all but the most trying of circumstances.' He held Isaac's eyes with a steely look.

'What do you mean?'

'What might you do for the king in order to return to Seville?' He widened his eyes. 'Where would your loyalty lie then?'

Isaac had no answer to that.

'You've discussed Cisneros with Abdul Rahman?'

'He's very concerned.'

'And Aisha's situation is precarious.'

Isaac chewed on the nail of his right forefinger.

'Abdul Rahman is a prominent, vocal critic of the Catholic hierarchy. I tolerate him, admire him even. Cisneros will take a different view. If he discovers Aisha converted to Islam to marry he will consider her an apostate.'

'I wish she'd stayed with her mother in Fez. But she's determined to return.'

'I wonder why?' Talavera arched an eyebrow.

Isaac felt himself redden.

'You're playing a dangerous game, Isaac. Abdul Rahman is no fool. When you told me of your deep affection for Aisha, I counselled you to leave the house.' He paused. 'It's been three months and you're still there. If you hadn't told me under the seal of confession, I'd give you an ultimatum.'

'I know, Your Grace. You're right, I should leave before I make a real fool of myself.'

'Making a fool of yourself will be the least of your worries if Abdul Rahman finds out how you really feel about his wife.' He paused. 'Not the calmest of men at the best of times,' he said with a wry smile. 'And these are nowhere near the best of times.' He paused. 'Three things are necessary for the salvation of man: to know what he ought to believe, to know what he ought to desire, and to know what he ought to do.'

'Thomas Aquinas?'

Talavera smiled. As he stood, he put the rosary away in his pocket. 'I have an audience with His Majesty this evening, I'll let you know on the morrow anything of use I'm able to share with you.'

'Thank you.'

'You'll let me know?'

'I'll pray on it, Your Grace.'

'The petition, Isaac, the petition,' the archbishop said, returning to his chamber.

Isaac paced his small office, wondering why the king wanted to see him. A vision of the caged bear that visited the city as part of a travelling fair last Easter sprang to his mind. Perhaps the king wanted to end his banishment and welcome him back to Seville as his senior adviser? It couldn't be that simple, nothing ever was with Ferdinand. In any case Alejandro now held that position. He chided himself for the resentment he felt towards his former deputy. It wasn't the only grudge he held against him. Even if there were no position on offer returning home would be enough. He felt his body warm at the prospect of being with his children again, of walking the *calles* of Seville. A relief from the hills of Granada.

He sat at his desk, poured another mug of water, and forced himself to focus on the petition. As he skimmed the lengthy document a depressingly familiar story emerged. Rumours of heresy regarding a wealthy local landowner had circulated. Rumours became accusations he had permitted *conversos* to hold clandestine Jewish prayer meetings on his property. The accusations became known to the *familiares* - the network of spies reporting to the 'Holy Office for the Propagation of the Faith.' More commonly known as The Inquisition. The Holy Office conducted what it claimed was a thorough investigation into the allegations. This would have been little more than a series of violent interrogations. Torture ensured the 'correct' evidence was obtained. The truth now established to the Church's satisfaction the Inquisition seized all the heretic's money and property, in this case a large silk farm on the road to Ávila. Why hadn't he been burnt at the stake? He must have repented or his connection to Talavera had saved him. He was now appealing to the archbishop for the return of his lands. It was a last resort and highly unlikely to succeed. But the owner must hope his families' connection with the archbishop would carry weight.

Hold on a minute. Ávila. A silk farm.

In his haste he had not read the specific details carefully. He scanned back to the beginning and there it was, 'Name of petitioner: Lorenzo Calderon.' The drunken oaf in Bar Aixa this morning. He'd expressed hatred of both Jews and *Mudéjar*. That was proof enough that he would not have allowed any non-believers to practice their religion on his property. The petition had merit and his recommendation was obvious. Still, he hesitated. Why should he support the plea of a bigot? These were the people perpetuating injustice and profiting from it. But if he didn't favour Calderon, he would be siding with the Inquisition. An impossible moral dilemma. Another one.

CHAPTER
SIX

*S*eville

'I'M TERRIBLY BUSY, SEÑORITA. I can only spare you a few minutes.'

Isabel was taken aback by the formality of Alejandro's greeting. Had she really expected a warmer welcome? Especially when she had interrupted him in his chambers at the Real Alcazar. But his face was just as she remembered it: fine skin drawn taut across high cheekbones, a Roman nose, thin lips and pale blue eyes. A delicate appearance underpinned by an aristocratic, almost haughty bearing. She was still deeply attracted to him.

'Their Majesties expect me in Granada within the week,' he said.

Where was the softness of voice and expression? She was tempted to just turn on her heel and walk out.

'My apologies, señorita.'

Sometimes her face's betrayal was helpful.

'Please do sit down,' he said gesturing towards one of the two chairs in front of his long, rectangular desk. 'Just one moment.' He made a small bow and walked to the back of the chamber to continue the discussion with a courtier that she had interrupted. Isabel looked around Papa's former room. It was much the same as when he'd occupied it. The walls were hung with the same richly painted tapestries, the furnishings luxurious, opulence fit for a royal palace. On the desk were two neat stacks of paper, a jug and two mugs. In Papa's time it would have been strewn with Indies trade contracts.

'Their Majesties have returned to Granada after many years. They never seem to stop travelling,' Alejandro said, walking past the chair facing her and sitting down behind his desk. 'Cardinal Cisneros has gone with them.'

She looked blankly at him.

'I'm sure you don't want to hear all that. What can I do for you?'

He was treating her like a bothersome supplicant. Two could play that game. She said nothing but glanced at the jug.

'Where are my manners?' Alejandro poured her a mug of water and handed it to her.

She deliberately took several slow sips then replaced the mug on the desk.

He crossed his arms and pushed out a cheek with his tongue. 'I trust you are suitably refreshed, señorita?'

Isabel gave him what she hoped he knew was an insincere smile.

He narrowed his eyes at her.

Good, he understood. 'How have you been, señor?' The muscles in his jaw tightened. He used to be more patient.

Alejandro held her gaze for a long moment and then grunted. Puffing out a long breath, he relaxed his arms and said, 'Isabel, it is good to see you and I would love to talk to you, but I really don't have time. If I can help, you only have to ask.'

She nodded, satisfied. 'It's about Papa.'

'How is he? I haven't heard from him in ages.'

'Neither had I for a month or so. But yesterday I received a letter from Ali. He seems to be fine.' Isabel hesitated; she was tempted to confide in him but decided she didn't want to reveal the apothecary's offer. 'But that's not the main reason I'm here.' She quickly recounted Alonso's visit, registering the look of alarm on his face when she repeated the friar's suspicion that Papa had murdered Torquemada.

'So that's why Alonso's been trying to see me for the last few months.' He thrummed his fingers on the desk.

Papa used to do that.

'He's so desperate to get his friend out of the Castillo he'd say anything. I could have him arrested.'

'What for?'

Alejandro looked around the chamber. 'I don't know, sedition, treason?'

'Papa no longer works for the king.'

'I don't need a reason, Isabel. Their Majesties have no regard for Alonso, not since the 'blood libel' nonsense.'

'Even so ...'

He raised his brows expectantly.

'There are elements of his story that are troubling.'

He leant forward. 'Go on.'

'Andreas would not commit murder. He has such a heavenly voice, and a beautiful soul.'

She ignored Alejandro's eye roll and ploughed on. 'I remember that there *was* a plot to poison Torquemada. The king commanded you and Papa to look into it.'

'That much is true, but it doesn't make your father a murderer,' Alejandro countered.

'No, I agree. But Alonso heard the rumours when he returned from the Indies last year. And he's spent the last six months investigating and turning it into an allegation.' Isabel hesitated. If she revealed what Alonso had said there was no going back. 'He's spoken to Ramos and Roja. Remember them?'

'Of course.' He could hardly have forgotten the two thugs that had caused so much distress to the family.

'They claim Papa suborned a member of Torquemada's household to poison him with arsenic that Papa took from Ali's shop.'

A puzzled look crossed his face, so she explained. 'When he returned from Granada, after hunting for the twins. Ali gave him the keys to the shop in Seville so that he could pack up the shop and send all his herbs and equipment to Granada? For his new shop.'

'Yes, I recall that now.' He paused. 'Even so, you surely don't believe Alonso?' He poured himself some water. He waggled the jug at her, but she shook her head.

She took a moment to answer. 'Of course not.'

The tightness went out of Alejandro's shoulders.

'But Alonso is on the way to Granada to repeat his lies to Their Majesties. They've refused to grant him an audience before but he's hoping that Cisneros' elevation will help him. They see eye-to-eye on most things, especially on forced conversion.'

'What does he hope to gain?'

She thought it was self-evident. 'Andreas' release and Papa's execution.'

He was silent.

'And Her Majesty will leap at the chance to pin the murder on Papa. She hasn't forgiven him for discovering the Inquisition's role in the blood libel. Thank the Lord His Majesty has more sympathy for him.' She looked away. 'It's the only reason he's still alive.' Why was Alejandro so slow to realise the obvious solution? She gave him a moment, but impatience got the better of her. 'We have to go to Granada, to warn Papa, and stop Alonso.'

He leant his head back against the chair and studied the ceiling. 'Is that the best course of action?'

Isabel jutted her lower jaw, she was barely containing her anger. 'What would you suggest?'

'Leave it with me.' He stood and beckoned towards someone.

She turned to see the courtier hovering in the doorway. Alejandro was about to dismiss her.

'If you ignore this what do you think will happen when Cisneros brings it to Their Majesties' attention?' she said, fixing him with a glare.

Her vehement tone had its intended effect.

Alejandro waved the courtier away and sat down. He looked away from her.

'That's right. They'll wonder why their senior advisor didn't warn them. And why he did nothing about an accusation regarding the murder of Her Majesty's confessor.' She paused. 'You'll be finished.'

He held her eyes for a long, calculating moment. 'A little strong, Isabel, but you're probably right. I can't ignore it. I'll discuss it with His Majesty the moment I arrive at the Alhambra.' He gestured towards the courtier.

'I'm coming with you,' she said.

He looked startled. 'It's too dangerous, Isabel.'

She didn't respond.

'Your father would never approve,' he added with a touch of frustration.

'He will understand when he realises I'm doing it to protect his interests.'

'Who will take care of the children?'

He sounded increasingly desperate to find any reason to prevent her from travelling to Granada. 'Juana and Martín are eleven not, they're not babies anymore. Catalina and Rodrigo are perfectly capable. And Gabriel is increasingly responsible.'

Alejandro held up his hands, whether as a barrier or in surrender she was unsure. But she didn't care. She would make the journey with or without him. Isabel was certain he understood that.

CHAPTER
SEVEN

 ranada

BY THE TIME ISSAC REALISED it was pointless to muse further about his dilemma the Nones bells had rung for late-afternoon prayers. He glanced in at Talavera's chamber, hoping to catch a word with him about Calderon. Empty – the archbishop must have gone to pray in the chapel before his audience with the king. Hopefully he would have good news for him on the morrow. Time to go home. Perhaps Aisha would have returned. He felt a pressure in his chest at the thought of seeing her again.

Isaac left the Alhambra and retraced his steps through the lanes that seemed unusually packed for early evening. He sensed a febrile energy in the air, an uncharacteristic urgency. He listened in to the surrounding chatter. It was not the usual relaxed pre-dinner singsong of "*Salaams.*" His

Arabic had become quite fluent, but he couldn't make out anything as everyone was talking even faster than usual in the thick accent of Granada. As he reached the fringes of the Albacín the crowd corralled him along the base of the citadel and drove him towards Plaza Nueva. He searched for a way out, but he was trapped by the sheer numbers of people in the narrow lanes. Why was he being swept along like this? He felt suffocated as the jostling escalated to shoving. Looking to his left he saw an alley that he thought led to Barrio Realejo. In desperation he wondered if he could force his way out to take refuge in a synagogue? Stupid idea, all the synagogues had been abandoned and locked up when Their Majesty's expelled the Jews almost a decade ago.

He glimpsed the red and yellow lettering of the Bar Aixa sign to his right and remembered his conversation with Calderon that morning. That was it, Isabella and Ferdinand were the cause of this madness. The crowds were flocking to see the arrival of the royal procession. He allowed himself to go with the flow. The fanfare of trumpets grew louder; the procession must be nearby. They suddenly spilled out into Plaza Nueva and Isaac could breathe more easily.

The plaza was lit by a string of torches mounted on stands - there must be more than a thousand. Now he was here he might as well get a good view. He pushed his way to the front and found himself less than ten paces away from the procession. A single file of soldiers led the way, each bearing a shield with the quartered escutcheon of the Catholic monarchs' individual kingdoms – the lion rampant of Isabella's Castile and the red and yellow stripe of Ferdinand's Aragon. The coat of arms symbolised their shared control, but he'd experienced just how powerful the queen really was. A train of horseman followed, scarlet cloaks covering their armour. Behind them rode a man wearing a bright red scapular. He sat tall in the saddle and looked directly ahead. Deep-set eyes, furrowed cheeks, and a bulbous nose. Cardinal Cisneros. He was preceded by a soldier bearing his ensign, a black raven. The cardinal had chosen the symbol of death.

A loud cheer to Isaac's left heralded the arrival of Their Majesties, sitting on high-backed chairs borne aloft on a single wooden platform shouldered by ten black slaves. The rostrum was flanked by soldiers on either side, each resting a hand on the hilt of his sword. Ferdinand and Isabella wore robes woven of gold lined with sable. The queen's unusually pale skin and fair hair glistened in the torchlight. The king appeared to have put on weight since Isaac had last seen him, his face even doughier than before. They greeted the crowd with slow waves and nods as they turned their heads from side to side. As they drew level Ferdinand turned towards Isaac. There was no surprise in his light brown eyes. But was that a wry smile of acknowledgement?

On the platform behind the monarchs was a girl who looked to be about fourteen. This must be the Infanta Catalina, Ferdinand, and Isabel's youngest child. She looked like her mother in both appearance and expression. Isaac had heard the rumours that she was more like her father: mischievous, less pious, and fearless. Her long auburn hair flowed freely from under a golden tiara and down over a fur stole. She wore a long white gown and looked confidently out over the crowd, turning her head from side to side, waving and smiling. The crowd cheered and called her name, she was clearly popular.

A loud cry of, 'Your Majesty, Your Majesty,' came from Isaac's right. He saw Ferdinand glance back toward the voice and then quickly away.

'Please grant me an audience,' a man was bellowing. 'I've lost everything.'

Isaac thought he recognised the voice.

'Shut up,' some chanted, and a ripple of disquiet spread through the crowd. But the man would not be silenced. 'Please Your Majesty, I beg of you.'

Two soldiers broke away from escorting the procession, unsheathed their swords and moved towards the disturbance. There was a collective gasp and the throng moved back. Isaac's instinct was to go to the man's aid. But why get involved? No good could come of it. There was a momentary hush followed by a collective groan. Isaac pushed his way towards the soldiers. A man lay face down, a pool of blood collecting around his head.

'Serves you right for disturbing Their Majesties like that,' a woman cradling a baby said. The crowd murmured their agreement.

The soldiers, satisfied the interruption was dealt with, sheathed their swords and rejoined the procession. Their Majesties left the plaza and continued on their way to the Alhambra. The crowd dispersed.

Isaac knelt and gently turned the man over. 'Thought I recognised your voice.'

Lorenzo Calderon held the sodden rag, now scarlet with the fool's blood, to his forehead. It was the first thing Teresa had laid hands on when Isaac stumbled into Bar Aixa, barely keeping Calderon upright. It was the nearest place he could think of. The bar was thankfully nearly empty, the entire city must have gone to witness the procession. He'd quickly told her what had happened.

'What were you thinking?' Teresa asked Calderon. 'If you were thinking at all.'

Calderon examined the bloody rag, groaned, and replaced it.

'Shouting at the king like that? What's wrong with you?'

'Perhaps a brandy?' Isaac suggested.

'Stupid man,' Teresa muttered as she hurried away to pour the drink.

'You're lucky they only used the butt of their swords,' Isaac said.

Calderon took the brandy, gulped it down and held out the glass.

Teresa said, 'No. One is medicinal, more and you'll be puking your guts up. Again.'

'Have mercy,' Calderon pleaded.

Isaac exchanged a glance with the barmaid, and she nodded. He was starting to question why he was bothering to help this bigot. He should have gone home to see if Aisha had returned. But something about Calderon's situation nagged at his conscience. Another victim of the Inquisition, accused of heresy. There were so many. This man had struck a chord with him, and he wasn't sure why. Perhaps he was taking pity on the version of himself he could have become.

Teresa slammed the shot of brandy down accompanied by a growl and returned to the bar. She glared at Calderon, who dispatched the second glass even quicker than the first.

'That's a nasty gash,' Isaac said, gently removing the rag.

Calderon hung his head and shook it. Blood spattered onto the floor.

'That's it, get him out of here,' Teresa bawled.

'Come on, I know a place,' Isaac said, helping Calderon to his feet.

As the Vesper bells signalled nightfall Isaac rapped on the door of the Apothecary. Calderon leant against the frame of the shop door, his head lolling on Isaac's shoulder. Isaac, panting from supporting the dead weight of the body, could see nothing through the small window in the door. He listened for movement. If Ali wasn't there he didn't know what to do. Returning to the bar wasn't an option, and walking the streets with someone who'd publicly berated the king was too dangerous. Perhaps he could just leave him in the doorway? He certainly wouldn't take him to Abdul Rahman's compound. The irascible spice merchant's hospitality would not extend to bigots. He'd probably throw them both out.

'Who is it? What do you want? I'm closed,' Ali called out.

'It's me, Isaac. Hurry, please.'

'*Ya Allah,*' Ali exclaimed as he opened the door and the body slumped through it.

They each grabbed Calderon under an armpit and dragged him over the flagstone floor towards the rear of the shop. Isaac held him up against the side of the counter as Ali cleared it of his weighing pan, ointment bottles and herb pouches. They hoisted him onto it.

'Who did this? No, tell me later. Let me attend to him. Make yourself useful and light some more lanterns.' Ali picked up a lit one and set it down next to Calderon's face. He lifted a hinged leaf at one end of the counter, went through to the other side and examined the patient.

Isaac held a candle to the wick of the lantern and lit several more, placing them along the counter. As he did so the Apothecary slowly revealed itself. Calderon was on a waist high wooden counter that ran the width of the shop, about ten paces across. The area between it and the doorway was empty, save for two high-backed chairs - where Ali normally examined patients, the ones who could sit upright. Although the shop was narrow the walls were high, about twice Isaac's height. Rough wooden shelves ran floor to ceiling on the rear and side walls behind the counter. On them sat neatly arranged rows of orange and blue earthenware jars decorated with geometric designs. Isaac grimaced at the large glass jar of slippery copper coloured leeches that occupied the end of the counter near Calderon's feet.

Ali went through the arched opening in the centre of the rear wall that led to a stockroom and beyond that a staircase giving access to a bedchamber Ali rarely used. He quickly returned with a small leather case.

'Will he recover?'

'Quiet,' Ali barked as he opened the case and took out two small wooden boxes and a glass jar. From the first he removed a pad of green, spongy material and dabbed the head wound with it. He looked up and gave Isaac a rueful smile. 'Sphagnum moss,' he explained, holding the pad up to the light, 'it soaks up the blood and has some healing properties.' Ali poured a few drops of golden liquid from the jar onto the wound. Even Isaac knew that honey could heal wounds. The apothecary opened the other box and removed a delicate white bundle.

'Cobwebs?' Isaac asked.

'Yes,' Ali said, as he began applying them to Calderon's forehead. 'You pack the open wound with them, and their natural stickiness knits the skin back together.' He pulled open a drawer beneath the counter and produced a narrow strip of linen. Ali gestured to Isaac to support Calderon's neck and wound the cloth around his forehead several times, finally knotting it securely. 'He'll wake up with a nasty headache. I'll prepare a poultice he can lay on the wound once it's closed.' They laid him down on a makeshift bed in the back of the storeroom that Ali occasionally used for his siesta. Then they sat facing each other in the two high-backed chairs.

'Who is he?' Ali asked.

'Lorenzo Calderon.'

Ali glared at him.

'A man I know who has problems.'

'By the state of his clothes I'd say he's near destitute. Where does he live?'

'I don't know.'

'Does he have family?'

'Yes, but they're in Seville.'

'It's late Isaac. I'm tired. I'm not a puller of teeth.'

He didn't want to tell Ali the story as he knew the Apothecary would question his motives – just as he did himself. But he'd exhausted his friend's patience, so he recounted the entire story, from meeting Calderon at Bar Aixa, reading the petition, and then the incident at the procession. The only thing he omitted were Calderon's views on Jews and the *Mudéjar*.

'I still don't understand why you're taking the risk of helping him.'

'Because he's another victim of the Inquisition and ...'

'And?'

Isaac shrugged. 'He's like me. Lost his status, his lands, and his family.'

Ali sighed and looked thoughtful.

'Can he stay here tonight?'

They placed a jug of water, a chamber pot, and a note – explaining they would return in the morning – beside the bed. Ali put the back of his hand to Calderon's forehead and said, 'I'll stay with him for a while, make sure there's no fever.' He held Isaac's gaze for a long moment. 'My brother sent word this afternoon that Aisha arrived.'

Issac felt the pressure in his chest return but said nothing.

CHAPTER
EIGHT

G*ranada*

THE BELLS FOR COMPLINE had long since signalled it was time to retire when Isaac reached Abdul Rahman's compound. The nightwatchman let him in. The courtyard was bathed by the light from a gibbous moon. On his way to his annexe he paused to trail his fingers in the pool, fracturing the moonlight into shards. Light from the same moon watched over Isabel, Gabriel, and the twins in Seville. What were they doing? He hadn't heard from Isabel for more than a month and hadn't seen the children in a year. He couldn't visit Seville and had forbidden Isabel from travelling as the journey was too dangerous. She'd protested but he'd insisted. It was not worth risking her life just to visit him. With a wry smile he remembered Gabriel was almost fifteen now and must be growing into his manhood - taller, stronger. In her last letter Isabel wrote with pride of how well he was coping with being the man of the house. Isaac hoped she was telling the truth, not just trying to make him feel better.

A noise came from somewhere above. He looked up at the balcony that fronted his host's bedchamber. There it was again – as though someone was softly clearing their throat. He peered into the shadows. A vague outline seemed to shrink further away the harder he looked. Was that the subtle flutter of a dress? Was Aisha watching him? Then her statuesque form emerged from the gloom into the moonlight. She wore a green, silk gown and a black mantilla draped loosely over her head and shoulders. Strands of brunette hair escaped from it onto her forehead, framing the large, brown eyes that reminded him of a cat. As she smiled, her eyes grew larger. What could he read in those eyes? Amusement? Pity? Love? His heart lurched. She threw back her head as though to laugh. He grinned and raised a hand. A dark shape launched itself from the balcony and hurtled towards him. A screech and a flapping of wings as it swooped down – barely missing his head – and then it banked steeply to rest in the uppermost branches of a palm tree. Curse those parrots. When he looked at the balcony again Aisha was gone.

As he unlatched the door to the annexe his mind was consumed by her. Had she deliberately drawn his attention? Or was he such a lovesick fool that he had conjured her? He had never revealed his true feelings to her. How could he when hardly dare admit them to himself. She was married for God's sake. To his benefactor to boot. The pressure in his chest, the floundering of his stomach, it must be love. The moment he admitted that the guilt surged through him. He still loved Maria; he was sure of that. And he saw his future with her in the afterlife. What was he supposed to do until then? And what would Isabel think if she found out?

Isaac removed his scabbard and sword and threw his cloak onto the chair. He relieved himself in the chamber pot and placed it by his bed – he would need it again before dawn. He washed his hands in the large earthenware bowl. A plate of hard cheese, a basket of rye bread and a carafe of *nabidh* had been placed on the small dining table. This thoughtful act only happened when Aisha was there to preside over the household. He was grateful, having eaten nothing since lunch with the brothers. Isaac sat down and ate, drinking water instead of the *nabidh*. He would pour that away outside later, to avoid having to admit to his hosts that he didn't care for it.

As he chewed on the bread he surveyed his meagre lodgings: one, small sparsely furnished room, the walls rendered with dark pink stucco. It often smelt of the adjoining stables. Opening the solitary window didn't help much. *'But you're a lucky man,'* he chided himself. *'You could be quartered in an Inquisition cell awaiting execution for heresy.'* This was a palace by comparison.

He undressed, levered off his boots, and pulled a nightshirt over his head. Feeling too restless to sleep he hauled out the wooden chest concealed under his bed. Abdul Rahman was tolerant of Issac's true faith, but that didn't equate to approval. And if anyone in the household were to inform the Inquisition of what was in the box they would both pay with their lives. Abdul Rahman's money and land would be seized. Not even his close relationship with Talavera would save the spice merchant and his family from ruin.

Isaac caressed the chest's smooth mahogany top, enjoying the coolness of the inlaid ivory against his fingertips. He unlocked it with the key he kept on a silver chain around his neck. Lifting the false base he removed the linen covered book hidden there. He sat cross-legged on the floor, unwrapped the Torah, and gently kissed it. He turned the pages until he found one of his favourite passages that restated God's covenant with the Jewish people. He swayed back and forth to the rhythm of the words as he whispered them:

And I will espouse you forever
I will espouse you with righteousness and justice,
And with goodness and mercy,
And I will espouse you with faithfulness;
Then you shall be devoted to the Lord.

The verse was a balm to his soul and his mind. Though his heart was still uneasy and confused. He replaced the Torah, locked the box, and put it back under the bed. He lay down on the soft straw mattress and closed his eyes. When he opened them on the morrow he hoped to see Aisha for real. But who would visit him in his dreams?

The following morning, as the sun began to warm the courtyard, Isaac perched on the edge of the fountain and looked up at the balcony. Had he really seen her? He'd hoped she would appear as he slept but he'd had an untroubled, dreamless night. Or perhaps he just didn't remember his dreams. A parrot squawked from the top of a palm tree. Was it mocking him? He let his fingers play in the cool water and thought about the day ahead in which Talavera loomed large. Had the archbishop discussed him with the king? And he needed to decide what to do about Calderon's petition. Calderon. Lost in his fascination for Aisha he'd forgotten all about him.

Ali came groggily down the staircase that led from the bedchambers. He waved a palm wearily and sat down at the table beneath the balcony. It was laden with fruit, a basket of bread and jugs of pomegranate juice,

'You look tired, old friend,' Isaac said taking a seat opposite him.

'Too old for all-night vigils,' the apothecary replied, shaking his head.

Isaac poured two mugs of juice and passed one to Ali, who drank thirstily.

'I stayed until I heard the bells for Matins and then came home to grab a few hours' sleep.'

'How is the patient?'

'He'll live. A nasty headache for a few days but he should recover fully. He's none too pleased to be taken care of by a "Moor."'

'He should be grateful. You probably saved his life.'

Ali tilted his head from side to side, noncommittal.

'Your brother's still sleeping?'

Ali nodded. Abdul Rahman was an owl.

Isaac hesitated before asking, 'Did you see her?' He aimed for a casual tone but the apothecary's look from beneath hooded eyes confirmed he had been too direct.

'No, by the time I returned Aisha was already asleep.' He paused. 'Did you?'

A loud rasp from the main gate disturbed them. He turned to see Khaled holding it wide open for two servant girls to pass through carrying large bags, returning from an early morning trip to the market.

'*Yallah*. Take those things to the kitchen. I will be there shortly,' said the tall woman in a green gown following them. Aisha's voice was gentle but commanding. Its timbre rich but delicate. Isaac felt the back of his neck prickle and his heartbeat quicken. This time there was no doubt.

Ali strode across the courtyard to greet his sister-in-law. She lifted the black mantilla from her face and folded it back over her hair.

'*Habibi*,' she cried out in delight.

He took hold of her hands and kissed her on each cheek. There was some rapid, excited talk in Arabic that Isaac could not follow and then she was walking towards him. He stood and bowed.

'Still so formal Isaac, after almost a year living in my house?' she said, arching a perfectly plucked eyebrow. Her deep brown eyes widened, and she smiled. 'You are family now.'

He hoped the warmth he felt flooding his cheeks was not apparent. She took his extended hand and drew him in to lightly touch each of his cheeks with her own. Her smooth skin scraped against his stubble, and he cursed himself for not shaving that morning. He smelt her oud – the musky perfume, woody and tantalising. She held him in her gaze for a long moment.

Ali cleared his throat.

They broke apart.

'I need to reestablish some order in the kitchen,' she said. 'I hear from my husband that you notice the difference when I'm away.' She cocked her head to one side.

Isaac managed a weak smile and a quiet, 'Yes.'

She waited, with an expectant expression.

Isaac understood. 'Thank you for the supper last night.'

'You are most welcome. We will have time to exchange stories over dinner. But now I must get on.'

Then she was gone, and Isaac was bereft.

Ali was looking at him thoughtfully.

'What is it?' Isaac asked.

'Nothing. It's good to have her back.'

'It is.' Isaac tried to contain his enthusiasm.

'But she shouldn't have returned.'

'Cisneros?'

'Correct,' Ali replied. Aisha's conversion from Christianity to marry Abdul Rahman made her a target. To Cisneros she was a traitor to the "one true faith." With the spice merchant's high profile in the community Cisneros would want to make an example of her. Apostates embodied doubt, and doubt was heretical.

'How can we protect her?' Isaac asked.

Ali snorted. 'We can't. All we can hope for is that she doesn't come to his attention.'

Isaac wondered whether Talavera was strong enough to have any influence.

Ali said, 'I must get on too. I'll take some of this for our patient's breakfast.' He put two slices of bread and an orange into his pocket. He hurried away calling back over his shoulder, 'I'll send word to the Alhambra should there be any change in his condition.'

Isaac glanced up at another shriek from the palm tree. Damn parrots. Out of the corner of his eye he caught a movement from the balcony. A figure in a red striped kaftan was disappearing through the door that led to Abdul Rahman's bedchamber. How much had he heard? No point in fretting over that now. He had to go to the Alhambra and make a decision about Calderon's petition.

CHAPTER
NINE

On the road from Seville to Granada

ISABEL AND ALEJANDRO began riding to Granada at sunrise on the day following their conversation at the Real Alcazar. They were accompanied by two red-cloaked royal guards. She thought this unnecessary but then recalled Papa's warnings about the dangers he'd faced on the journey the previous year. They changed to fresh horses at lunchtime, otherwise they would not complete the journey before sunset the following day.

Isabel was grateful Alejandro had not prevented her from accompanying him, though she didn't tell him so. She would have travelled alone if she'd had to, despite the danger from the *Mudéjares* who had taken refuge from Granada in the mountains. They had refused to convert to Christianity but did not want to join the many who had fled to Fez. They were increasingly well organised. She wondered if their bloody reputation for decapitating travellers was exaggerated. Surely they were just after food and money for survival. And Ali and his brother were *Mudéjares* but she couldn't imagine them committing such barbaric acts. Abdul Rahman had assisted Papa and taken him in after his exile. Christian monks had attacked Papa, not Muslim thieves.

They were now almost halfway to Granada and ambling down a narrow track to the village of Palma del Rîo. Isabel watched as the sun departing behind the Alpujarra mountains left a rich orange glow that would soon disappear. By the time they entered the Hostería del Infante in the village square night was falling and she was exhausted.

'Good evening, señor,' said the large man standing behind the counter in the dimly lit inn. His tone was far from welcoming.

'Good evening, Señor Mora,' Alejandro replied.

She was amused by the shocked expression that passed over the innkeeper's face.

'Do I know you?' Mora said, squinting at them.

She tried to remain patient as Alejandro reminded the innkeeper that he and Papa had stayed last year. She just wanted to lie down.

The innkeeper tapped an index finger on his lips. 'You had that Moor with you, didn't you?'

Alejandro nodded.

Isabel was too tired to object to the offensive word Mora used to describe Ali. But she was annoyed with Alejandro for not challenging it.

'Two rooms?' Mora asked, raising an eyebrow suggestively.

'Yes.' Alejandro touched his hand to the hilt of his rapier.

Isabel gently pulled it away. The man's insolence was not worth it.

'And your guards will sleep in the stable with the horses.'

The innkeeper's daughter showed them up the rickety stairs to their chambers, which Isabel was dismayed to find were adjoining one another. The girl must have caught the look that passed between her and Alejandro as she said, 'Them's the only two decent rooms we have. The others are in the attic, under the eaves.'

Alejandro gave a small bow and disappeared into his bedchamber.

The room was simple, but it would do. A trestle bed with a straw mattress, a table with an earthenware bowl and a mirror above it. Her face was flushed. How could Alejandro find her attractive like this? She poured water from the jug into the bowl and washed her face, letting the cool water revive her. She chided herself for her vanity. Another deadly sin. The girl returned with Isabel's bag and stood expectantly in the doorway. Did she want a coin for her trouble? Then she saw the look of wonder on the girl's face and realised it was admiration. There couldn't be many ladies from Seville who stayed at the inn. She smiled at the girl, who mumbled that supper would be ready shortly, and fled.

Isabel sat on the bed gingerly, she hadn't ever ridden for a whole day and her thigh muscles ached. It had been an odd journey. They had been galloping too fast to maintain a conversation. She was both grateful and frustrated by that. Isabel didn't want to talk about her feelings for him, didn't want to reveal anything. Or to risk confirming that he no longer reciprocated her feelings. She wondered whether he now thought of her as more sister than potential wife. He cared; she knew he wanted to protect her. She trusted him. But she wanted to talk to him about Papa and Alonso's accusations. She needed to discover what more he knew.

Isabel took Mama's Bible out of her bag and thought for a moment about her father's heresy which had resulted in his exile. She knew he still practiced Judaism and read the Torah in secret. It had become an uncomfortable shared secret that they never discussed. His beliefs were sincere, and she'd decided that had to be good enough for her. It hadn't always been. She'd first suspected around five years before, when she was twelve – about the same age as the innkeeper's daughter — and had been so appalled at her father she'd considered informing the Inquisition. She was glad she hadn't. Judaism was in his soul the way Mama still was. It was heartfelt. It was love. She'd learnt to tolerate it, which didn't mean she approved. During his absence she had almost forgotten she was the daughter of a heretic. When he'd been forced to admit it last year it was only the king's kindness in exiling him that saved him from the pyre. She leafed through the fragile pages of the Bible until she found the passage from Romans:

For I am convinced that neither death nor life, neither angels nor demons, neither the present nor the future, nor any powers, neither height nor depth, nor anything else in all creation, will be able to separate us from the love of God that is in Christ Jesus our Lord.

Hearing the words as she read them aloud calmed her. Angels and demons. Were people like that, one or the other? Which was she? Certainly no angel, but she refused to believe she was a demon. Torquemada' had been worse – a demon masquerading as an angel. And what of Alonso? Did his confession, his service in saving the souls of savages in the Indies make him an angel? Who was she to decide? She was taking the place of The Almighty - yet another sin. She put the Bible under her pillow, knelt at the side of the bed and prayed for absolution.

Isabel sat opposite Alejandro at a rough-hewn table in front of an empty fireplace. She was alone with him, there were no other guests, and the bodyguards were eating their food in the stable. The girl served them each a plate of hearty looking stew and placed a basket of rye bread, a carafe of red wine and a jug of water in the centre of the table. Isabel thanked her and leant forward to savour the aroma of the stew.

'Rabbit,' the girl said. 'Fresh caught this morning.'

'I remember it from last year, it was delicious,' Alejandro said, giving the girl a smile.

Isabel was amused to see the girls' cheeks redden as she scuttled away to her position behind the counter, which she vigorously wiped down. Isabel exchanged a knowing look with Alejandro. They ate in silence, dipping hunks of bread into the unctuous sauce.

He pushed his empty plate away and drank some wine. Grimacing, he hastily gulped a mouthful of water.

'That bad?' Isabel asked.

The girl returned, cleared their plates, and left a plate of hard, white cheese. 'From our own goats,' she said, quickly withdrawing. Alejandro sliced a sliver of the cheese, put it in his mouth and grunted his satisfaction. He offered the knife to Isabel. She shook her head.

They shared a comfortable silence which Alejandro eventually broke.

'Tomorrow will be more dangerous. The nearer we get to Granada the more likely we are to encounter bandits.'

'Surely they won't attack royal bodyguards?'

'Probably not, but we need to be watchful.' He raised his glass, sniffed the wine, shook his head, and put it down.

'What do you actually think, Alejandro?'

He studied her face before replying. 'About what?' he asked.

'Alonso's story?' She saw relief wash over him. Had he assumed she meant what did he think about her, about them?

He looked away from her, into the empty hearth, as though carefully crafting his response. 'I don't think Andreas did it. I met the fellow once and I agree with you, he's a gentle soul incapable of murder.' He met her gaze. 'That doesn't mean your father had anything to do with it.' He snorted. 'Absolutely absurd idea.'

'But the rumours ...'

'Seville is run on lies and half-truths, most of them spread by The Holy Office for the Propagation of the True Faith.' His voice dripped with contempt as he gave the Inquisition its formal title.

'But he had cause.'

Alejandro cocked his head, waiting for her to explain.

'Mama.'

'True. But why wait so long?'

She didn't need to say anything. They exchanged a knowing look; they knew just how stubborn and patient her father could be. With 'her father could be both patient and stubborn.'

He tried a different tack. 'Your father is a courageous man. Not a coward who would stoop to poison.'

His vehemence sounded odd. She knew him well enough to detect a false note. What was he not telling her? It was late, she was tired, and they had an early start the next day. She could be patient too. She bid him goodnight.

She hadn't slept well, her mind racing with what Papa may have done and what Alejandro was holding back. Her body had burnt at the thought of him sleeping so close to her. After a hasty breakfast and a sour-faced farewell from Mora they were back in the saddle. She rode behind Alejandro's stallion through the cobbled lanes shrouded by early morning mist with a king's man guarding the front and rear. They soon emerged onto a grass plateau and whipped the horses into a gallop. They made good time as sunlight cut through the mist to reveal the jagged peaks of the Alpujarra mountains ahead of them.

As the sun reached its peak they paused in the hilltop town of Baena just long enough to acquire fresh horses. The guards were on high alert as bandits had recently raided the town. She wanted to rest in a tavern to escape the heat, but Alejandro insisted they press on. If they didn't they would have to sleep out in the open.

They rode on into the afternoon over narrow tracks and through desolate gullies. She had never felt so thirsty. They stopped all too briefly to fill their water bottles from streams and allow the horses to drink. She splashed her cheeks with water, but the relief was only temporary.

As, blessedly, the heat seeped out of the day they travelled over hillsides covered with fig, quince, and citrus orchards. Such a difference from the alluvial plains surrounding Seville. She would have to teach the children about that when she returned. They rode past seemingly endless smallholdings of mulberry trees. She knew the *Mudéjares* tended the trees which produced the silk used by the tailors of the Albaicín. Another teaching point for the children.

Just as she thought she couldn't take any more, the track began to descend. After trotting through a densely wooded copse they brought the horses to a halt at the edge of a steep drop. They were looking out over a lush green valley. On the far side Isabel had her first sight of The Alhambra framed against the snow-capped peaks of the Sierra Nevadas. At first, it seemed to her to be just a massive, solid block of red stone supported by brick ramparts towering hundreds of feet above the river below. Looking more closely she picked out the many towers and huge entrance gates that made it an unassailable fortress. As the setting sun bathed its red walls in a saffron light windows, porticoes and turrets emerged. Then lanterns and candelabras began to glow and flicker from inside the red citadel, and it shimmered equally in the light from within and without. She couldn't decide whether it was more castle or palace.

'It's extraordinary,' she said.

'Wait until you see inside,' Alejandro replied as he coaxed his stallion forward.

The horses nimbly picked their way down the steep slope. They crossed the riverbed and began the ascent to Granada as the call to prayer from both cathedral bells and the muezzin drifted across the valley.

CHAPTER
TEN

ISAAC SQUINTED AT THE PAPER. It was mid-morning but gloomy in his windowless chamber at the Alhambra. He didn't see why he should have to go to the trouble of lighting another lantern at this time of the day. He should ask Talavera for a better chamber, one with windows for a start. His annoyance was intensified by the sound of muffled banging coming from nearby.

'Isaac.'

Being summoned by Talavera's bark was one of the few things about working for the archbishop that he found irritating. He put down Calderon's petition. As he opened the door that led to the adjoining chamber the banging grew louder.

'How much longer?' Talavera asked Isaac as he stood

looking out of a large, mullioned window which filled the room with light. He would have no problem reading in here, Isaac thought. Without turning around the archbishop beckoned him with a forefinger. They looked out onto the Court of Lions. Several stonemasons were working with chisels and hammers to repair the twelve sculpted lions and ornate marble fountain that formed the centrepiece of the courtyard. The king wanted them restored to their former glory after the damage his own soldiers had done when the Alhambra was recaptured from the Moors.

'I don't know, Your Grace. The destruction was quite extensive.'

Talavera turned his head and fixed him with a puzzled expression. 'The petition, Isaac. Not the repairs.'

He was beginning to think the archbishop enjoyed deliberately sowing confusion in his mind. It happened too often to be coincidence. And he might be getting on, but he wasn't stupid or senile.

A smile played across Talavera's thin lips and blue eyes. He raised his brows expectantly.

'It's a difficult one, Your Grace.'

The smile disappeared from Talavera's face. The sun went behind the clouds. Another of his affectations.

'In short, Calderon's claim appears justified. The evidence is the usual thin mix of rumour and conjecture. I've spoken with him ...'

'How? When?'

He recounted the nature of his two encounters with

Calderon and his current condition.

Talavera nodded in what Isaac took to be approval.

'The man is a bigot,' Isaac continued, 'though not unusual, it certainly helps his case. He would not have permitted *converso* prayer meetings on his property. The Inquisition acted unjustly.'

'The right thing to do is to return his property?'

The archbishop's eyes drilled into him. 'Yes, that would be the righteous course of action.'

'But?'

'Is it politically expedient, Your Grace? At this moment?'

'With Their Majesties here?' He folded his arms. 'What would Cisneros say?' Talavera sneered.

'Exactly, Your Grace.'

'I will pray on it.' He returned his gaze to the courtyard.

'There was one other matter. If I may, Your Grace.'

The nod was almost imperceptible.

'Did you raise my case with His Majesty?'

'Yes, you'll be hearing something quite soon.'

Bowing his head – he would get nothing further from the conversation – he made to leave.

'Isaac.' He paused. 'Be prepared for the unexpected.'

When had he not been?

After enjoying a brief drink at Bar Aixa and fielding Teresa's questions regarding Calderon's whereabouts with vague answers - why was she so interested? - Isaac decided to pay a call on the patient. A visit to the Apothecary would make a welcome diversion. He was conflicted. He was desperate to see Aisha but apprehensive about what Abdul Rahman might have thought he witnessed from the balcony that morning. Ali might warn him about anything his brother might have said. Though why he thought that a possibility felt ridiculous. He had lost his heart, was he losing his mind?

He pushed open the door to the shop and stumbled through the gloom. Calderon was sitting in one of the high-backed chairs positioned in front of the counter. Why wasn't he lying down? As he approached he could see Calderon's chin was resting on his chest. Was he dead?

'Who's there?' Calderon called out in a weak voice.

'Isaac Alvarez,' he said sitting in the other chair.

'Mmm. Water?'

Calderon gulped from the mug Isaac had filled from the earthenware jug on the table.

'How are you?'

'Damned uncomfortable. The apothecary told me to stay upright. Says it'll help my brain recover.' He didn't sound convinced.

'You can trust Ali's advice.'

Calderon snorted. 'Trust a Moor?'

'That "Moor" saved your life. That "Moor" was up half the night at your bedside. That "Moor" gave you refuge after you harangued His Majesty in public.'

Calderon's jaw tightened.

Isaac held his gaze. 'You would be dead without him.'

Calderon exhaled sharply and he looked down at the floor.

'I wasn't expecting you,' Ali said, appearing from behind the counter. He lifted the hinged flap. 'I was in the stockroom.' He brought a three-legged stool and perched between them.

'I was passing, thought I'd see how well you're looking after the patient.' Isaac glanced at Calderon who did not meet his eyes. 'He seems to be recovering well. Under your excellent care.'

Calderon looked up and said, 'Thank you, apothecary.' He bowed his head in acknowledgement.

'You're most welcome,' Ali said, with evident surprise.

Isaac briefly clasped Calderon's shoulder. It was time to tell the truth. 'There's something you should know.' As Isaac revealed who he worked for and what he knew of his petition, Calderon's face betrayed a range of emotions: surprise, disbelief and then what seemed to be gratitude. But as the power Isaac had to help him became apparent a cunning look appeared. 'What have you advised the archbishop?'

'Frankly?'

'Of course.'

'That as you're an obvious bigot,' Isaac paused, allowing the word to sink in, 'it is highly unlikely you would have permitted *conversos* to worship on your property.'

Calderon was stunned into a state that Isaac didn't think happened very often to him: silence. His eyes moved back and forth as he thought through the implications of this information. All three of them knew that Isaac's characterisation might get his property back and even save his life. Isaac studied the range of feelings flickering across Calderon's face: anger, as he clenched his jaw; offense, as his eyes darkened; and then, as his features softened, he was surprised to see what looked like gratitude. After thanking Isaac, the sly glint returned. 'Talavera will sanction the return of my property?'

Isaac tipped his head from side to side. 'He's considering it. But there are political implications.'

Ali said, 'Cisneros?'

'Of course.'

'Damn him,' Calderon said.

'I thought you would be a supporter?' Ali said. 'With his zealotry for our forced conversion to the 'One True Faith'?'

Calderon opened his mouth, but no words emerged.

Isaac exchanged a knowing look with Ali.

'Señors,' Calderon said, placing a hand on each of their shoulders, 'I'm grateful to both of you, but there is only one way to settle this.' He paused. 'Wine!'

After they made their excuses - Ali did not drink alcohol and Isaac was too busy - Calderon repeated his thanks to both and staggered off to Bar Aixa.

'Only one drink,' Ali called out as Calderon slammed the door shut.

'Does he seem like someone who listens to advice?'

'Sounds like the pot calling the kettle black, my friend.'

Isaac grunted.

'Remind me why we're doing this?' Ali asked.

'Because you took an oath to "give help and succour alike to all."'

'And you?' Ali held out a palm.

Isaac jutted his lower lip. 'Because he reminds me of myself. Because I love a lost cause. Because I'm a fool.' He smiled. 'You choose.'

'Perhaps all three?'

He decided against asking Ali whether his brother had mentioned anything about him and Aisha. He may as well return home and find out for himself.

The main door to the compound rasped as Khaled pushed it open to allow Isaac to enter. The noise did not disturb the two figures seated under the balcony. He stood just inside the doorway and observed them as they leant towards each other, foreheads almost touching, hands gesticulating. He could hardly believe it. Aisha and Isabel? His heart thumped erratically. Was he imagining things, again? Perhaps he had – what did Ali call it? – "a choleric imbalance" that was disturbing his mind. He took a step back into the shade of a palm tree. Their smiles were broad, their eyes dancing as they touched each other's arms and knees with ease. They seemed like old friends. Was this a good or a bad thing? What were they saying about him? He came out from the shadows.

'Isabel?'

'Papa!'

For a moment he thought she might run to him as she had

when she was little. He imagined sweeping her up and holding her close. Instead, she waited for him, held his hands in hers and kissed him softly on each cheek.

He shook his head, still bewildered.

Aisha said, 'You look as if you've seen a ghost.'

He glanced from one to the other, both smiling, enjoying his confusion.

Before he could respond Aisha said, 'You have a wonderful daughter. I have learnt many things from her in such a short time.' She raised her brows. 'She has big plans; I like an ambitious woman. I'll have lunch brought out to you. You have a lot to catch up on.'

Her smile melted his burgeoning anger. She took her leave, promising to see them for dinner.

They sat next to each other facing the courtyard.

He wanted to ask her what Aisha meant about her plans, but there were more important questions. 'How did you get here? Why?'

'Wait, Papa.' She insisted on telling the whole story from the beginning. The servants filled the table with platters of saffron roasted chicken, couscous, and grilled peppers. Isaac's impatience grew as the retelling of her journey with Alejandro was interrupted as she stopped to savour the food and comment on how delicious it was. Eventually, as trays of filo pastry sweets were brought, she completed her account.

'Let me understand, Isabel. You left behind your responsibilities to the children and undertook a highly dangerous journey just to prevent Alonso telling the king I murdered Torquemada?' His surprise had given way to anger.

Her eyes narrowed to slits, lips pinched. 'Aren't you happy to see me?'

'Of course, my dear, but that isn't what's most important.' He took a breath. 'I can't bear the thought of losing you.'

'Nor I you.'

They exchanged rueful smiles. The fountain burbled, the afternoon was becoming hotter, the parrots were blessedly silent.

Isabel said, 'Aisha is lovely.'

He gave a thin smile; if he was too expressive he would incriminate himself. But, knowing his daughter, saying too little would be equally revealing. 'Yes, she's been a very gracious host. The food is wonderful. I've been very lucky.'

She held his eyes and he felt her search his face. Pursing her lips she said, 'A welcome change from Catalina's fare.'

They diverted into domestic news, he was eager to hear how well Gabriel was assuming his role as man of the house and pleased that the twins were thriving. But inevitably they circled back to more immediate matters.

'Alejandro will speak to His Majesty regarding Alonso's claims?' he asked.

'He thinks it's for the best. "Getting your retaliation in early," he called it. To head off Cardinal Cisneros, whom he thinks Alonso is sure to ally with.' She looked up at the sudden squawk from the parrots clattering through the tops of the palm trees. 'Of course it's all nonsense and His Majesty will understand that.' She turned to face him. 'It is all nonsense isn't it?'

'Of course.' He chose his next words carefully, his lawyerly instinct coming to the fore. 'As much as I wished that old devil dead a thousand times I had nothing to do with his actual death.' Mercifully Alejandro had not revealed to her their plot to poison Torquemada. It was not in Alejandro's best interests to, unless he blamed everything on him. He refused to believe his old deputy was capable of such disloyalty. But his daughter was exceptionally intuitive, he must be careful. If she found out the truth of what he had done he could not be certain of her reaction. Would she consider it just, righteous?

Isabel said, 'Alejandro believes that once he has discussed it with him, His Majesty will consider it to be unworthy of his time and refuse to meet with Alonso.'

'That may be, but Her Majesty will not be so easily diverted from the truth about the death of her beloved confessor. And she was never my biggest supporter.'

Isabel nodded in agreement.

He hesitated before asking, 'And how are things between you and Alejandro?'

'There is nothing between us except friendship.'

This lacked conviction but he did not pursue it. He was about to ask her how long she intended to stay and what she would do to fill her time when there was banging at the outside door. Khaled opened it to admit a royal messenger who bowed, confirmed Isaac's identity, and handed him a roll of parchment secured with a red ribbon. Isaac untied and unfurled it, and silently read the letter. He dismissed the messenger.

'It's a summons. I'm to go to the Court of Lions first thing tomorrow morning.'

Alejandro must have already discussed Alonso's accusations with Ferdinand. How would this affect the chance of his exile being lifted? If the king believed Alonso he could have him executed. Isabel's smile was intended to be encouraging, but a summons from His Majesty always brought to mind the old Hebrew verse:

You are caught in his tongs:
With one hand he brings you into the flames
While protecting you from the fire
Which with both hands he sets against you.

How would Ferdinand balance the competing needs of his queen, his Kingdom, and his faith? Isaac knew one thing for sure: his own needs would only become important if they serviced the king's. Sleep would be elusive tonight.

ELEVEN

THE FIGURE that turned towards Issac as he approached the fountain in the centre of the Court of Lions was not the one he'd expected.

Alejandro stepped forward and held out his hand. 'Isaac, it's been too long.'

No, "Señor"? His old deputy was clearly in a confident mood. He hesitated before holding out a hand to receive a warm shake and a clasp on his forearm.

Alejandro said, 'Shall we walk?'

They strolled side by side under the colonnade surrounding the courtyard. It was in a state of disrepair. Work had not yet begun on restoring the delicate geometric filigree design and Arabic script that adorned the upper part of the columns. The stonemasons he'd seen working yesterday from Talavera's chamber had disappeared. There were no courtiers in attendance. They were completely alone. Alejandro didn't want them to be overheard. It must be a delicate matter.

'His Majesty sends his apologies. He was called away on urgent business.'

'Don't give me that shit. We've known each other too long.'

Alejandro raised an eyebrow, and then dipped his head in acknowledgement.

'His Majesty has sent you to do his dirty work.' Isaac shook his head in disgust. 'He won't tell me in person that I can't return to Seville?'

'No.' Alejandro smiled. 'You've got it wrong, old friend.'

'Don't "old friend" me,' he sneered. 'What kind of friend doesn't keep his promises?'

'I'd hoped we'd put that behind us. I carried out my part of ...' Alejandro looked around to make sure nobody was listening, '... of the plan to ... dispatch our, our enemy but it just didn't happen.'

Isaac snorted.

'Perhaps the servant got the dose wrong. I don't know, and I certainly didn't investigate. The time after your exile was dangerous enough without it coming to Her Majesty's attention that —' his voice dropped to a whisper, 'I was snooping around asking questions about Torquemada's health.'

'And heaven forbid anything would prevent your advancement.' He deliberately raised his voice.

'That's really what this is about isn't it?'

Isaac didn't reply.

'Your anger, your disappointment ... your *jealousy* over my appointment.'

Isaac felt his anger grow as he recognised the truth of this. He turned away to look at the half-reconstructed lions. If only it was so easy to repair broken relationships. What was the equivalent of a chisel and hammer for that?

'Did you honestly expect me to turn it down? Would you have?' Alejandro asked.

Isaac was silent for a long moment. 'No,' he eventually admitted.

Alejandro put a hand on his elbow, and they stopped. 'We went through too much together,' he said with tenderness.

Why was it so hard to let go, to forgive? He turned to face Alejandro. 'Tell me why I'm really here. The business with Alonso?'

They began to walk again.

'No. The king regards the accusation of murder against you as nonsense but is grateful to Isabel for ensuring he heard of it quickly. He knows Cisneros will make use of it somehow. He shares the same intolerant views as Torquemada when it comes to Jews and *Mudéjares.*'

'Which is why Her Majesty wanted him appointed here?'

'Correct. Whilst the king might share their diagnosis of the problem he's certainly not in favour of their more barbaric methods of conversion.' He paused. 'The king holds Isabel in high regard. He was impressed by her honesty and integrity when she stood up for you against Torquemada. He has plans for her.'

Isaac noted the tinge of sadness that had entered his voice.

'But I'm getting ahead of myself,' Alejandro said.

'She's a wonderful daughter, I couldn't ask for better.' He gave Alejandro a rueful look. 'Make someone a wonderful wife one day.'

Alejandro returned a wry smile. 'That ship sailed long ago.'

'Most of them return you know,' he said.

Alejandro was puzzled.

He smiled. 'Ships? After long voyages. They return to port, come home.'

Alejandro pursed his lips.

Isaac saw a momentary flicker of longing pass over Alejandro's face. Then he felt his fury returning. 'Why am I here? I don't suppose His Majesty intends to rescind my exile? If it was good news he would give it in person.'

Alejandro nodded. 'Though you're only half-right.'

'Tell me.'

'His Majesty is concerned about the threat from the rebels. He sees them as a serious security threat to the Kingdom. They're no longer just bandits in the hills. They're increasingly well organised under a new leader.' Alejandro raised his brows.

Isaac assumed he was inviting him to supply the name. 'I don't know who you mean.'

'Your host, the spice merchant.'

'That's absurd. His religious, political views wouldn't surprise you, but to become commander of a group of rebels? No.'

'Yet we have proof. Written instructions to the bandit leaders in the hills intercepted with his signature and seal on them.'

'If you have the evidence arrest him.'

'His Majesty believes that will only inflame the situation and increase the probability of a costly war. He sees the *Mudéjares* as potential sources of revenue. He would like to convince Abdul Rahman to lead the rebels to reconciliation.'

'Appointing Cisneros is a pretty odd way of going about it.'

'Yes, that's unfortunate. Her Majesty ...' He didn't need to explain further. Isabella and Ferdinand shared the power but in religious matters the queen had the final say.

'So, what's my part in all of this?' Isaac asked.

'Isn't it obvious?'

'Nothing is obvious when it comes to His Majesty. Spell it out.'

'He wants you to gather intelligence from Abdul Rahman and persuade him to back away from armed rebellion and agree a negotiated settlement.'

'And if I can't get him to do that?'

'There will be an insurrection which His Majesty will use all his imperial force to quell.' He paused. 'Many will die, on both sides.'

'You want me to become a spy?'

Alejandro shook his head. 'It's for the benefit of the Kingdom.'

'And if I refuse?'

'His Majesty hopes you will see the benefit of his continued protection from the Inquisition.'

Isaac's frustration turned to fury, but it was pointless to argue further. He turned away and hurried through the maze of the Alhambra's courtyards, Alejandro's words ringing in his ears.

'You have until tomorrow morning to decide.'

'You haven't told him yet?' Ali was incredulous.

'No, we had so much else to discuss and Papa was distracted by His Majesty's summons,' Isabel replied. 'I didn't want to give him anything else to fret about. You know how much he worries.'

She was sitting next to Ali on the stone wall that surrounded the fountain in the courtyard. The air was still cool. She tilted her face to the sun rising over the high walls of the compound and basked in its warmth. Papa had just left for the Alhambra. He'd been taciturn, always a sign he was nervous. This was the first chance she'd had to talk privately with Ali since her arrival. The previous evening's dinner had been convivial but full of small talk. She'd enjoyed Abdul Rahman's warm welcome, though his embrace disconcerted her. When he noticed her discomfort he held her at arms' length and cried out, 'You're my sister now!', and hugged her again. Isabel missed Juana and Martîn at home in Seville and was disappointed that their hosts' three children were still with their grandmother in Fez. She would have liked to talk and play with them. The food was exceptional and Aisha had been very attentive, though she hardly spoke to Papa. Had they fallen out? Was her arrival the cause?

'You will have to discuss it with him before you can work with me.'

'I'll speak to him this evening, and we can begin tomorrow?'

Ali tipped his head from side to side, noncommittal.

Isabel was unconcerned, she would make it happen.

'How does your Papa seem to you?'

She played her fingers through the cold water of the pool, weighing her reply. 'Physically, he seems very well. The cooler mountain air suits him. Seville is too hot. He's put on a little weight; he obviously enjoys Aisha's cooking.'

Ali looked away from her.

'You don't agree?'

He said, 'I think you're right about his physical condition.'

She remained silent, it paid to be patient with Ali. And to listen very carefully for what he didn't say.

'He misses you all terribly, more than he will admit.' Ali crossed his ankles. 'And your dear Mama, of course.' He took her hand, and she gently squeezed his in return.

'Ali.' She waited until he looked at her. 'You would tell me if there was something important happening to Papa that I needed to know?' She saw something flicker across his brown eyes as he released her hand.

He was silent for a long moment. 'If I felt it was my place to tell you, of course I would, my dear.'

She was perplexed by the way he'd chosen to phrase his answer. Before she could challenge him Aisha appeared, took them both by the hand and led them to the table for breakfast. Yet more food. She would have to be careful, or her waistline would succumb to Aisha's generosity, just as Papa's had. She was feeding them the way mothers fed their children. It was how some women expressed their love.

God have mercy! That was why Aisha ignored him last night. That's what Ali was hinting at. Did she love him? She seemed very happy with her husband; she'd clearly missed him. So it was more likely Papa had fallen for her. Foolish man. She wondered if Abdul Rahman knew. Ali would never tell him; she was quite sure of that. But the spice merchant was not stupid. Her mind raced with so many questions and possibilities, none of them good. Most of all, what would Mama think?

Was he to become no better than one of the Inquisition's *familiares*? To spy on the man who had given him a home; the brother of his oldest friend. Alejandro could dress it up as 'gathering intelligence', but it was still a betrayal.

Isaac stumbled over someone or something and a voice called out, 'Watch it, señor.' He'd ended up in the heart of the Albacîn, so deep in thought he hadn't realised where he was. Mumbling an apology he hastened on. But where to? Not to the compound before he'd thought this through. He couldn't face any of them. He found a quiet corner in Bar Aixa. He was thankful Teresa knew him well enough not to engage him in conversation. One look at his face must have told her all she needed to know. She left him alone with a carafe of red wine.

Isaac had spent long enough with the king over the years to know what he was up to. If he provided Ferdinand with accurate intelligence he could put the rebellion down before it even started. If he tried to play a game and give the king false information then he risked planting seeds of discontent amongst the rebels that would lead to its breakup. Either way the king won. He was most definitely caught in his tongs. And if he refused the Royal command? Ferdinand would reluctantly allow Cisneros to ramp up the forced conversions and evil would reign in Granada the way it had in Seville under Torquemada. And Ferdinand would allow the Inquisition to do what it wanted with him. He would burn.

He could hide. There were rumours of caves in the hills at Sacromonte where the rebels took refuge. It wasn't an appealing prospect and was only a short-term fix. He could run. Get on a ship bound for Lisbon or London. As so many Jews had over the past decade. Like Maria had wanted them to do all those years ago. If only he'd listened to her. He took a long draught of wine. What would she tell him to do now? But he felt the same hard nugget of resistance, of pride, of stubbornness – call it what you will – deep inside that prevented him from running then, and he would not do it now. He could not abandon his children and his faith.

He finished the wine and toyed with the idea of another, but getting drunk wouldn't help him to make better decisions. He refused to end up a sot like Calderon. There seemed no good way out of his predicament. Hell really was having to choose between terrible things. He made to leave and took a silver coin from the pouch at his waist. It glinted in the midday sunlight that had crept into the bar. He held it up and turned it from side to side, Ferdinand on one, Isabella on the reverse.

To represent the equal distribution of power. That gave him an idea. He balanced the coin on a thumb and flicked it into the air and watched as the two pictures tumbled over one another. He trapped it on the table under his palm. Yes, there might be another way. And perhaps a price to be exacted as well.

BOOK II

Five months later ...
Granada
December, 1499

CHAPTER
TWELVE

ISAAC WAS HORRIFIED. He stood with Ali in the cathedral plaza amid a crowd that filled the square. They covered their mouths and noses with handkerchiefs in a vain attempt to keep out the acrid smell of the fire. Ali muttered, 'Ya Allah, Ya Allah,' as the plumes of black smoke rose into the salmon pink evening sky. For the past hour they had watched the wagons draw up every few minutes. Soldiers tossed the cargo down a line to feed the bonfire in the centre of the plaza. It had grown to be taller than two men, glowing orange at its base and from its peak sputtering fumes heavenward. There were ripples of applause as the *Mudéjar* holy books fed the inferno. Celebrating as centuries of knowledge and wisdom vanished in a cloud of smoke.

Isaac scanned the faces of the mob. Some eyes shone fiercely. He wasn't sure whether it was a reflection of the heat from the fire or their delight. Perhaps both. Others were wide-eyed or grimacing with horror. About half of them, they must be the *Mudéjares*, were quiet. The remainder became raucous when the fire popped and crackled. Children danced near the edge of the bonfire, screaming as the sparks flew. Then Isaac locked eyes with someone he thought he knew. The man touched the edge of his wide-brimmed hat. It was Lorenzo Calderon. He hadn't seen him for months, not since he'd given him the news that Talavera had granted his petition and returned his lands, though the archbishop had retained half of the money the Inquisition had confiscated. A clever way to mitigate his decision should Cisneros find out. Calderon held Issac's gaze, shook his head and pursed his lips. Isaac nodded his understanding. If there was one Catholic who disapproved of this barbarism there must be others. Or so he hoped.

Isaac turned his head at a loud cheer from the people nearest to the cathedral. A raised platform had been constructed in front of the cathedral steps. Then he saw the reason for the jubilation: a cloaked figure was ascending the stairs to the dais. When he reached the top he removed his cowl and Isaac recognised Cardinal Cisneros. A neatly groomed tonsure garlanded his bald skull. His eyes were dark and hooded as he stared down at the bonfire, his thin lips pressed tightly. He stood in the centre of the dais and crossed himself. There were a few muted 'boos' amongst the cheers. Cisneros surveyed the crowd with his piercing eyes as though seeking out the malcontents.

Issac glanced at Ali, jutted his jaw at the cardinal and said, 'He's given himself a prime view.'

Ali emitted a deep growl. He was barely containing his anger.

'He doesn't appear to be enjoying it,' Isaac said in a low voice.

'Does he have any joy in his life?' Ali spat in reply. 'The only consolation is I'm told he's made an exception for medical books. Avicenna will survive.'

Cisneros clutched the railing and leant dangerously far forward. If he toppled he would fall into the throng. The suppressed rage of those *Mudéjares* who watched in silence would surely get the better of them and they would tear him to pieces. The red-cloaked queen's guards stationed at the base of the platform would have their work cut out to save him. Perhaps he wanted a closer look at the conflagration. Or to consume the expressions of fear of so many in the crowd. Or to hear pages crackle and bindings snap as the sacred books of the *Mudéjar* were cremated. Did he know the bindings were lined with pearls, the pages perfumed and inscribed with beautiful coloured inks? If he did, he didn't care.

Isaac noticed a man in a blue kaftan with his arm around a boy who looked to be of a similar age to Gabriel. The man was shaking his head and muttering into the lad's ear. Perhaps he was explaining what was happening or consoling the boy. Isaac couldn't imagine sharing a rational explanation with Gabriel should they witness Bibles or Torahs being publicly burnt. A wagon driver threw down more books that the soldiers slung down the row. A sudden roar from the fire raised screams of delight from the children.

'Have you ever seen anything like this?' Ali whispered.

Isaac removed his handkerchief to reply and accidentally

inhaled a lungful of bitter smoke. He coughed. Now he knew what burning, wood, parchment and ink tasted like. A strange notion occurred to him, that those words and thoughts were now a part of him. 'No.' He looked down. 'Not quite like this.'

'I'm sorry, my friend,' Ali said, touching Isaac's upper arm. 'I forgot. Watching a friend burn is far worse.'

Was it? The sight of Juan's body melting into the inferno had haunted Isaac for four years. But this was an attempt to wipe out the legacy of thousands of scholars over hundreds of years. Just because they were worshippers of Allah. This would have far more effect on the city, on the Kingdom than the death of one man.

As yet another wagon arrived to feed the flames something shifted in the section of the people in front of Isaac. Women began to wail. A chant of, '*Allahu Akbar*,' began softly but quickly became louder. The captain of the guards pointed into the throng, and then turned to look up at Cisneros, who waved him forward with the back of his hand. The captain and two other guards waded into the mob, which parted as the soldiers swung their swords. They were heading towards Isaac and Ali.

'Let's go,' Isaac said.

They began to shove their way out when a loud crack, followed by a shared gasp made them turn back. They watched as the guards dragged the man in the blue kaftan out of the crowd, his son screaming after him, 'Abu, Abu.' They hurled him at the base of the platform. There was a sickening thud as the boy's father slammed into the cobbles. He didn't move, only a low moan confirmed he was still alive. Ali instinctively made to go and help but Isaac caught him by the arm and shook his head. It was pointless, he would just be arrested. The captain glanced up at Cisneros for guidance. He stared down with dead eyes. The man's son was being restrained by other men in kaftans as he cried out, 'Mercy. Mercy. Please.' Cisneros flicked a glance at the boy.

Isaac thought he was going to order the man's execution there and then.

But Cisneros shook his head and the captain gestured to his two comrades to take the man away. Perhaps even Cisneros understood that a public execution was a step too far. He made the sign of the cross, pulled his cowl over his skull, and descended from the platform. A phalanx of soldiers quickly surrounded him and shepherded him away. The boy broke free and ran after his father.

Ali tugged at Isaac's sleeve. 'We should go before this gets out of hand. There's nothing we can do here.'

Chants of, 'Allahu Akbar' followed them as they made their way into the Albacîn.

'What is Cisneros thinking?' Ali asked.

'He's ensuring "accelerated conversion" to Christianity sticks,' Isaac replied. 'He doesn't want any of the "New Christians" to slip back. If there are no copies of the Holy Quran left they can't return to their former beliefs.'

'It's pure fucking evil,' Ali said.

Isaac had never heard his friend curse.

'Allah alone knows how my brother is going to react. Hurry, let's get home before he acts without thinking.'

'You go on ahead. I'm going to make sure Isabel is safe.'

Isabel loved being alone in the Apothecary, especially at night. She'd established a routine. She lit as many lanterns as she wanted to – ignoring Ali's advice to save money – and settled in the chair in front of the counter to read. Ali had given her an extensive list, but she especially liked Avicenna. Isabel was amazed by how much someone writing five hundred years ago understood about the human body. Then she prepared precise measures of powder on the brass weighing scales and created cures using the pestle and mortar. Some of them were actual remedies that would be collected in the morning. They were the simpler ones that Ali trusted her to prepare. But she also practiced making the more complicated mixtures. She did this without Ali's permission. She wasn't doing anything wrong but did feel a little guilty about the waste of herbs and powders. Ali didn't seem to notice, or he pretended not to. Sometimes she composed letters to Gabriel and the children. She couldn't wait to see them in just two weeks' time.

Isabel had been irritated by Papa who had burst in a little while ago anxiously asking her if she was safe. Of course she was. He'd said something about a book burning in the cathedral square. Isabel hadn't really listened properly, still absorbed in Avicenna. She got rid of him by agreeing to return home under the escort of one of Abdul Rahman's men. As Papa left he was mumbling something about the spice merchant being angry. She was sure he would sort it out. Isabel didn't want to be involved, she wanted to lose herself in learning how to heal. She'd locked and bolted the door behind him and put up the, 'Closed' sign.

She took a deep lungful of the sandalwood incense that she routinely burnt now. In Seville it was dismissed as the "smell of the Moors." She'd grown to love the rich, woody aroma. Isabel was startled by a loud rap at the door followed by the thump of someone shoving at it. 'We're closed. Come back on the morrow,' she called out in a deliberately forceful voice. She pushed her hand through the slit in her gown to make sure the dagger she concealed at the top of her thigh was there.

A cultured, female voice said, 'You're useless, step aside.' Isabel couldn't hear the reply from whoever else was there.

'Lady Apothecary, you needn't be afraid. Please open up.' The politeness of the request and the gentleness of the tone persuaded Isabel to move towards the door.

'Who's there?'

'I'm here on a ... royal matter. I need to talk to you privately.'

Isabel remained silent. Waiting for more.

'If he were here Señor Alejandro would vouch for me,' the lady said.

Curiosity got the better of Isabel. She turned the key in the lock and pulled the top and bottom bolts. She wasn't prepared for who stepped through the door.

CHAPTER
THIRTEEN

ONCE ISAAC HAD PERSUADED ISABEL to accept that Khaled would escort her back to the compound in an hour – and extracting a promise that in the meantime she would keep the door locked – he returned home. Abdul Rahman's reaction was exactly as Ali feared it would be. He was pacing up and down the courtyard, kicking at stones, shouting at the servants, telling the parrots to, 'shut the fuck up' in his thick Granadino accent. Isaac was glad Isabel was at the Apothecary and Aisha was visiting a friend. Women should not have to witness such rage or hear such foul language. The rest of what he said was largely incoherent, but the emotion was unmistakable. His brother walked alongside him, talking in a low tone. Finally, the spice merchant fell to his knees, sobbing. He looked up at Isaac, tears falling freely, and said between jagged sobs, 'Why did I listen to you?'

Isaac opened his mouth to reply but Ali shook his head vehemently. He knew Ali was right: he couldn't offer consolation or explanation. This was how the man in the square must have felt as he'd tried to explain to his son the terrible things happening right in front of them.

'Patience?' Abdul Rahman screamed. He got to his feet and advanced on Isaac. Ali gestured at Khaled and together they tried to restrain the spice merchant. But his natural strength coupled with his anguish made it impossible. He jabbed Isaac in the chest. 'What are you?' he growled.

Isaac stood his ground. 'I'm truly sorry, Abdul Rahman. I didn't think Cisneros would go this far. I had no idea.'

'You have no ideas and no faith.' He pushed his face forward, his forehead almost touching Isaac's. He could smell the sweetness of pomegranate mixed with something bitter. 'You're no better than a *kafir*.'

He'd been called a lot of things, a bloody Jew, a heretic, a murderer but never an unbeliever. Isaac knew it was the worst insult Abdul Rahman could think of. He opened his mouth, but before he could say something to placate the spice merchant the cry of the *muezzin* calling Isha prayers drifted across the courtyard.

Ali and Khaled each took one of Abdul Rahman's arms and pulled him away. Ali said, 'Brother, let us pray.'

Abdul Rahman looked up and shouted, '*Allahu Akbar.*' He repeated it as Ali led him upstairs to his chamber. Ali turned his head to give Isaac a mournful look and mouthed, 'I'm sorry.' But there was no need to apologise. Isaac would have felt the same if the sacred books of the Jews had been incinerated.

After instructing Khaled to go and bring Isabel back, Isaac went to his apartment, sat on the bed and thought. Since the summer, life had settled into a peaceful rhythm. His unease at

Isabel becoming an apprentice to Ali – was it really a suitable job for a young woman? – had given way to pride at how fast she was learning new skills. Though Isabel's talk of bringing the children and making the move to Granada permanent made him uneasy. He remained hopeful the king would let him return to Seville. Isaac was looking forward to their visit for Christmas in two weeks. It would be wonderful to see Juana and Martîn, but he missed Gabriel the most. The infrequent letters from Catalina - almost illegible - and from Gabriel - too brief - encouraged him to believe his son was growing into a fine young man. Isaac consoled himself that perhaps his absence had enabled Gabriel to mature, out of his shadow. But were they telling the truth? And there was no mention of what Gabriel intended to do with his life once he was eighteen.

He'd pushed his feelings for Aisha to the back of his mind, on most days. His fear that Cisneros would target her as a convert from Christianity to Islam had so far proven unfounded. After his meeting with Alejandro he'd accepted the king's commission to provide information about Abdul Rahman's part in the rebellion. Isaac had exacted a promise from Alejandro that, in return for his cooperation, he would petition the king to protect Aisha, if the need arose. Isaac minimised the risk to everyone by advising the truculent spice merchant to exercise patience and caution. Abdul Rahman respected Isaac's advice, he was a former royal advisor after all. And he was supported in this by Ali – who had no appetite for revolution – and Talavera, who still believed in peaceful, not forced, conversion. As a result, the rebellion had gathered little momentum over the past few months. This reduced Isaac's sense of betrayal as he convinced himself he was peacemaker, not spy. He could truthfully report to Alejandro that Abdul Rahman was only one of the leaders of a loose collective of *Mudéjar* who held a range of views from insurrection to peaceful acceptance of conversion. The most vocal of the malcontents appeared to have fled to Fez to join the exiled King Baobadil. He passed along some other tidbits of information. According to Alejandro, Ferdinand was satisfied with the status quo: the *Mudéjar* merchants were paying their taxes and the bandits in the hills were relatively quiet.

For the first time in a long while there had been a degree of sweetness to his life. But Cisneros had changed everything. It was a senseless act of provocation and could not remain unanswered as it marked the beginning of a new phase of the cardinal's war against the *Mudéjar*. Issac was sure that even after Abdul Rahman had calmed down he would not be placated, could not be prevented from acting. But if the situation in Granada worsened the children could not visit. He would not see the young man his son had grown into. His optimistic mood rapidly deteriorated.

A sudden thump at the door interrupted his maudlin reverie.

'Open up!'

He recognised the voice.

A tall and imposing figure walked past Isabel and entered

the Apothecary, her face obscured by the hood of her cloak. She held up a hand and the two guards accompanying her remained outside, taking up a position either side of the entrance. Isabel bolted the door and saw that the woman had removed her cloak and thrown it on the counter. Isabel admired the coppery hair cascading over her shoulders, gleaming in the candlelight. It was pulled tightly back to form a neat centre parting. She wore a brocaded yellow gown and a gold-decorated crimson scarf. Isabel couldn't help but feel a twinge of jealousy. Whoever this woman was, she was beautiful and important.

'I apologize for the intrusion at the late hour, Lady Apothecary,' the woman said, her voice soft and musical. 'I am in urgent need of your services.'

With a shock she realised it was the Infanta, Catalina of Aragon, Their Majesties' youngest child. She curtsied deeply. 'My apologies for not immediately recognising Your Majesty.' She felt herself redden. 'I was taken up with my work.'

The princess put her hands on her hips and surveyed the shop. She took in the shelves behind the counter. 'How fascinating. All those jars of special herbs and powders.' She gave Isabel a broad smile and said, 'Normally the apothecary comes to us, so I've never seen inside a shop before.'

Isabel was stunned. She'd met the king and the queen before, and rather liked Ferdinand, but something about this beautiful young woman unnerved her. 'What can I do for you, Your Majesty?' Isabel asked, trying to keep her voice even.

'I have something that needs to be tested, and I have been

told you can help me.'

Isabel felt a knot form in her stomach. This was not the kind of request she was used to. She furrowed her brow in confusion.

'No need to look so puzzled. One of my ladies-in-waiting took a love potion from you a couple of weeks ago, and it worked like a charm.' She smiled. 'She didn't want to see the old man who owns the shop. Neither do I. That's why I'm here now.'

'Tested? What is it you have? Your Majesty.'

The Infanta reached inside the pocket of her gown and produced a vial filled with silver powder. Isabel took it and peered closely but couldn't immediately determine what it was.

'I could try to test it, but I'm not that experienced ...'

'Nonsense, I'm sure you've learnt a lot,' she waved a hand at the pile of books on the table.

'Yes, Your Majesty, but perhaps ...' she hesitated, 'you would like me to ask Señor Abu Ali Sina to attend you at the Alhambra?'

She swatted the question away with the back of her hand. 'No, I don't want him to know anything about this. I suggest you work on it immediately,' she said, a hint of steel creeping into her voice. 'I'll wait.'

'I can certainly try,' Isabel said, motioning the princess to follow her to the counter.

'What do you think it is?' Isabel asked, as she lifted the hinged flap and went behind the counter. She put on a white apron.

The Infanta was leaning her elbows on the other side of the counter. 'I need to know if it's poison, arsenic.'

Isabel felt a sudden twinge of fear. Arsenic? How had the princess got hold of it? She decided it was better not to ask. Isabel knew the basic tests for identifying it. 'You might want to take a seat Your Majesty. It will take some time.'

'It's quite alright. It's fascinating to watch.' The princess steepled her elbows and rested her chin on her interlaced fingers.

Isabel took down a jar of arsenic powder from the shelf behind her and carefully poured a small quantity into a brass pan. Then she tipped the powder the princess had given her into another pan and set them side by side and studied them. She sniffed each of the pans, being careful not to inhale any of the powder.

'I thought arsenic didn't smell?' the Infanta said.

'It doesn't, I'm trying to detect a difference between the two. Your powder does have a slight odour, but that might come from being stored and then exposed to air. They look quite similar, Your Majesty, but your powder is paler, it's not as metallic looking.'

'It's not arsenic?'

'Probably not,' Isabel said. 'Let me do one more test.' She lit a nugget of wood in an incense burner and placed the pan with the princesses' powder on top. 'Arsenic does not melt when heated like most solids do, Your Majesty.'

At first the powder did not change, and Isabel thought that

perhaps she was wrong. Then it melted to a viscous yellow slime.

'It's definitely not arsenic,' Isabel said. 'It could be one of the rarer poisons, but I'd suggest that was unlikely.'

'Very good.'

'If you wanted to be completely certain perhaps you could give some to one of your dogs?' Isabel said with a raised brow.

She felt the Infanta surveying her coolly but held her gaze.

'I don't think that will be necessary,' the princess replied. She held out her hand and Isabel returned the vial with what remained of the powder. The princess took out three silver coins from the leather pouch at her waist and laid them on the counter. 'For your trouble.'

Isabel dipped her head in thanks. 'Will that be all, Your Majesty?'

'For the moment.'

The Infanta picked up her cloak and draped it around her shoulders. She pulled up the hood and moved towards the door. Isabel unbolted and opened it.

'We will meet again, very soon,' the princess whispered as she swept out.

Isabel secured the door and slumped back against it, relieved the visit was over but thrilled to have met the Infanta. She was engaged to be married to the next king of England. Isabel was even more thrilled by the prospect of meeting her again. Surely it was too stupid to contemplate that they might even become friends? She had made no real female friends since Mama's death. Catalina was more like a mother to her.

And she'd spent all her time being a governess to the children. She didn't resent that; it had been her duty. But now she wanted to do more of the things that interested her. To study, to travel, to really live. Perhaps the princess would be a part of that. It might be just a dream, but she was allowed to dream, wasn't she?

CHAPTER
FOURTEEN

'DAMN THE MAN, HE'S GONE TOO FAR THIS TIME,' Alejandro said, striding through the open door to Isaac's apartment without waiting for an invitation. He threw his hat onto the bed and paced. He grimaced as he massaged the back of his neck.

Isaac poured himself a mug of water and offered Alejandro one, but he declined with a vehement shake of his head. Isaac sat in the only chair in the room and waited. He recalled the old days in Seville when he'd been exasperated about something one of the monarchs had done, he too would pace in his chambers at the Alcazar. And Alejandro would sit and listen patiently, waiting for him to calm down. It was interesting to witness this, entertaining even.

'What's there to smile about?' Alejandro snapped.

'Very little in the here and now. I was just thinking about how our roles have become reversed.'

Alejandro stopped moving for a moment and looked thoughtful. He gave a small, smile of understanding and his posture relaxed a little.

'I assume you're talking about Cisneros?'

'Who else?' Alejandro spat back. He closed his eyes and took a deep breath. 'Apologies, Isaac, apologies,' he said making a small bow.

Isaac acknowledged the conciliatory gesture with a dip of his head. 'You're not the only one who's been angry with me this evening.'

Alejandro sighed heavily. 'I'm sure the spice merchant is not best pleased.' He paused. 'But why is he angry with you?'

'Because I counselled patience. Urged him to have faith in Talavera and the king. Told him Ferdinand wanted to avoid the cost of putting down a rebellion and was happy to keep taxing the *Mudéjar*.'

'All true. And His Majesty feels almost the same way about the cardinal as Abdul Rahman does.'

'Tell me.'

'He's livid with Cisneros. Doesn't understand what's to be gained by inciting hatred.'

'Doesn't want all the *Mudéjar* to flee as it will reduce his tax take,' Isaac countered. 'Won't stand up to the queen and insist their religious freedoms are maintained.' He narrowed his eyes at Alejandro. 'Greedy and spineless.'

'I didn't expect you to have much sympathy for him, but that's harsh.' He paused. 'He's the only reason the Inquisition hasn't burnt you as a heretic.'

'It might be a blessed relief if they did. I could be with Maria and leave all this mayhem behind.'

'You don't mean that,' Alejandro said softly. 'You wouldn't

leave Isabel and the children bereft. Not for a while longer.'

'I'm just exhausted. Tired of being thought of as a heretic, a murderer, and a spy.' He wiped a palm across his face. 'Abdul Rahman just called me a *kafir*, an unbeliever.' He paused. 'I'm none of those things.'

Alejandro sat down on the bed. 'That's one of the reasons I'm here.'

'Let me guess. His Majesty wants a report on how Abdul Rahman intends to react?'

Alejandro nodded.

'Tell him he can go to hell. I haven't a clue and I wouldn't tell him if I had.'

'It's not that. It's Alonso, or more accurately Cisneros.' Alejandro explained that the friar had persuaded the cardinal of the validity of the allegation against Isaac for the murder of Torquemada. The cardinal hadn't been difficult to convince; he and Alonso shared the view that the *Mudéjar* should be forced to convert. And if the claim was proven, Andreas, a fellow cleric, would have to be released.

Isaac asked, 'I thought you said the king didn't care about Alonso's accusations?'

'*He* doesn't.'

So Cisneros had her Majesty's ear. And given her enmity towards him, Isaac knew it wouldn't have taken much to convince her that he was to blame for her beloved confessor's death.

Alejandro continued, 'She wanted to arrest you, but was persuaded by His Majesty to "invite" you for questioning.'

'When?'

'Tomorrow morning.'

'You know I'm not responsible for Torquemada's death,' Isaac said quietly.

Alejandro was silent for a long moment. 'I know you wanted him dead, and you involved me in the plot.'

'I didn't force you. You were willing enough.'

Alejandro held Isaac's eyes. 'Yes, I was.'

'But for whatever reason our plan didn't succeed. And when else would I have had the opportunity?' Nobody knew about what had happened in Torquemada's bedchamber at Avila that night a year ago and Isaac was not about to reveal it now.

Alejandro said, 'You can't defend yourself by admitting a failed plot. It would be foolish.' He paused, his lower jaw shifting, left and right. 'There is, of course, another option ...'

'Run?'

Alejandro dipped his head.

He snorted. 'I didn't do it before. I've faced worse.'

Alejandro puffed out a long breath. 'Then all I can do is state my belief in you to Their Majesties.'

'You'll be a character witness?'

'You might call it that. For all the good it'll do.' Alejandro cleared his throat and leant forward, clutching his knees. 'I need to tell you something that's been troubling me for a long time.'

'Go on.'

'It's a confession really.'

Isaac smiled wryly. 'In that case you want a priest. A heretic is hardly the right person to hear a confession.'

'I wouldn't trust any of those priests. They report everything back to the Inquisition. You're the only person I *can* tell.'

Isaac waited. He had no idea what his previous deputy, old friend and former future son-in-law was about to reveal.

After Isabel had gotten over her excitement she couldn't shake off the feeling of unease that had lingered in her chest after the Infanta left. For some reason she couldn't quite pin down her last words – "We will meet again, very soon" – now sounded more like a threat than a promise. If the Infanta was up to something Isabel was afraid of being dragged into it. She was beginning to understand what Papa had endured for all those years with the king: you never quite knew where you were with royalty. Their priorities and allegiances shifted with the wind.

She was glad when Khaled arrived to escort her home. They made their way through the darkened streets. It was close to midnight and there were only a few candles alight in the houses. Strange figures lurked at every corner; no doubt whipped up by the book burnings. She tried to brush off her apprehension, telling herself it was just her imagination running wild. She was grateful Papa had insisted on sending Khaled. He kept a deferential one step behind her, but whenever they neared a noisy group he walked alongside her with his right hand placed on the scabbard of his sword. This was reassuring. She had her dagger and was confident she could cope with a single assailant, but not a group of drunken young men. As he drew alongside her for the third time she considered asking him about the book burning. He would be distraught, and she decided there was no point in making him talk about it.

As they entered the narrow *calles* of the Albaicîn Isabel quickened her pace, her heart rate quickening.

'Nearly there,' Khaled whispered.

She heard footsteps. Khaled was fast to react, drawing his sword as he turned. Isabel saw the silhouette of a man gaining rapidly. She tightened her grip on the dagger. But as the man drew nearer, Isabel recognized him. It was Ibrahim, another of Abdul Rahman's men. He was disheveled and his eyes were bloodshot. Khaled lowered his sword.

She rushed to Ibrahim's side, taking his arm to steady him. 'What happened? she asked.

'The burnings. They got my younger brother, Omar,' he said.

She felt a lump in her throat. Cisneros' barbarism was hitting close to home now. Ibrahim's brother was a brilliant scholar and a gentle man.

'He was protesting so they arrested him.'

'I'm so sorry,' she said, her voice barely above a whisper.

'I don't know where he is,' Ibrahim said, his voice cracking.

Khaled said, 'We must hurry. It's not safe to be out.' He put an arm around Ibrahim and led him on. They walked in silence, each lost in their thoughts. When they reached the compound, Isabel said, 'I hope you will have better news of your brother tomorrow.'

Isabel was enveloped by sadness. The burnings had a human cost as well as an intellectual one. She had a lot to discuss with Papa. What would he make of it all? Especially her encounter with the princess.

CHAPTER
FIFTEEN

ISAAC WAS STUNNED INTO SILENCE by what Alejandro revealed. He splashed his face with water from the washbasin. Then he took a step towards Alejandro who was still sitting on the bed. 'You deliberately sabotaged my plans to send Torquemada to hell?'

'Are you certain that's where he would've ended up?'

'What on earth do you mean?'

'By murdering him you would have martyred him. And all martyrs go to heaven.'

'That's not for you and me to decide.'

Alejandro stood up. 'I didn't do what you asked, I didn't pass the poison on.'

'You lied to me about it?'

'I did, for the greater prize.'

Isaac snorted with laughter. 'What on earth would that be?'

'Your soul. Your opportunity to spend eternity with Maria.'

Isaac looked away from him.

'I could not allow you to commit the mortal sin of murder.' He clasped Isaac's shoulder. 'It would have been you in hell, not him.'

Isaac pushed his hand away, sat down and put his head in his hands. 'I trusted you,' he growled.

'I did what I thought was right.' He paused. 'He was old, I thought it was wiser to let nature take its course. But I knew you couldn't be argued out of it.'

He looked up at Alejandro and sneered. 'That's exactly what Torquemada claimed as his reason for torture and murder. He was "saving their souls." Much comfort that was to their families.'

Alejandro picked up his hat. 'You were impatient. Torquemada was old and dying. Vengeance might have brought you satisfaction, but it would have cost you too much.' He paused. 'Can you not see that?'

'It's a betrayal, Alejandro. Why tell me now? After keeping it secret for so long.'

'I fear events are about to overwhelm us.' He turned his hat in his hands. 'I wondered when, if, I might get another chance.'

He might be right, Isaac thought. The queen had him in her grasp again. Ferdinand might not choose to defend him this time. The rational part of him should acknowledge that Alejandro had done what he considered to be the right thing. Wasn't that what he was always trying to do? He should embrace Alejandro and thank him. But something dark rose up from deep inside and he said, 'Get out.'

Alejandro put on his hat. 'I will see you on the morrow in

the queen's chambers at the Alhambra. I will defend you as best I can.'

Isaac said nothing. He stared at Alejandro as he made his way towards the door. The man had been his closest ally, his friend for years. Yet, he had kept such a monumental secret from him. He couldn't contain his anger and he lunged at Alejandro, tackling him to the floor. Alejandro grappled with him, trying to push him off.

'What did you do to me?' Isaac snarled, his eyes flashing with fury, as he pinned Alejandro to the floor.

'I didn't do anything to you,' Alejandro replied, struggling to breathe.

'You made a decision about my life, my soul, without my consent. His hands tightened around Alejandro's throat. He had never felt so betrayed in his life. Alejandro had been a source of strength, a constant in an unpredictable world.

'Stop,' Alejandro gasped, 'you'll kill me.'

Isaac looked down at his friend, his breath coming in short, angry jabs. What was he doing? Killing Alejandro wouldn't make anything better. His grip loosened slightly. 'You're right,' he muttered, pulling himself away.

Alejandro coughed, rubbing his sore throat. He got up, dusting himself off.

Isaac shook his head, 'I let my anger get the better of me.'

'We've been through so much. I couldn't bear to think of you suffering for an eternity.'

Isaac looked at him, the fire in his eyes slowly extinguishing.

Alejandro placed a hand on his friend's shoulder, 'Doing

the right thing isn't always easy.'

Isaac sighed heavily.

'Will you be alright?'

'I just need time to think.'

As Alejandro left, Isaac collapsed onto the bed. He had saved him from damnation, but it still hurt that he had kept it a secret for so long. Could he ever fully trust him again? He needed to focus on defending himself against the accusations and intrigues of the queen's court. And perhaps, in time, he could learn to forgive Alejandro.

Khaled sat Ibrahim down on the bench outside the compound then pushed open the door for Isabel. She saw someone advancing from the darkness of the courtyard. She took a step back towards Khaled. She slipped a hand through the pocket in her gown and began to unsheathe the dagger. The figure materialised and said, 'Good evening, Isabel.'

She exhaled. 'Oh, it's only you.' She removed her hand and held it out for him to kiss.

'No need to sound so disappointed,' Alejandro replied, removing his hat and lightly brushing his lips against the back of her hand. His tone was curt, and he looked distracted, upset even.

'My apologies, it was relief more than anything. Events have unnerved me tonight.'

He gave a tight-lipped smile and made to move past her.

'Have you been visiting Papa?'

'Yes.'

'Would you have time to talk? I've just had a visitor at the Apothecary I'd like to discuss with you.'

He seemed reluctant, but she held his eyes, and he nodded his acquiescence. She thanked Khaled and before he returned to his guard post outside the compound he lit the four lanterns that stood sentry at each corner of the fountain. They sat side by side on the stone plinth that surrounded the pool, facing the house which was in total darkness. The courtyard was eerily silent, even the parrots were quiet. Was the whole of the city in a state of shock?

Isabel realised that this was the first time they'd spent any time alone together since their arrival in Granada. She had been busy learning her new craft, whilst he, no doubt, was trying to keep His Majesty happy. Sitting with him in the moonlight she realised something. She missed him.

'I've just had a royal visitor at the Apothecary.'

'The princess?'

She swatted his knee playfully. 'How did you know?'

'It's just the kind of thing she would do, sneak out of the Alhambra. She's very bored.'

'You could have let me tell the story,' she said, looking directly at him.

He smiled, and this time it was broad and genuine. She felt the drum of her heartbeat. She glanced away from him.

'What did she want?'

'I can't tell you the specifics, that's confidential.' She hoped that didn't sound as pompous as it felt.

'Love potion?'

She shook her head.

'Poison?'

'No, I won't tell you. Stop it,' she said with a small laugh. 'I wanted you to know in case you think His Majesty should be aware. I didn't want to hide something that might be useful to you.'

He took a moment to answer. 'Secrets will always get you into trouble, eventually,' he said.

'Sounds as though you speak from experience.'

Alejandro gave her a sidelong glance. He tipped his head to one side and moved a little closer to her. Was he going to hold her, to kiss her? Then a dark look passed over his face and he withdrew. She'd seen that expression before; he was hiding something.

'What were you discussing with Papa?' Her tone was cold, the playfulness eaten up by disappointment.

'He'll tell you, I'm sure ...'

She sat up straighter and brushed a strand of hair away from her face. 'What is it?'

He looked over his shoulder as if someone might be listening. 'Alonso is in Granada.'

She raised her brows.

'Yes, for quite some time apparently. He's convinced Cisneros that there's some validity to his accusation that your Papa murdered Torquemada.'

'Curse Alonso.' She shook her head. 'Will he never stop causing trouble to this family?'

'Your Papa's summoned by Her Majesty on the morrow.' He ran a hand through his hair and exhaled slowly before speaking again. 'I've told your father I will do what I can to support him.' He grasped her hand for a moment.

Too briefly, she thought. 'What's the worst that can happen?'

He looked away from her.

Isabel didn't press, it had been a foolish question. Few survived a royal questioning. 'I'd better go and speak with him.' She stood up. 'We've been through an interrogation by Their Majesties before and lived to tell the tale.'

Alejandro stood up and took her hands in his. 'Yes, you did. I'm sure your father will remain stoic and dignified. No matter what Alonso throws at him.' He leant forward and brushed his lips against her cheek. She leant into his lips, hoping he would embrace her and kiss her properly. But he moved away, squeezed her hands, gave a small bow and was gone.

CHAPTER
SIXTEEN

ISAAC OPENED HIS EYES THE NEXT MORNING sensing he'd been disturbed by something. It was still dark, so it wasn't the daylight that had jarred him awake. Pushing himself up on his elbows he peered into the blackness. Nothing, nobody materialised. Then the insistent tapping at his door broke through into his consciousness. He lay back down, determined to ignore whoever it was. It couldn't be Isabel. They had talked into the early hours about how to handle the queen and Alonso. He was concerned by the information she'd shared with him. It clearly troubled her conscience to reveal it. But it might make the difference between his life and his death. If he had to, he would use it.

Tap, tap, tap.

She'd agreed to accompany him to the Alhambra. His Majesty had a soft spot for Isabel. And after Catalina's visit to the Apothecary last night they might have another royal ally. She was Queen Isabella's favourite child after all.

Tap, tap, tap.

'Go away,' he hissed.

Tap, tap, tap.

Isaac threw the bedcovers aside and stomped to the door. Whoever was on the other side of it would regret intruding on him at such an ungodly hour. He didn't care that he was only wearing a nightshirt. He pulled back the bolts, threw the door open and made to reprimand the untimely visitor. Then he saw who it was. His mouth remained open, in complete surprise. Then he became embarrassed. To hide his undress he closed the door halfway, peering from behind it.

'I know how this looks, but I must speak to you in private,' Aisha whispered from behind her lacy veil.

For a long moment he didn't know what to do. Or how he felt: shock, delight, anticipation, or dread? Eventually he gathered himself and held up a forefinger, indicating she should wait. He closed the door, threw on trousers, and covered his nightshirt with a cloak. It would have to do. If Aisha was seen standing outside his apartment it would be almost as unseemly as her entering it. He quickly lit three candles and placed them on the low table in front of the chair. If it was important enough to come so early she wouldn't easily be got rid of. Not that he wanted her to go.

He let her in, gave a small bow and gestured towards the solitary chair. She wore the same green, silk gown cinched about the waist, that he had seen in the vision of her on the balcony. What was the appropriate thing for him to do? Was it worse manners to stand, or to sit on the bed? He involuntarily emitted a quiet chuckle.

Aisha drew back her black lace mantilla to reveal her brunette hair and said, 'What do you find amusing?' Her voice was quiet and husky.

He shook his head. 'I was wondering whether it would offend you more if I remained standing or sat on the bed.'

'As you like, Isaac. In the circumstances, it hardly matters.' The candlelight glinted against the flecks of yellow and green in her irises. She sat back and laced her fingers over her stomach.

He settled himself on the bed, the straw mattress crunching under his weight. Even in his dreams he'd never imagined she would be in his chamber. He'd had visions of them being together. Mainly it was innocent – walking through the patios of the Alhambra discussing the art and history of the *Mudéjar*. Once or twice his imagination had led him to dream of acts that he found both delightful and, on awaking, shockingly traitorous to the memory of Maria. He was ashamed of himself.

'Tell me,' he said, suddenly businesslike. In a few hours he would be fighting for his life. This conversation needed to be over quickly, for all sorts of reasons.

'If it wasn't vital I wouldn't be here. Anything else I would confide in Ali, but I'm afraid of what he might say.'

He didn't know what to say, so remained silent.

'I've been up most of the night with my husband.' She compressed her full lips into a tight line. 'He's alternated between praying and weeping,' she said in a low voice. Isaac leant closer.

'He wants vengeance.' She looked at him through tightened eyes. 'You know that feeling.'

'Is he still angry with me?'

'Less so. I think he regrets insulting you.'

'That's not important now.'

'He intends to assassinate Cisneros.' Her voice was softened with shock. 'Today.'

He closed his eyes. This was almost too much to bear. Then it occurred to him that the cardinal's death could solve his problems as well. It very well might but it would signal the end of the *Mudéjar* in Granada. Their Majesties response would be savage. They would slaughter every single one of them, including Aisha.

'Has he considered what that will mean for you? You're already vulnerable.'

'He wants me to leave Granada immediately.'

His stomach lurched.

The *muezzin's* call signalled the dawn prayers, and a soft light filtered through the shutters, playing across Aisha's lustrous hair.

'Where would you go?' he said curtly.

Aisha gave him a puzzled look. He realised she had misinterpreted his tone, he had sounded harsh to reprimand himself, not her. 'To Fez. To be with my mother and my children.' She unlaced her fingers and covered her face with her palms. 'I thought they could return here.' A wave of sadness rippled over her face as she dropped her hands. I don't want to leave. There are many people I care about here.' As she smiled at him her eyes widened and the candlelight danced across them.

He felt himself falling, wanting her. He forced himself to focus on the problem. 'What do you think I can do that you and Ali cannot?'

Before she could answer there was a single knock at the door. They exchanged furtive glances. He looked for a hiding place. Could she get under the bed? Ridiculous. A louder rap. If it was her husband it wouldn't matter what Isaac said to appease him, he would still kill him. His rage at Cisneros already had him at boiling point. And he couldn't defend himself against Abdul Rahman and his men. Aisha stood and arranged her mantilla to cover her face. Three crisp raps and a low call of, 'Isaac, open up. Now.'

He opened the door a crack and looked out into the rapidly receding gloom. Ali pushed at the door, hurriedly entered, and closed it behind him. He looked at each of them in turn, his face a curious mixture of disdain and empathy.

'I can explain,' Aisha said, as she drew back her mantilla.

Ali held up a palm. 'No need. I'm sure the only reason you've come here in the dead of night is to seek Isaac's advice whilst my brother remains asleep.' He glared at them.

Isaac wasn't sure if it was sarcasm he heard in Ali's voice. Was he about to accuse them? Then he would have both brothers against him, and he would have lost his oldest friend.

Ali continued, 'Lucky him. He kept me up most of the night with his wailing and shouting. I could hear almost every word he said.'

Isaac raised his brows, taken aback by the lack of sympathy in Ali's tone.

'No need to look surprised, my friend. My brother has always tended to the histrionic.' He looked hard at Aisha. 'I don't blame you for seeking advice from Isaac. Foolishly inappropriate time and place, but in the circumstances ...' He gestured for them to sit, and he took his place next to Isaac on the bed. Aisha sat back down with a long sigh. '... although I would have preferred you had come to me.'

Aisha began to explain but Ali cut her off, 'I know you think I share my brother's view, and I do. The word of Allah, the legacy of our historians and scientists has been destroyed. It's an unspeakable tragedy. I just don't share his idea of the solution. Assassinate the cardinal!' He shook his head. 'Idiot,' he said with vehemence, 'It would be the end for all of us.'

Isaac poured two mugs of water and gave them each one.

Ali gulped his down. 'Apologies, sister, for my intemperate language.'

Aisha smiled. 'He's your brother as well as my husband. You have the right.'

Ali grunted. 'So what have you two cooked up between you?'

'We didn't get that far,' Isaac replied. 'Whatever we decide,' he looked at each of them, 'needs to be done quickly, before he wakes up.'

Ali said, 'There's little immediate danger of that, you can almost hear his snoring from here.'

Aisha smiled.

Isaac decided against revealing that he had his own life to defend in just a few hours. There would be time enough later.

Or so he hoped.

'Fortunately, I have a solution.' Ali paused. He reached into the inside pocket of his cloak and withdrew a small leather pouch tied securely with string. It was the kind of bag Isaac had seen him use for remedies to give to customers.

Aisha put her hand to her mouth.

Isaac said, 'You're not serious?'

Ali snorted. 'I'm not intending to kill him, we just need to knock him out.' He reached inside the pouch and showed them the small glass vial of white powder. 'Temporarily of course. Put him in a deep sleep where he can do no harm. We'll do as much as we can to deal with the crisis before he wakes up. It will keep us all safe, at least for a while.'

Aisha looked at Isaac uncertainly. She hesitated for a moment. 'This is an extreme measure, Ali,' she said. 'Are you certain there aren't any other ways? This could be dangerous for him if things go wrong.'

Isaac kept quiet, watching as Ali thought over Aisha's words before responding with a solemn bow of his head.

'I understand," Ali said slowly, 'but I'm confident this is our best hope. I've used this same draught myself. I'm still very much alive.' He glanced between them before continuing, 'It will give us time to come up with another solution and prevent my brother from doing irreparable damage.' He held each of their eyes in turn, 'To the family, to Granada, to himself.'

Aisha sighed heavily and exchanged a long look with Isaac before nodding her agreement. 'I will help you administer the draught,' she said to Ali, as she drew the mantilla over her face.

As she made to leave she touched Isaac briefly at the elbow and dipped her head. He wondered whether, depending on how things went later that morning, he would ever see her again. She gave him a puzzled look. His anguish must have made its way onto his face.

'I have some urgent business to attend to at the Alhambra,' Isaac said, aware of the weakness in his voice.

Ali narrowed his eyes at him questioningly.

'I'm just tired Ali. That's all.'

After they'd gone he turned his mind to the next ordeal. Whilst they had been debating what to do about Abdul Rahman the bells for the Prime service had rung. Isabel would soon arrive to accompany him to the red citadel.

CHAPTER
SEVENTEEN

THAT THEIR MAJESTIES would keep Isaac and Isabel waiting was to be expected. A courtier showed them to the patio adjoining the Hall of Kings. He gave no indication as to how long they would wait or any apology for the delay. Isaac knew they were being put in their place. Isabel squeezed his hand as they stood at the end of a long rectangular pool. He took a deep lungful of *azahar*, the orange and lemon blossom that perfumed the citadel. Would this be the last time he would smell it? Isabel must have noticed the worry etched on his face as she leaned in to whisper, 'We'll get through this together.'

Isaac smiled, grateful for her comforting presence. Hopefully, the information she'd given him last night would be enough to save him. He tried to calm himself by focussing on the beauty of the geometric tiles and the soothing sound of the fountain. But he couldn't distract himself from the dark thoughts which threatened to overwhelm him. Footsteps approached and he turned to see a man in royal robes with a serious expression.

'Isaac Camarino Alvarez,' he said in a commanding voice. 'Their Majesties will see you now.'

They followed him into the Hall of Kings where Isaac immediately sensed a tense atmosphere. It was at least a hundred paces long and lined by pillars of rich blue and vermillion tiles, topped by arches of intricate filigreed stucco work. They had to walk past the members of the royal court crammed in on each side of the hall. They stared and whispered at them as they made their way towards Their Majesties at the far end. Ferdinand and Isabella were seated in their thrones on a dais, with Cardinal Cisneros standing on their right and Friar Alonso to their left. Isaac scanned the room for Alejandro. He'd promised to be here, but Isaac couldn't see him.

He looked up at a painting on the ceiling that appeared to have been recently restored. It was of a *Mudéjar* soldier killing a rival with a spear before the beseeching gesture of a lady watching the tournament from a tower. Her expression looked ambiguous: was she indicating mercy or death?

Eventually they stood before Their Majesties. Isaac bowed deeply and Isabel curtsied. Queen Isabella was dressed entirely in black. Gone were the wealth of vibrant colours she wore in Seville. He felt a twinge of sadness recalling she was in mourning for the death of her two children and a grandchild in the past three years. It must be difficult to maintain a public air of regal calm whilst coping with such private grief. She looked down at Isaac with stony, brown eyes and said, 'We've been here before.' Her voice was imperious.

'Yes, Your Majesty,' Isaac said.

'This must be the third occasion you've come before us to defend yourself against very serious accusations.' She arched an expectant eyebrow.

Isaac lowered his head in acknowledgement.

'Heresy. Betrayal. And now murder.' She smiled. 'How are you still alive?' Her voice dripped with scorn. There was a ripple of laughter from the court. She glanced across at her husband.

Isaac, head still bowed, raised his eyes to the king. His expression was stoic and unreadable. Isaac glanced at Cisneros, his bony face lit up by a glint from his deep brown eyes. He looked pleased with himself. He had gathered confidence from the book burnings. That he was standing alongside Their Majesties demonstrated Isabella's strength over Ferdinand's fury at the cardinal's actions. She was more of a religious zealot than her husband and Isaac knew she would approve of the incineration of the *Mudéjar* holy books. Alonso stood with his hands clasped over his stomach, his gimlet eyes giving nothing away. He was more stooped than when Isaac had last seen him, he seemed much older.

'Well?' demanded the queen.

Isaac looked directly at her and said, 'At Your Majesty's pleasure.'

The queen snorted. She turned her attention to Isabel. 'I thought better of you, my dear.'

'Your Majesty?' Isabel replied.

'Defending your dear Papa yet again. Do you really believe there can be continuous smoke without fire?' The queen glared.

Before she could answer Isabella pointed at a courtier who led Isabel away to sit in a chair to the right of the dais. Isaac gave her a weak smile which she returned. They both knew she had no choice but to be silent.

The king leant across to his wife and muttered something that Isaac could not hear.

'Very well,' Isabella said. 'Let us begin.'

Isaac tried to keep his composure as the questioning began, a wrong word could cost him his life. The queen's questions came first, sharp and probing, forcing him to defend himself at every turn.

'You stand here accused of murdering Tomás de Torquemada, my confessor and the Grand Inquisitor of All Spain.' She paused. 'Do you deny it?'

'I do, Your Majesty, in the strongest possible terms.'

'Liar,' shouted a man from behind him.

'Silence!' shouted Ferdinand, 'or I'll have the hall cleared.'

A hush descended. Isaac stood tall, head held high, eyes locked on Alonso. The accusation was grave, but he knew the truth and he would defend himself to the death if necessary. He had nothing to lose. His anger grew. He'd been accused of crimes he had not committed, and all the while the true wrongdoers went unpunished. One of whom was standing before him. Alonso had committed heinous acts in the name of religion. He was tired of this game, sick of being at the mercy of these ruthless monarchs and their cronies.

'Your Majesty,' Isaac said trying to keep his voice steady, 'I have endured many accusations and trials, and I have always defended myself with honor and dignity. But this is far more serious. Today, I stand accused of murder. I ask you, Your Majesty, to do me the honor of hearing me out fully.'

The room fell silent, and even the king leaned forward, apparently intrigued.

Isaac took a deep breath, gathering his thoughts. 'Friar Alonso, I am innocent of this vile accusation. I may not have agreed with the Grand Inquisitor's methods, but I would never resort to murder.'

Alonso sneered. 'You dare to speak against the Grand Inquisitor's methods? You are a heretic, Isaac. And a liar,' he spat.

The king said, 'We are not here to put on trial the methods of the Inquisition. We're gathered to listen to the evidence that Isaac Camarino Alvarez murdered Tomás de Torquemada.' He turned to the queen, who nodded. 'Let us confine ourselves to that. Alonso, make your case and make it concisely. Then, Isaac, you will have an opportunity for a rebuttal.'

Alonso descended the steps from the dais, nearly stumbling on the final one. He stood before Their Majesties, hands clasped behind his back. 'It is no secret,' he began in a solemn tone that sounded insincere to Isaac, 'that Señor Alvarez is a heretic.' This was accompanied by murmurs of assent from the onlookers. 'A Jew pretending to be a Christian.' Alonso looked satisfied as the court erupted into chaos, nobles and courtiers all talking at once. The king silenced them with a wave of his hand.

Once they were quiet Alonso said, 'That he has been spared

the pyre is a great testament to Their Majesties' mercy.' He looked directly at the king, making it clear he understood the queen would not have been so generous.

That's brave, thought Isaac. He must be very sure of the strength of his relationship with Cisneros, and of the cardinal's with Her Majesty.

Alonso continued, 'Your Majesties, members of the court, we stand here to bring justice to a heinous crime committed against the church and the people of Spain.' The friar's voice grew louder with every word.

Isaac took a deep breath, steeling himself for what was to come.

'Tomás de Torquemada was a great man,' Alonso said, 'a martyr, who fought tirelessly to rid our country of heresy and ensure our people have a place in Heaven. And yet, his life was snuffed out by the very man who stands before us today.'

Isaac listened intently, his mind racing. None of this was true, but he knew it would be difficult to prove his innocence. Who had set him up? And why?

'He had a motive,' Alonso said, 'as he was always at odds with the Grand Inquisitor. And let's not forget his long history of heresy and betrayal.' He finished with a self-satisfied smirk.

Isaac stepped forward, his voice calm and measured. 'Your Majesties, I know this appears damning. However, it's all conjecture.' He turned towards Alonso and asked, 'What is your actual evidence, friar?

Alonso grinned, clearly relishing the moment. 'Evidence?' he scoffed. 'Surely, you know as well as I do, Señor Alvarez, that in matters of faith, evidence is not always necessary.' The onlookers murmured their agreement.

Isaac's eyes narrowed. This was not looking good. But he refused to give up hope. 'I ask again, what evidence do you have that I murdered Tomás de Torquemada?'

Alonso looked taken aback by his directness, but quickly regained his composure. 'We have eyewitness accounts, who saw you leaving the Grand Inquisitor's chambers in the convent of Avila on the early morning of September 16th, 1498, the day of his death.'

Another ripple of shock coursed through the court.

'And who are these eyewitnesses?'

'We cannot reveal their identities for their own safety,' Alonso replied smoothly.

'And yet you expect me to accept their testimony without question?' Isaac said, his voice tinged with sarcasm.

'Their credibility has been verified,' Alonso replied.

'By whom?' Isaac pressed.

'By me,' Cisneros answered, speaking for the first time. Tight-lipped and sanctimonious.

The queen smiled at the cardinal. His assurances were clearly good enough for her.

Alonso continued, 'The fact remains that you had both motive and opportunity to carry out this wicked crime.'

Isaac shook his head. 'That is simply not true. I may have disagreed with the Grand Inquisitor, but I would never resort to murder. And as for opportunity, I was nowhere near his chambers on the night in question.'

'How can you prove that?' the queen asked, her skeptical tone matching her expression.

Isaac paused, considering his options. He knew it would be difficult to prove his innocence without concrete evidence, but he had one last card to play.

'I will answer that Your Majesty. If I may I would like to ask Friar Alonso something about his motives.'

The queen scowled but dipped her head in assent.

Isaac turned to face Alonso. He had only one chance to get this right. One chance to use the information Isabel had reluctantly shared with him to save his life. He looked over Alonso's shoulder at his daughter and held her gaze for a long moment. Seeking permission. Isabel glanced away and when she looked back she dipped her head in assent. Time to attack.

CHAPTER
EIGHTEEN

'ISN'T IT A FACT THAT YOU CONCOCTED THIS ACCUSATION based on rumour in order to save your best friend's life?' Isaac said.

A wave of astonishment rippled through the court.

Alonso took a step towards Issac. 'How dare you!' he shouted.

Isaac spoke rapidly, 'Brother Andreas, your childhood friend from the Monasterio de San Reyes, is accused of the murder and held in the Torre del Oro in Seville. Am I correct?'

Alonso clenched his fists and his jaw. 'What of it?'

'Isn't it also true that Brother Andreas was sent away from the monastery after Father Bartolome accused you both of inappropriate behaviour?'

There was uproar in the court. Isaac raised his voice. 'And Bartolome is Prior at the convent in Avila that Torquemada built for his retirement?'

Alonso stared at Isabel for a long moment.

Isaac couldn't see his expression, but he saw its effect on her.

Isabel was stricken. She had broken both Alonso and Andreas' confidences.

Alonso turned back to Issac, crossed himself and said, 'May the Lord forgive you.' He turned to the queen. 'Your Majesty, what Señor Alvarez says is true.' There were murmurs of surprise from the crowd. 'I love Brother Andreas, and he loves me,' he said in almost a whisper.

'Shame,' someone called out.

'We sinned. We were guilty, and I *am* ashamed of what we did.'

There was silence in the hall.

'We shared a deep bond, based on our families' histories. We both grew up not knowing our fathers. Out of youthful stupidity, we were disrespectful to Father Bartolome. We made fun of him, repeatedly. He reported it to the Prior, who sent Andreas away. I thought I would never see him again.' He turned to face the crowd. 'Our love was pure, fraternal and platonic.'

There was some laughter and jeering from a few in the court.

Alonso bowed his head.

It was a powerful performance, Isaac thought – it seemed sincere. Before he could question Alonso further Cisneros spoke.

'Your Majesties, I would like a witness to address you.' He beckoned to the back of the hall with a bony index finger.

Isaac turned to see who the cardinal was gesturing to. An old man in a plain brown robe, was making his way down the length of the hall. He moved slowly with the aid of a cane, but with purpose. He stood before the dais and said, 'I am Brother Bartolome.' There was a gasp from the crowd. Isaac felt a surge of hope as the old monk approached. Was this his chance for salvation? But then he realised Cisneros must have arranged this. Alonso was even cleverer than he had given him credit for. They had foreseen what Isaac might say.

'Brother,' the Cardinal said softly, 'thank you for coming all this way. Tell us what you need to say.'

Bartolome rested both hands on his cane. Isaac saw it twitching as his hands trembled.

'I was the Master at the Monasterio de San Reyes when the incident involving Friar Alonso and Brother Andreas occurred,' the old priest began calmly.

'Yes, we are aware,' Queen Isabella said. 'And we hear you do a fine job taking care of our beloved confessor's legacy at the convent in Avila. But what does that have to do with –'

'Everything, Your Majesty,' Bartolome interrupted. 'Because,' he looked down, 'it is a lie.'

The room fell silent as Bartolome took a deep breath. 'I deeply regret what I did back then,' he said, his voice choked with emotion. 'I allowed my anger at Alonso and Andreas' disrespect to cloud my judgment.' He swallowed. 'I accused two innocent young men of a crime they did not commit. It was my mistake, and I have carried that guilt with me for years.'

There were murmurs of surprise as Alonso glared at the monk in fury. Isaac wondered why he was angry. Surely Alonso knew this was going to happen? It must all be part of the act.

Bartolome made the sign of the cross, fell awkwardly to his knees and chanted, 'Mea culpa.'

A memory flashed through Isaac's mind of witnessing Alonso doing the same thing in front of Their Majesties four years ago in Seville. Had that been an act too?

Alonso helped Bartolome to his feet, held his hands and said, 'I forgive you.'

The old monk appeared to be crying as a courtier led him away. The hall erupted into chaos.

What a performance, and how convenient, Isaac thought.

The king thundered, 'Silence!' Order was immediately restored.

Isaac said, 'I don't see how this makes the slightest difference.'

Ferdinand nodded, apparently in agreement.

Isaac said, 'If anything Friar Alonso has just admitted how strong his desire is to see his *friend* found innocent by accusing me.' He glanced across at Isabel and saw her wince. Part of him instantly regretted the implied slur in the way he had sneered 'friend.' But he was fighting for his life, and if it meant impugning the integrity of an evil man like Alonso, so be it.

'I tend to agree with Señor Alvarez,' the queen said.

Isaac looked at her with astonishment. What was she playing at?

'It makes no difference what the nature of Alonso and this other monk's relationship was. If there was anything sinful,' she looked down at Alonso, 'then they'll burn in hell.

However, I find Father Bartolome's evidence that it was a purely platonic relationship convincing. And his contrition very moving,' her voice breaking on the last word. 'We have a credible, attested witness that can put Isaac Alvarez at my dear departed confessor's chambers on the night of his death. If there's nothing else, I'll move to judgement.'

Isaac gave the king a pleading look, but Ferdinand ignored him. He'd saved him twice before, there clearly wasn't to be a third occasion.

Isaac's mind raced. Isabella's twisted logic was impenetrable. He had no answer. She was going to sentence him to death there and then. He looked wildly around for an escape. If he ran the members of the court would stop him, even if the guards didn't. He could confess and throw himself on Their Majesties' mercy, but all that would earn him would be a less torturous death.

'Wait!' a voice called out from the right of the dais. 'Your Majesties, I beg your indulgence.' The crowd shifted aside to allow someone to shoulder their way through. As Alejandro emerged he paused briefly to clasp Isabel's shoulder. He stood before the monarchs, next to Isaac, and bowed deeply.

The king looked back and forth from Isaac to Alejandro with a sardonic grin.

Alonso ascended the stairs of the dais to return to his place beside the queen.

Cisneros scowled.

'I did not give you leave to address us. Guards,' Isabella said. Two red-cloaked soldiers advanced on Alejandro.

Isaac wondered what his former deputy was playing at. It was too late for a character witness to have any effect on the queen's decision.

'Please, Your Majesty,' Alejandro said, lowering his head, 'allow me just a few moments.'

Isabella glanced across at her husband who raised his eyes heavenward, puffed out his cheeks and shrugged his shoulders.

The queen raised a palm to halt the guards. 'Proceed. Rapidly.'

I was with Señor Alvarez, all night on the 15th of September 1498, and the following day,'

The crowd murmured.

'He could not have committed the murder of Tomás de Torquemada.'

Isabella studied Alejandro closely through tightened eyes.

He did not flinch or look away.

She said in a deliberate, steely tone, 'Why did you not come forward sooner?'

I'd very much like to know that too, Isaac thought.

'Because I was embarrassed of where we were and,' Alejandro broke eye contact with the queen, gave Isabel a sidelong glance and then looked down at the floor, 'what we were doing.' He paused. 'I'd hoped it wouldn't be necessary to reveal it. I didn't want to bring shame to Señor Alvarez and his daughter.' He dipped his head towards Isabel who scowled at him.

The king leant forward, a knowing grin on his face.

Isaac was dumbfounded.

There was silence in the hall as everyone waited for Alejandro's next words. Isaac had no idea of what he was about to say, but felt a glimmer of hope.

Alejandro puffed out his cheeks and continued, 'We were in a brothel, Your Majesty.'

The court erupted into scandalised whispers, and the queen's face contorted in revulsion. Alonso and Cisneros exchanged looks of disgust. Isaac glanced over at Isabel who had covered her face with her hands.

'I didn't want to admit to being there, but I see it is the only way to prove Señor Alvarez's innocence. He was with me all night long.'

Cisneros said, 'And how do you remember the exact date so clearly?'

Isaac turned to look at Alejandro. Had he prepared an answer to this?

Alejandro bit his bottom lip and rubbed his palms together. 'Because, Your Majesty,' he paused, 'we were in Salamanca when –'

'That's three days ride from here,' Isabella interrupted, sounding scornful.

'Yes, Your Majesty, we were at a reunion of university friends, we are both law graduates of Salamanca. We were still there on the night of the 16th when the sad news of the Grand Inquisitor's death reached us.' He paused. 'That's why I remember it so well.'

Isabel flashed Alejandro an angry look.

The sound of a slow handclap cut through the silence. It was Cisneros. 'Well played, Señor, well played. Salamanca is far enough away for it to be difficult for us to find witnesses but near enough to Avila to make your story plausible.'

The king studied Cisneros. Isaac knew Ferdinand was weighing his options. Up to this point the queen had been in full control of Isaac's fate. But now his senior adviser had provided evidence that could tip the scales in his favour. Isaac felt his shoulders tighten. There was doubt on the king's face, and he knew that this could go either way. He held his breath as Ferdinand deliberated his decision. Would he side with his wife or choose to believe his senior advisor and the man who could provide him with inside information on the *Mudéjar* rebellion?

CHAPTER
NINETEEN

'WHEN THE KING SAID THAT YOUR,' Isabel said glancing at Alejandro, 'testimony provided reasonable doubt as to your,' she looked at her father, 'guilt I couldn't believe it. And when he released you I've never felt such a sense of relief.'

It was an hour after the court had declared Isaac free. Cisneros had insisted that this be conditional on the result of further investigations. The queen supported his demand, and the king had no choice but to agree. Alonso had also gotten what he wanted. The queen declared herself so moved by Bartolome's contrition and Alonso's forgiveness that she decreed it was only fair to free Andreas. Nobody dared challenge the garbled logic of this. Isaac assumed the king would be relieved his wife had found a way to exert her power.

They had returned to Isaac's apartment, having decided it was too dangerous to discuss the matter anywhere else. The Inquisition's spies were everywhere. Isaac was propped up on the bed, exhausted. Isabel sat next to him dabbing his brow with a washcloth. Alejandro stood with his back to the door.

'And the pair of you,' Isabel said, 'should be utterly ashamed of yourselves.'

Alejandro exchanged a glance with each of them and burst out laughing. Isaac and Isabel immediately joined in.

'The very idea of you in a brothel, Papa,' Isabel said once she'd controlled herself.

He gave her a stern look and raised an eyebrow.

She held his gaze and raised a brow in return.

They smiled.

'It was a brilliant story though,' she said.

Alejandro bowed with a flourish of his arm.

Isaac said, 'As Cisneros and Ferdinand both suspected.'

'It suited His Majesty to believe it,' Alejandro said. 'He doesn't want you dead, Isaac. If nothing else, he's amused by your escapades.'

Isaac gave him a mock, deadpan scowl.

'If he'd called me a liar in public he would have had to declare me a traitor and execute me as well.' Alejandro's face tightened and his tone became more serious. 'There are still dark days ahead of us. The rebels must respond to the burnings and Cisneros won't stop, especially when he has the queen on his side. His Majesty needs the support of every loyal man in the Kingdom. And whatever else he might say about you, Isaac, he knows he has your loyalty.'

'But at least someone's happy,' Isabel said.

'Who?' Isaac and Alejandro chorused.

'Alonso. Andreas has been released.'

Isaac shook his head in disgust.

'We should be happy for them, Papa. They share a genuine love.'

'Love?' Alejandro asked sardonically.

'It is possible for two men to love each other chastely,' Isabel said, smiling at each of them. They did not look at each other.

'Anyway ... ,' Isaac said, 'I have to tell you both something,' They regarded him intently.

'About Torquemada's death.' He inhaled deeply and let his words tumble out as he exhaled, 'I was at the convent on September 16th, the night Torquemada died. In his bedchamber.'

Isabel stopped dabbing his brow with the washcloth and screwed up her face in anguish.

Alejandro stood at the end of the bed and stared darkly down at Isaac. 'Explain,' he demanded.

Isaac sat up on the edge of the bed and held Isabel's hand. He looked into her eyes and said, 'What I'm about to say is the truth. I swear it on your mother's life.' He purposefully didn't say it was the whole truth.

'Go on,' she replied.

Isaac glanced up at Alejandro, 'I can never repay you for the risk you took for me. But you deserve to know what really happened.' He held Isabel's eyes, 'You both do.'

He was interrupted by three loud, rhythmic thumps on the door. His first thought was that Cisneros had "discovered" some new evidence and had sent his men to arrest him.

'Isaac Alvarez,' came a deep voice, 'open up.'

Alejandro's hand went to the hilt of his sword and he motioned Isabel to get behind him. Isaac opened the door to reveal a bear of a man filling the doorway.

'With your permission,' Abdul Rahman said with a dip of his head. He had to adjust his body slightly sideways to enter the room. He took a step towards Isaac.

Alejandro shifted the rapier a notch out of its scabbard. Isaac wasn't sure what was happening. Had Abdul Rahman come here to hurt him?

'Tell your friend to stand down, Isaac, I mean no harm,' the spice merchant said. 'At least not to anyone in this room,' he said laughing loudly. But Isaac thought he registered a hollowness.

Alejandro held up his palms. Isabel came out from behind him and took one of Abdul Rahman's paws in both her hands and said, 'I'm so sorry.'

'Thank you, my dear,' he said and embraced her. 'Council of war my friends, council of war,' the spice merchant roared, beckoning them to follow him out of the apartment.

Abdul Rahman took up his customary position at the head of the long dining table under the balcony. Ali sat to his right, Khaled to his left. Abdul Rahman gestured for Isaac to sit next to Khaled. *So, I've been demoted*, Isaac thought. He considered it a small price to pay in the circumstances. Isabel sat opposite him, with Aisha next to her. Alejandro loitered at the other end of the table, seemingly uncertain of his position. Abdul

Rahman did not invite him to sit.

'Señor Alejandro,' the spice merchant said, 'I'm in two minds about you.'

Isaac opened his mouth to reply but Abdul Rahman silenced him with a dark stare.

Alejandro replied, 'I understand you might not be confident of where my loyalties lie. But I have the ear of the king and I can assure you he was almost as outraged as you by Cisneros' actions.'

Abdul Rahman banged his fist on the table, 'I doubt that, and not for the same reasons.'

'No,' Alejandro replied confidently, 'not for the same reasons. He wants peace in the Kingdom because war is costly. It suits him for the *Mudéjar* to be prosperous so that you continue to pay taxes.'

Abdul Rahman gave a derisive grunt.

'You'll recall that after the fall of Granada the *Mudéjar* were treated far more favourably than the Jews.' He gave Isaac a meaningful look. 'If you permit me to stay I will give you the best advice I can. You may think I'm conflicted, but your interests are more closely aligned with the king's than you fully appreciate. The real danger is that the Kingdom wastes its newfound prosperity on war with its own people.'

Isaac and Ali exchanged glances, nodding their agreement.

Abdul Rahman narrowed his eyes at Alejandro. 'If you betray me I will cut out your entrails, roast them and eat them.'

There was a long moment of shocked silence. Then Abdul Rahman roared with laughter and gestured for Alejandro to take his place next to Isaac.

Aisha said, 'You must forgive my husband, he has a peculiar sense of humour.'

Abdul Rahman ignored her and said, 'Around this table are the people I love and trust most.' He stared at Alejandro. 'I have to thank my brother,' he held Ali's hand, 'for having the wisdom to ensure I had the rest I needed to moderate my rage.'

Isaac sensed that the spice merchant's anger had shifted from explosive to something altogether more menacing. Its intensity was frightening.

'But now,' Abdul Rahman paused, 'is the time for action. We cannot allow this outrage to stand. Our religion, our culture, our heritage has been irreparably harmed.'

There were murmurs of agreement from around the table.

'What do you suggest, brother?' Ali asked.

'War.' He looked at each of them. 'I will bring all our brothers in from the mountains. We will blockade the city until they hand Cisneros over. We will do to him what he did to the words of Allah.' He paused. 'An eye for an eye, a tooth for a tooth.'

Isaac decided that if this was Abdul Rahman's considered suggestion when he was calm there was no point in arguing against it directly. Instead he asked, 'Do you command enough men to sustain the blockade?'

'Of course, and more will rally to our cause from Africa.'

'Ferdinand will respond by bringing in soldiers from across Spain,' Isaac said. 'Then he will ask the English king to support him. They don't need an excuse to start another religious crusade against the "Moors."' He turned towards Alejandro who nodded his agreement. 'The Infanta is promised to Henry, the Kingdoms are already becoming united.'

Ali said, 'This makes much sense, brother. It is wise counsel.'

Abdul Rahman growled and shook his head. 'Khaled, what do you say?'

The trusted retainer held his master's eyes and tightened his lips. It was confirmation enough.

'If,' Abdul Rahman emphasised the word, 'if I decide not to fight what is the alternative?' His tone was sarcastic.

Alejandro said, 'If I may?'

Abdul Rahman gestured to him with an open palm, 'Most welcome.'

'What you really want is revenge on Cisneros?' Alejandro began. Receiving no denial he went on, 'Then ask for his removal and the restoration of Bishop Talavera.'

Clever, Isaac thought. Ferdinand would get rid of Cisneros and without having to spend a ducat.

Alejandro continued, 'I will inform His Majesty that you have graciously offered this as a conciliatory gesture in order to maintain the peace. I will lend it my strongest support.'

Abdul Rahman ran his fingers through his beard. 'And what about the queen? Cisneros is her creature,' he said.

'I'll admit that Her Majesty's view is a concern. But even she can be persuaded to take a realistic view.'

'My love?' Abdul Rahman said to Aisha.

'It is worth trying,' she replied quietly.

Isaac wondered why her tone was so tentative. She had been against the assassination of Cisneros. Surely this was a compromise she should endorse. Was she scared of her husband? Isaac said, 'It will allow you to prepare your troops whilst you await an answer. You will be seen as conciliatory. And if His Majesty says no, then you can bring your men down from the mountains. It costs you nothing to make the offer.'

Parrots squawked in the palm trees and Abdul Rahman looked up at them. The chatter of the Albacîn residents going about their daily business outside the compound drifted across the table.

'What do they want?' He pointed a finger at the gate that opened on to the street.

'Many of them want the same as you, revenge, violence and death,' Ali said. 'But that doesn't mean it's the right thing to do, brother. You are an important leader of our community. That gives you the responsibility of making a carefully considered decision, not an easy one.' He clasped his brother's shoulder and smiled.

'Your words are wise, Isaac,' Abdul Rahman said. 'Alejandro, make the offer. I will stay my hand for one day. Now I must pray.' He left the table and Khaled, Ali and Aisha followed. She smiled at Isaac before she left. He felt his heart warm.

Isaac said, 'I'm going to speak to Talavera, to see what else he knows.'

'Before you do,' Alejandro said, 'we need to finish our conversation.' He looked at Isabel. 'It's best I have all the information before I go to speak with His Majesty. He's no fool.'

CHAPTER
TWENTY

ISAAC BOLTED THE DOOR to his apartment saying, 'We won't be disturbed this time.'

Isabel sat in the chair with her arms crossed, Alejandro remained standing.

Isaac poured himself a mug of water and took a long draught. 'You both deserve to know the truth.' He recounted the story of the night he'd visited Torquemada in Avila.

Isabel listened with her face twisted in agony, while Alejandro stood in silence, his expression unreadable.

It was still so vivid in Isaac's mind. It had been the dead of night. He'd kept watch on the convent from the seclusion of the forest and was surprised how easy it had been to gain access to it. He remembered wondering why there were no royal bodyguards – had Torquemada lost the queen's favour? Or did he consider he had all the protection he needed from The Almighty? He recalled the moments of doubt about his intentions. He could still feel the odd scent in his nostrils of incense mixed with rotting flowers as he entered the bedchamber. Still see the decanter of sherry on the side table and the memory it had evoked of the time he'd shared a glass with the Grand Inquisitor. When he was trying to save Maria.

'He was asleep when I entered. Snoring like an animal. He'd gotten fat.' Isaac saw the crackling fire throwing shadows over Torquemada's face. 'He looked awful, his face reflected what he truly was, hideous.' He shook his head. 'I was determined to kill him, but I hesitated, considering the best way to do it –'

'Oh, Papa,' Isabel said, the anguish clear in her voice.

'He murdered your mother.' Isaac held her eyes for a long moment.

'Go on,' Alejandro said, breaking the spell.

'I'd just unsheathed my dagger when the old devil suddenly woke up and looked at me.' Isaac paused, lost in memory.

'And?' Isabel said sharply.

'He said to me, "you can do it, but it won't bring you the satisfaction you desire." Then he said, "Trust me, I know."' Isaac shook his head, still amazed that Torquemada could come up with such words in the circumstances.

'Then?' Isabel demanded.

'Then we talked.'

'About what?' Alejandro asked.

'That his physician had given him a very brief time to live. Something about gout poisoning his body. He tried to assure me that his main concern had always been to save the souls of his flock. That even though I was a heretic I could still avoid hell by recanting, but not if I killed him. He said how much he admired your mother and he talked of other things and –'

'What other things?' Isabel said.

Isaac hesitated before replying, 'I can't recall exactly. By the time he finished it was daylight, the convent was stirring, and I left.'

'You expect us to believe this?' Isabel said, her voice rising.

'I swear it on your mother's memory.'

'Why didn't you tell me before?'

'I was embarrassed. I thought it would be the last thing you needed to hear. I haven't been hiding the truth, I've been trying to spare you from it.'

'Why tell us now?' Isabel said.

'The weight is too great, I need to unburden myself. Both of you have risked so much for me, I couldn't bear to carry my deceit any longer.'

There was a long moment of stillness before Isabel spoke. 'Torquemada was clever, appealing to your piety and love for Mama in order to save his own life.'

'But he knew he was dying,' Isaac replied.

'So he claimed,' Alejandro said.

Isabel said, 'We'll never know the truth. He did sincerely believe that the torture and the burnings would save souls from damnation.' She paused. 'If he's right then you and Mama will be together again, in heaven.' She gave her father a weak smile.

Isaac didn't know how to respond. The logic was irrefutable, but it was a logic that justified the abomination of the Inquisition.

'What else did he say?' Isabel asked.

He hesitated. 'Nothing.' He held her eyes as she searched his face.

Alejandro broke the deep silence. 'You shouldn't have gone,' he said in a quiet voice. 'It was reckless.'

'I had to do something,' Isaac replied.

'Are you sure you weren't seen?' Alejandro asked.

'There were no guards in attendance. And I didn't come across any of the sisters on the way in or out. If I'd been seen someone would have come forward by now.'

'Probably true,' said Alejandro.

'I'm glad you told us,' Isabel replied softly. 'But what are we going to do now?'

Isabel threaded the large tortoiseshell *peineta* through the hair on the crown of her head, scraped it back and covered it with a red mantilla. Twisting her neck back and forth, she studied her reflection in the mirror. The arrangement made her look taller and emphasised her forehead pleasingly. She looked almost regal. She just needed to pluck out those hairs dotting her brows. Should she keep her hair loose or hold it in place with the *peineta?* It was a style that was even more fashionable in Granada than Seville. Which would Alejandro prefer? She was using this as a distraction from the shock of what Papa had just revealed.

After a brief word with Alejandro before he rushed off to put Abdul Rahman's proposal to the king she'd come up to her bedroom. To be alone, to think. Did she believe Papa?

Alejandro seemed to. But his loyalty to Papa had always been absolute. It was so reverent that it was almost as if Alejandro worshipped him. There was something about the story that didn't totally convince her. Why didn't Papa finish what he went to do after travelling all that way and taking the risk of entering the convent at the dead of night? He'd had three years to stew on his thoughts of revenge. But then Papa's major fault had always been prevarication. As she'd gotten older she'd realised it was borne of an intellectual, philosophical bent of mind to see matters from both sides. That was how he practiced Judaism whilst pretending to be a Catholic. When she was younger she was disgusted by what she believed was his hypocrisy. Now she could understand it as pragmatism, even though it exposed the family to danger. She still didn't agree with him, but she understood. She no longer blamed him for Mama's death. That sin was all Torquemada's.

'My dear, you look wonderful.'

She whirled round to see who had entered her chamber without knocking – a custom of the house she could not get used to – and found Aisha admiring her.

'If you will allow me?' Aisha said, advancing on her. She gently pushed the *peineta* back so that it pulled Isabel's hair even tighter, then drew the mantilla forward so that it framed Isabel's face more closely. 'Perfect,' Aisha said, holding Isabel's shoulders at arm's length.

Isabel looked in the mirror. 'I'm not at all sure it suits me.'

'Nonsense, my dear. You look wonderful. You will attract many admiring glances.' Aisha smiled mischievously.

'Especially from Señor Alejandro.'

Isabel felt the heat in her cheeks and turned away. She clawed the *peineta* out of her hair and tossed it onto the drawer, letting the mantilla fall to the floor.

Aisha picked it up and laid it carefully on the bed. 'I'm sorry,' she said, 'that was overly familiar of me.' She paused. 'I just came to ask if you knew where your Papa was?'

'He's gone to the Alhambra, to talk to Talavera. He wants his advice.' Isabel folded her arms and stood with her back to Aisha.

'My dear. I am sorry.'

She knew she should stop being rude. Shaking her head, she turned and embraced Aisha. 'I am too.'

They sat facing each other on either side of the bed. Aisha began, 'I felt exactly the same when I first met Abdul Rahman. I was young, shy, easily embarrassed, confused.'

Isabel smiled.

'And with everything else that's going on it's no wonder you're confused and distressed. These stupid men, their arguments, their wars. They claim it's for the glory of Allah.' She paused. 'Maybe for some it is, but for too many of them it's all about money and power. My husband has ridden off into the hills to gather his men for the blockade.'

'Abdul Rahman doesn't have confidence in Alejandro?'

'He thinks he can trust him, but he doubts the king can persuade Her Majesty. Ali is with him, hopefully he'll be able to restrain him from whipping up the men too much.'

Isabel hadn't spoken to another woman so openly since

Mama died. 'It's not just the men though is it? Isabella is no better.'

'That's true, and it's a shame. She should use her femininity, her wiles, and her better nature to bring peace.'

Isabel thought this view a little naive. But it said much of Aisha's kind nature. 'What did you want to see Papa about?'

'To enquire whether he would be with us for lunch.'

This was an odd answer. Aisha didn't usually enquire how many would be eating as she just had the servants prepare ample amounts of food. Was Aisha fonder of Papa than she'd realised? She'd thought that it was only her father making a fool of himself. 'How do you feel about him?' Isabel blurted out before she'd thought it through.

Aisha's eyes tightened and her lips pursed. She fussed with her mantilla. 'Not as I think he feels about me, my dear.' She paused. 'Not as you and Alejandro feel about each other.' '

Isabel nodded in acknowledgement. She couldn't keep on denying what was obvious.

'Your Papa is like a brother to me.'

It sounded sincere. Isabel smiled. 'What will you do?'

'About your Papa? My husband? The king?' Aisha laughed. 'Men, it's all about the men. We need to think about ourselves, what do we want?'

Before Isabel could reply Khaled appeared at the door, bowed his head, and held up a roll of parchment bound with a red cord. 'Apologies, but the messenger said it was very urgent.'

'For me?' asked Isabel.

'No, senorita,' Khaled said as he handed the missive to Aisha.

As she untied the cord Isabel saw the scroll was sealed with the symbol of a black raven.

Aisha's face crumpled. She tossed the paper over to Isabel.

A summons from Cardinal Cisneros.

CHAPTER
TWENTY-ONE

WHEN ISAAC RETURNED TO THE COMPOUND after meeting Talavera he was greeted by Aisha and Isabel. The discussion with the archbishop had been a waste of time and he was feeling depressed. His mood was not improved when he saw Aisha and Isabel's drawn faces. What had happened now? Aisha put her finger to her lips and led the way to a small, bare room adjacent to the courtyard. It was normally used as a staging post for food on its way from the kitchen to the dining table. The spicy aroma of *ras-al-hanout* lingered in the air. There was nowhere to sit, so they huddled in the centre of the room. Aisha thrusted a roll of parchment at Isaac.

He unfurled it, quickly scanned its contents, and read aloud, 'Cisneros invites you to discuss some "matters of religious importance" –'

'Isaac, please,' Aisha said putting her finger to her lips again.

He had been reading as though he were a herald making an important announcement. Nodding he continued in a low tone, 'at his chamber in the Alhambra, tomorrow morning.' No wonder they'd looked distraught. He wanted to pace, as he always did when he needed to think, but the room was too small. He suggested continuing their conversation in the courtyard, but Aisha did not want any of the servants to overhear.

'What do you think, Papa?'

This was no time for nicety and prevarication. 'He's a cunning dog. He's taking advantage of Abdul Rahman being out of the city; relying on you to be too scared to refuse.'

Aisha said, 'He doesn't know me very well.'

Isaac exchanged a knowing smile with Isabel.

'I'll face him. He won't touch me.'

'I wouldn't be too sure of that,' Isaac said. 'Talavera made it clear that Cisneros now has all the power. He can't do anything to help me. Until a few days ago Talavera was the most influential man in Granada. The book burnings – and Their Majesties apparent acquiescence – have changed everything.'

And it had made Isaac's situation even worse. Implicit in the deal with Ferdinand was that the information Isaac provided on the rebels would keep a lid on the boiling pot in Granada. And the royal coffers would continue to fill with tax revenue. Unless Their Majesties agreed to Abdul Rahman's demand that Cisneros leave his position immediately a *Mudéjar* uprising was inevitable. The city would be in ruins as would Isaac's dreams of returning home to Seville.

'What does he mean by "religious matters?"' Aisha asked.

'Your conversion from Christianity to Islam makes you an

apostate in his eyes. As things stood in Granada before his arrival you had done nothing wrong, particularly if you were a sincere, observant *Mudéjar*. Which you are.'

Aisha said thoughtfully. 'But?'

'He will question you in such a way as to prove that you are insincere. Then he will arrest you.' He paused to allow this to sink in.

Aisha gasped.

'Even if he doesn't arrest you he's being deliberately provocative. He's hoping that Abdul Rahman will rush back, overreact and then he can arrest him. You can't go. It's a trap.'

Aisha opened her mouth as if to argue but Isabel took hold of her hand and squeezed. 'Go on Papa,' she said.

'You need to hide for a couple of days. Until Alejandro has spoken to the king. If he agrees to get rid of Cisneros then this summons is moot,' he waved the parchment in the air. 'If His Majesty is determined not to compromise then it's best that you are already safe. I've no doubt Abdul Rahman will carry out his threat to blockade the city. And if there is no option but to accede to Cisneros' "request" it will give me time to negotiate with His Majesty. To make sure you are accompanied when you see him and that he guarantees you will not be arrested.'

'You think the king will agree?' Aisha asked.

'I don't know, but if he doesn't then you're well out of it.'

'When and where?' Aisha asked.

'Now and somewhere you'll be safe. My apologies, the place I have in mind will not be as comfortable as you would like.'

Aisha dipped her head and thanked him.

Isaac raised a brow at Isabel who responded, 'Of course I'll go. I'd be delighted to.' He was glad he had not had to argue with her. She'd realised that she could not stay in the compound by herself, and that Aisha would be glad of the company.

'Khaled will take you. I'll send word to Cisneros that you've already left the city to accompany your husband on a business matter.'

'Will he believe it?' Aisha asked, her voice wavering. He'd never seen her this nervous.

'Probably not,' he replied, 'but it will buy us a day or two. And I don't see any other choice.'

He wasn't sure if this was the right thing to do but he was certain that to do nothing would be disastrous.

Isabel stood at the back wall of the cave and peered into the gloom. She could just make out Khaled on guard at the entrance in the late afternoon sunlight. If she stretched her hands out She could almost touch both side walls simultaneously by stretching her hands out. It was cold and smelt of damp earth and livestock. Khaled had told them it was part of a complex the rebels had discovered in the Sacromonte hills. It was only two hours ride to the north of the Albacîn. Nothing was known of their origin, though Isabel imagined that maybe the rebels from the Roman Empire had taken refuge here. Even now still thinking of teaching points for the children.

They passed about a dozen caves as they'd ridden up the narrow track. Khaled had confidently taken the lead, he'd clearly been before. He told them that the rebels had dug out and enlarged each of the caves to make them inhabitable. They passed a few residents on the way. The children were unwashed and dressed in rags. The adults said, "Salaam" to Khaled but avoided eye contact with herself and Aisha. Goats and dogs wandered freely.

'I know Papa said we might not have the comfort we're used to but I didn't think it would be so ... rustic,' Isabel said. At least the ceiling was high enough for them to stand up. It was just about its only redeeming feature.

'It's spacious enough for us, my dear,' Aisha replied as she spread some woolen blankets on the hard ground.

'We won't get much sleep on those,' Isabel said with a shrug. 'Did you know about these caves?'

'My dear husband never said a word.' She paused. 'Perhaps he didn't want to worry me.' She sat down on the blanket. 'Or didn't trust me enough.' She patted the space next to her.

Isabel joined her with a grimace as her buttocks met the stony ground. She took Aisha's hand. 'We'll be safe here. That's what matters.' She wanted to be more reassuring but couldn't find the words. She wanted to share more with Aisha about her longing for Alejandro, and the guilt she carried for rejecting him. But she didn't want to burden her when she was so worried about her own safety, and her husband's. Everything was so uncertain. Papa's plan was for them to hide and wait for the king's response to Abdul Rahman's demand for Cisneros to step down. But what if the response didn't come? Or if it was not what they hoped for?

Aisha lay down and closed her eyes. Isabel walked over to Khaled and whispered, 'Do you think we're safe here?'

'As safe as anywhere,' Khaled said with a shrug. 'No one knows about this place, except for us.'

Isabel was not entirely convinced, but it was better than nothing. At least they were not being followed.

Suddenly, there was a commotion from lower down the track. Khaled drew his sword and ran outside. Isabel and Aisha followed closely behind.

A group of twenty or so men and women were arguing in Arabic. They were dressed in rags and were unwashed. They must have been hiding out in the caves for a long time. Isabel couldn't understand what they were saying, but their postures and gestures were aggressive. Khaled tried to calm them, but it wasn't working.

'What's going on?' Isabel asked, stepping forward.

One man turned to her and spat out a string of words that she didn't understand. The others started shouting too, pointing at Isabel and Aisha.

'What are they saying?' Aisha asked, her voice strong.

Khaled said, 'They are worried about you being here. They think you bring danger.' He paused. 'They want you to leave.'

Isabel exchanged a worried glance with Aisha.

'I've told them who you are and that you are under the protection of our leader Abdul Rahman, but they're insistent. They fear the king's men will come at any moment.'

Aisha stepped forward and spoke. She began softly by introducing herself – Isabel understood that much. Then her voice rose and became guttural and to Isabel's ears aggressive. Aisha gesticulated wildly and her facial expressions were fierce. The crowd were spellbound. Khaled was smiling. There were murmurs of '*Allah hu Akbar*.' Her tone suddenly softened, and her gestures became gentler. Then the crowd seemed to melt away into the twilight.

'What did you say to them,' Isabel whispered.

'That I was named after the third wife of the Prophet, peace be upon him, and that they should be ashamed of themselves. I reminded them that the Prophet said, "There is no good in the one who is not hospitable."'

'I'm relieved it worked,' Isabel said.

'They're simple people. We'll be safe for tonight. But your father better come up with a plan. We'll have to leave at first light.'

CHAPTER
TWENTY-TWO

THE SUN WAS SETTING as Isaac situated himself in the darkest corner of Bar Aixa and waited for Alejandro to arrive. It was quiet and Teresa quickly brought him a glass of sherry, but he declined her offer of food. He couldn't eat, his stomach was roiling with worry. Mercifully she didn't engage him in any further discussion, she understood his mood. He hoped Aisha and Isabel were safely at the caves by now. He trusted Khaled, perhaps more than he trusted his old friend. It was an unnerving thought, especially now. But surely after the lies Alejandro had told Their Majesties to save his skin he had to have faith in him. So why did something in his gut say otherwise? Just as Isaac was about to try and answer that question someone occupied the stool on the other side of the table.

'That place is taken,' Isaac growled.

'That's how you greet an old friend?'

He recognised the voice and looked up. It was Lorenzo Calderon. For a moment he considered telling him to get lost, but he didn't deserve such rudeness. He shook Calderon's outstretched hand.

'Are we?' Isaac said.

Calderon gave him a puzzled look.

'Old friends.'

'That's how I think of you. After the great service you did me. I wouldn't have my estate and my family back without you.'

He gave a dismissive snort.

'I am genuinely grateful. I'm in your debt, Isaac.'

'You have a strange way of showing it. I've hardly heard from you.'

'Given the risk you took for me and with Cisneros' new regime I thought it best if I kept some distance.' He paused. 'For both our sakes. And I've been busy settling my family back on their return from Seville.'

He studied Calderon. There was a lightness to his expression, he looked younger. The face of someone who had found a measure of happiness. Calderon was right. It had been wise not to be seen together immediately after Talavera had decided the petition in his favour. Cisneros had eyes everywhere and if he heard even a rumour that Talavera had gone easy on a heretic he would use it against the archbishop. He realised that part of his reason for treating Calderon this way was jealousy. Isaac wanted what the silk merchant had: home and family. He should stop letting his darker emotions get the best of him. But why had Calderon chosen this moment?

'So, what do you want now?' Isaac folded his arms and leant back.

'Nothing. I just wanted to say hello. And ...', Calderon hesitated. 'I'd heard about what happened at the court. I thought you could do with as many friends as possible right now.'

Isaac thought for a long moment. 'You owe me a debt, you say?'

'I do.'

'I might need it to be repaid very soon.'

'You only have to ask.'

'It might be dangerous.'

Calderon smiled. 'What isn't nowadays? I won't promise to do whatever you ask me but if it's within my power and my family won't suffer consider it done.'

Isaac looked over Calderon's shoulder and saw Alejandro approaching. 'I have an important meeting now. Come and see me at Abdul Rahman's compound early tomorrow morning.'

Calderon stood, bowed his head and left.

'Who was that?' Alejandro asked as he took the empty stool.

Isaac quickly told him Calderon's story.

'Almost a happy ending. That's rare,' Alejandro said.

'Enough of him. What's your news?'

'Not good. His Majesty would be only too willing to get rid of Cisneros but Her Majesty ...', Alejandro's words trailed away.

'As expected,' Isaac said. 'And Cisneros has upped the stakes, he's called Aisha in for questioning.'

Alejandro let out a long breath.

'A good thing I got her out of the city.'

'Where is she?' Alejandro said, surprised.

Isaac hesitated. Could he trust Alejandro? He saw his former deputy's eyes tighten in concern. 'In the Sacromonte caves.'

'Really? I can't see her being too pleased about that,' Alejandro replied with a smile.

He decided not to tell Alejandro that Isabel had accompanied her. He felt the need to withhold something. It made him feel more in control.

'Aisha can bear a little discomfort. It's only for a night or two whilst we decide what she should do.'

'Her options are?'

'Go Fez to be with her family or take her chances with Cisneros.'

Alejandro did not respond. He gave Isaac an expectant look.

'What is it?' Isaac asked. 'Spit it out.'

'Why are you so concerned about her?'

He looked down at the table and pushed his empty sherry glass from side to side. Dare he trust Alejandro?

'They've been so generous to me.'

'There's more to it than that.'

He thumped the sherry glass down on the table. 'So what if there is?' he hissed.

Alejandro reached across and clasped Isaac's hand. 'You *can* trust me.'

He squeezed his old friend's hand in return and smiled.

Alejandro leaned in; his expression attentive.

'Aisha is not just any woman. She's important to me.' He paused, searching his friend's eyes for understanding. 'I don't know how to explain it, but when I look at her, I feel ... something that I haven't felt for a long while.'

Alejandro's eyes widened. 'You *love* her?'

'Yes, I think I do'

Isaac saw empathy in Alejandro's eyes. He must feel the same way about Isabel.

Alejandro said, 'It's difficult to deny the heart what it desires.' He drank the remains of his sherry. 'But you don't need me to tell you how messy this is.' He continued softly, 'The wife of the rebel leader?'

Isaac shrugged. 'Let alone the guilt I feel about Maria.'

'Do you think,' Alejandro hesitated, 'that perhaps part of the attraction is that she reminds you of Maria?'

Isaac was startled into silence. *Damn it, he might be right.*

'I'm sorry I didn't mean to – '

'No, Alejandro, it's fine. I'd never thought of it that way.'

'Does Isabel know?'

'I think she might have guessed.'

'Not much eludes her notice.'

He smiled in acknowledgement of his daughter's perceptive nature. He gestured at Teresa for more drinks, and she brought a plate of cheese and a basket of rye bread. As she turned to go she gave Alejandro a long, lingering look. Isaac shook his head and wagged his finger playfully at Alejandro who shrugged and smiled as if to say, "What am I supposed to do?"

Isaac took a slice of cheese, put it atop a hunk of bread and took a large bite. He had an appetite now that he'd decided what to do.

'What's your next move?' Alejandro asked.

'Calderon,' he said decisively. 'He owes me a debt, and he's got connections in Fez. He could help us get Aisha there.'

A skeptical look crossed Alejandro's face. 'Are you sure you can trust Calderon?'

'How can we be sure of anyone?' Isaac replied. 'Besides, what other choices are there?'

'If she flees she looks guilty, and Cisneros will ensure she's never allowed to return. There's no guarantee he won't send his people after her. He's vindictive enough.'

'But if she stays he'll kill her.'

Alejandro chewed some bread thoughtfully. 'What if I ask His Majesty to extract a promise from Cisneros that if she agrees to be questioned he guarantees her freedom.' He gulped some wine.

'And what if Ferdinand asks why she's so important?'

'That's easy. She's Abdul Rahman's wife. I'll tell him it's a way of keeping the peace in the city for a while longer, to keep the tax revenues flowing.'

He could see the sense in Alejandro's plan. 'You deal with the king. I'll put Calderon on alert when he comes to see me tomorrow morning.'

As the bar filled, noisy chatter made it almost impossible for them to continue their conversation without raising their voices. But he was exhausted anyway. From planning and plotting, from thinking about his feelings, but most of all from longing: for Maria, for Aisha, for his children, for Seville. Dear God, when would it end? And how?

CHAPTER
TWENTY-THREE

AFTER A RESTLESS NIGHT Isaac was already awake when the cry of the *muezzin* punctuated the dawn. He enjoyed the lilting, almost melancholic call to prayer. How much longer would Cisneros permit it? He hastily fumbled at the buttons on his doublet and smashed his feet into his boots. There was no time to waste. During the sleepless night he realised he'd made a mistake sending the women away. It would be easier to keep them safe in the city; maybe a night at the Apothecary and then they could leave for Fez.

A cold breeze greeted him as he opened his apartment door. 'Damn.' He went back inside and put on his cloak. Isaac strode across the still moonlit courtyard towards the gate where Ibrahim was on watch. He greeted him and asked after the health of his brother, who had been caught up in the aftermath of the book burnings. He remembered Isabel's horrifying account of how Cisneros' guards had treated him.

'Omar's still in prison, señor. I don't think he has long to live.'

'I'm sorry to hear that Ibrahim. Let us pray to God for better days.'

'*Inshallah*, señor.'

Isaac hoped God was willing too. 'Ibrahim I need you to go on an errand for me.' He beckoned the young man closer and whispered instructions into his ear.

Isabel knew Aisha was right, they needed to leave the caves as early as possible the next morning. They couldn't risk staying in one place for too long, not when Cisneros' men could be hunting them. And now the inhabitants of the caves, who she'd thought would be on their side, had made it plain they didn't want them there. She pushed aside her worries, focusing instead on the warmth of the fire Khaled had lit and the safety of the cave. Sitting down next to Aisha she leant her head against her shoulder and felt a sense of calm flow through her.

As the night settled in, she listened to the drip of water, the rustling of livestock, the soft murmur of Khaled's voice. There was nobody there, he must be speaking to himself. To stay awake? She felt cocooned by the darkness, but knew she wasn't really safe. As her mind emptied for sleep she felt a sudden ache in her heart. For Alejandro. She wondered what he was doing right now. Was he thinking of her?

She must have drifted off but was returned to consciousness by a noise from outside. A soft, scraping sound, like a footstep on the rocky ground. She sat up slowly, her heart pounding.

She glanced over to Aisha, who seemed to be sleeping soundly. Khaled was already standing and unsheathing his sword. He moved towards the mouth of the cave, sword raised. Isabel slowly got to her feet, trying to make as little noise as possible. She followed Khaled, stationed herself behind him and peered into the darkness.

At first, she couldn't see anything. But then she spotted movement, a crouching figure coming quickly and quietly towards the cave. She backed away, not wanting to be seen. Khaled advanced and Isabel watched as he brandished his sword and engaged in a silent battle with the intruder. He jabbed at the stranger forcing him to move backwards. As they got further away Isabel emerged from the cave. She still had her dagger and if Khaled became injured she was ready to engage the prowler. Better to scare him off out here than for him to trap them in the cave. Finally, with a swift motion, Khaled knocked him down and stood over him with his sword raised high ready to kill.

Then there was laughter.

After dispatching Ibrahim on his errand Isaac settled himself at the long dining table beneath the balcony. A slight breeze played across his face. Orange sunlight shimmered across the pool at the centre of the courtyard. Roosters crowed from the surrounding streets. Their cries were returned by the screeching parrots in the swaying palm trees inside the compound. Pans clattered and doors banged as the servants prepared breakfast in the kitchen. The Albacín and the house were getting ready to greet a new day.

Isaac found comfort in the routine of this domesticity, and he drifted off. The next thing he knew someone was pushing his shoulder and calling his name. As he opened his eyes his hand moved instinctively towards his rapier, but he'd left it in his room.

'It's alright, Isaac. It's me, your friend. You asked me to come?' Calderon's tone was gentle.

Isaac shook his hand without standing and gestured for him to sit. He worried at his eyes with the heels of his palms to wake himself up. He loosened his cloak as the early morning chill had dissipated. A servant girl brought a tray of hot mint tea, a plate of pastries and a bowl of almonds.

'Thank you for coming, Calderon.'

'I'm at your service, señor.'

Isaac studied the silk merchant's face for any signs of insincerity. Seeing none he took a sip of tea. It was very sweet, the way Abdul Rahman liked it, but still refreshing.

'How good are your contacts with Fez?' Isaac asked, deciding he had no time for small talk.

Calderon sipped his tea before responding. 'Excellent. We send a shipment almost every month. First to Seville, then by ship to Rabat and finally overland to Fez. About fifteen days in total.' He took a handful of almonds and popped one in his mouth. 'The next one is due in a few days' time. Can I ask why?'

'I may need an extremely precious package delivered there. Quickly, safely and completely confidentially.' Isaac stared at

Calderon, trying to gauge his reaction. His face gave nothing away.

'Of course, I'd be delighted to help.'

Isaac took a bite of warm pastry and savoured the sweet spicy tang of honey and cinnamon.

'Would this ...,' Calderon hesitated, 'be a living package?'

Isaac glanced away to give himself a moment to consider how much he should reveal. If Aisha was to be concealed in a wagon and aboard a ship for two weeks preparations would have to be made. 'Yes. Alive.'

'And female?' Calderon raised an enquiring brow.

Arrangements for a woman would be more complex than for a man. 'Yes.'

'It can be done.'

Loud thumping at the external door interrupted further discussion. No-one had replaced Khaled or Ibrahim on guard duty as the rest of the men were away with Abdul Rahman. Isaac unbolted the door and Alejandro stepped over the sill. He put an arm around Isaac's shoulder and tried to lead him back towards the table.

'Tell me,' Isaac said, shrugging him off and turning to face him.

'I've just come from His Majesty.' He took a deep breath. 'He will offer his protection to Aisha when she's questioned by Cisneros.'

'Everything's fine then.' His relief was short-lived as he saw the pain in Alejandro's face. 'Tell me.'

'It'll be moot if what the king told me is true.'

Calderon had joined them, quickly shaking hands with Alejandro.

'Word has reached him,' Alejandro paused, 'that Cisneros has an informer amongst Abdul Rahman's men.'

'Who?' Isaac asked.

'He didn't have the name. Just that Cisneros knows where Aisha is, and he's sent his men to return her to the city.'

'Damn. He'll accuse her of contempt of the Inquisition, that's enough for him to imprison her,' Isaac said.

Alejandro nodded.

'The rest is inevitable.' Isaac paused, knowing he must add to his friends' distress. 'Alejandro,' he said clasping shoulder, 'there's something I didn't tell you.'

Alejandro looked from Isaac to Calderon, searching their faces.

'Isabel is with Aisha.'

Alejandro set his jaw and Isaac saw a vicious gleam enter his eyes. For a moment Isaac thought he was setting himself to throw a punch. Calderon must have had the same thought as he took a step towards Alejandro. Then the tension suddenly left his body and he said, 'So, what's the plan?'

CHAPTER
TWENTY-FOUR

'WHY ARE YOU LAUGHING?' Isabel hissed at Khaled and the intruder.

Khaled hauled the other man to his feet and led him to the mouth of the cave. Isabel narrowed her eyes and studied his face. 'It's Ibrahim isn't it?'

'Yes, señorita,' Ibrahim said, making a deep bow.

She had not spoken to him since Khaled had escorted her back to the compound from the Apothecary on the night of the book burnings. She felt a twinge of guilt for not asking after his brother since then. Now was not the right time.

'The idiot should have announced himself,' Khaled said giving Ibrahim a playful punch on the shoulder.

Ibrahim said, 'My apologies for startling you señorita, but your father sent me to bring you back to the compound.'

'Did he say why?'

'No, only that it was important you both come right away.'

Isabel glanced at Khaled, hoping he might know what was going on, but he just shrugged. She explained the situation to

Aisha and told her she had no idea why Papa was asking them to return. They quickly packed up and mounted their horses for the two-hour ride back to the city. There was a gentle mist hanging in the air as Khaled led them down the narrow track with Ibrahim covering the rear. The few cave dwellers they passed did not greet or make eye contact with them. They must be relieved to see the back of them. Isabel could understand that.

It was warmer by the time they reached the base of the hill and the mist had been burnt away by the sun. As the track became wider they galloped and made good time. Isabel had to concentrate hard to keep up as she wasn't as proficient a rider as the others. She was impressed by Aisha who stayed in the saddle effortlessly. They entered a wooded area and slowed to a trot. It was good to be in the shade. The track was broad enough for them to ride two abreast, Khaled with Aisha and Isabel with Ibrahim. This gave her the opportunity to ask him what had happened to his younger brother.

'Omar is still in jail, señorita. The last time I saw him he was in a terrible way.'

'I'm so sorry, Ibrahim.'

'Thank you, señorita. He was a brilliant scholar, he had a bright future.' He looked off into the distance and she thought he might cry. 'I'm not sure how much longer he will last. Conditions are very bad.'

'I'll visit him, I'll make sure they treat him well. And I will speak to Santa Alfaqui about his case.'

Ibrahim glanced across at her and grinned.

Would it be better to talk to the princess? Talavera's influence was waning, and he might want to avoid involvement with an arrest connected to Cisneros' book burnings. But the Infanta would have her father's ear.

They were nearly out of the woods when they came upon a pond surrounded on three sides by tall reeds. Sunlight sparkled across the surface and a family of ducks paddled in the shallows searching for food. What an idyllic spot. It was now very warm, and Isabel was grateful to stop and rest. Khaled dismounted, cupped a hand into the water and tasted. He told them to refill their leather water pouches and let the horses drink.

Isabel leant against a tree and closed her eyes. At first she thought the faint rumbling sound was in her mind. Then she wondered whether it was thunder. Perhaps it would rain? But when she opened her eyes she saw the alarm on Khaled and Ibrahim's faces. It had been a kind of thunder, the thunder of hooves.

'What *was* the plan?' Isaac thought. Without responding to Alejandro's question he returned to his place at the head of the dining table. A servant appeared with fresh glasses of mint tea. Isaac took a long gulp and let the hot liquid scald his tongue. Calderon and Alejandro sat on either side of him. He registered the concern on their faces.

Placing his glass firmly on the table he said, 'I've already sent Ibrahim out to bring them back. But Cisneros' men might get there before him. We have two choices. One, we gather as many men as we can and ride out to the caves to prevent Isabel and Aisha's capture.'

Calderon seemed to agree.

Alejandro's expression did not change.

Isaac continued, 'But by the time get on the trail to Sacromonte Cisneros' men may already have their prisoners and be returning to the city. They'll be armed and well trained. I don't like our chances.'

Alejandro murmured his agreement.

'Even if by some miracle we get away with it where will we go? We can't come back here. We'll be rebels. We'll have no choice but to join Abdul Rahman in the mountains.'

Calderon's expression was one of alarm. 'I won't do that Isaac, I'm sorry.'

'I don't expect you to, Lorenzo.' Isaac turned to look at Alejandro and they locked eyes for a long moment.

'I'll return to His Majesty,' Alejandro said, 'I'll secure a letter offering his protection to Aisha. Cisneros will still question her, but we'll be present, and he won't be able to arrest her.'

'It's the best we can do,' Isaac said, 'as a first step.'

'I'll meet you at the city gates,' Alejandro said, 'we'll wait for Cisneros' men, give them the letter and escort them to the Alhambra.'

Calderon said, 'I will make discreet arrangements for a female to be transported to Fez on the next ship.'

'Do you have room for another?' Isaac asked.

'You?' Calderon asked.

'No, Isabel.'

Isaac was about to ask Alejandro to find out more about Cisneros' informer, but did not get the chance. Alejandro got up without another word. He slammed the door to the compound so hard it sent the roosting parrots roosting into agitated flight.

'It's a long story,' Isaac said in response to Calderon's puzzled look.

A group of horsemen were galloping directly at them. Isabel's heart thudded so loudly she thought it would explode from her chest. The riders were still too far away to see who they were, but she could tell they were heavily armed. Khaled told Ibrahim to ensure the horses were securely tethered. He motioned for them to position themselves at the edge of the wood with the pond at their backs. Their horses whinnied and pulled at their ropes. Isabel considered riding away and escaping through the woods with Aisha. But there were too many horsemen, and they would make quick work of Khaled and Ibrahim and then easily hunt them down.

'What do we do?' Aisha asked.

Isabel had never seen her so distressed.

'We fight,' Khaled said, gripping the hilt of his sword.

The horsemen drew closer, a dozen of them wearing the colours of the Cardinal. They were hopelessly outmatched. How had Cisneros' men discovered where they were so quickly? She had experienced real danger before but nothing like this. Isabel told herself to stay calm as the horsemen drew closer.

Khaled and Ibrahim positioned themselves in front of her and Aisha, Khaled's scimitar flashing in the sunlight. Ibrahim stood just behind his comrade, pulled out his bow and arrows, ready to fight from a distance. Isabel glanced at Aisha who was muttering furiously and holding cupped hands in front of her face. She was praying to Allah to save them.

The horseman drew to a halt about fifty paces away. They assembled in an arrow shaped formation, ready to charge but prepared to defend. The leading horseman took off his helmet and tucked it under an arm. He was a burly man with a thick beard. He announced, 'I am Captain Leon. We are not here to harm you. Our instructions are to escort you back to the city and Cardinal Cisneros' custody.'

Isabel saw that Ibrahim had notched an arrow into his bow but kept it down at his side. Would his desire to avenge his brother help or provoke an unnecessary fight? The captain put his helmet back on and gestured his men forward with a forefinger. Isabel expected them to charge but they slowly trotted towards them. Her mouth went dry as she prepared to defend herself. She took out her dagger. It would be useless against a broadsword but if she could get in close she could so some damage.

When the horses had drawn close enough to see the sweat on their flanks the captain held up his fore and middle finger. The two soldiers on either side of him dismounted, grasped the hilts of their swords, and strode forward. Khaled charged towards them, his scimitar held high. Isabel drew Aisha to her and put an arm around her. Aisha was muttering, 'Ya Allah, Ya Allah.' God's intervention might be their only chance, Isabel thought.

Aisha cried out, 'If they take me they'll kill me.' She began to sob. 'I'll never see my children again.'

Isabel could not offer any false assurances. She hugged Aisha tightly. As the men clashed, she saw that Khaled was a skilled fighter, and he held the swordsman at bay for longer than she dared hope. She'd expected Ibrahim to have rained arrows down on the rest of the soldiers, making it harder for them to advance. But he'd lowered his bow. The soldiers circled Khaled. He turned continuously, whirling his scimitar to fend them off.

The captain's voice boomed out, 'Tell your man to stand down. Otherwise I will instruct my men to finish him.'

Isabel called out, 'Khaled, enough. Do as he says.'

Isabel would never know if he heard her. Khaled let out a guttural scream and ran straight at one of the soldiers, his blade raised above his head. As he brought it down the soldier knocked it aside with his shield and in the same movement thrust his sword deep into Khaled's stomach. He fell to his knees and then toppled over, his face smashing into the ground with a sickening thud.

Isabel heard Aisha's scream then the world went silent. She watched Aisha run across and kneel beside Khaled's body. Her face distorted by anguish, mouth opening and closing but Isabel heard nothing. There was an exchange of looks between the captain and Ibrahim, who dropped his bow and ran. Isabel thought it odd that the soldiers did not chase after him. The captain dismounted and walked towards her. He was saying something to her, but she couldn't hear. Isabel thrust her dagger at him but he caught her by the wrist and forced her to let go of the blade. She braced herself for the blows, but he took her arm with surprising gentleness. Then she blacked out.

CHAPTER
TWENTY-FIVE

ISAAC WAS FRUSTRATED that the Albacîn was so packed that he had to lead his black stallion through the lanes. It was always busy, but he could usually mount and trot, the residents well used to avoiding collisions with horses, goats and cattle. He racked his brains for why there should be so many people on the streets. But there was no festival or celebration that he could recall. Then he noticed the groups of young men huddled together, some whispering conspiratorially, some shouting in the guttural Arabic of Granada which he couldn't fully understand. He could pick out words like, "Satan" and phrases like, "son of a dog." Instead of the usual, "Salaam," he was greeted by hard, angry stares or blank expressions. There was a febrile, ugly atmosphere that he'd never felt before in Granada. All because Cisneros refused to honour the religious freedoms Their Majesties had agreed to in the Alhambra Treaty. Put more simply: the cardinal wanted to eviscerate every trace of Islam.

He prayed that Alejandro would be waiting at the Puerta de

Elvira with the king's letter offering his protection to Aisha. This was one of the main gates to the city and Cisneros' men would have to pass through it from Sacromonte on their way to the cardinal's chambers at the Alhambra. If His Majesty had reneged on his promise there would only be two choices: fight, or trust that Cisneros would deal with Aisha justly. It wasn't really a choice. As he approached the fringes of the city he mounted his horse and began to trot. This lightened his mood a little.

The sun was at its peak and as the horse moved faster Isaac felt the sweat pooling at his lower back. He stopped, removed his hat and wiped his brow with the back of the sleeve of his tunic. It seemed to be getting darker. Was it about to rain? He hadn't heard any thunder. As he looked up, shading his eyes with a palm, he saw the reason: the sun was disappearing. At first he thought it was a bank of black clouds. Then he realised it was the moon passing over the face of the sun. He watched as the moon seemed to devour the sun, leaving smaller and smaller crescents of sunlight. He had heard Ali talk of this phenomenon - an eclipse. A eerie hush descended over the city. No dogs barked, no parrots screeched, no roosters crowed. Then a bright flash as the moon almost completely covered the sun, leaving just a sliver of light around its edges. For a few seconds there was nearly complete darkness. As the moon completed its transit the sun began to reappear accompanied by loud howls and shrieks from the residents of the Albacín. He remembered Ali telling him that the *Mudéjar* holy book said that eclipses were a natural manifestation of Allah's power. But, according to Ali, too many interpreted it superstitiously and regarded it as an omen foretelling an evil event. A shiver ran through him. He replaced his hat and cantered on. He didn't have time for the supernatural, too much was happening in the real world.

As he descended a steep lane the crenellations atop the sandstone wall of the Puerta de Elvira came into view. He passed through the tall horseshoe shaped gate. The guards did not stop him, they were not bothered by who was leaving the city, only who was entering. Just beyond was Ibn Malik cemetery, where he had agreed to meet Alejandro. He trotted around the graveyard, but he wasn't there. Isaac stood tall in his spurs to look over the walls and saw a man in a red and white striped kaftan kneeling by a gravestone, his head bowed. He got stiffly to his feet and rubbed the small of his back. Isaac knew that feeling, all part of the pleasure of getting old.

Isaac called out, 'Señor, have you seen a man in the last hour?'

The man turned. His face was deeply lined, his cheeks hollow. 'You mean since the eclipse?'

Isaac nodded.

'That's my wife,' he gestured at the gravestone behind him.

'I'm sorry,' Isaac said, bowing his head. 'But if you could –'

'And both my sons.' He looked directly at Isaac, his face empty and haunted. 'And my three daughters.'

He didn't know what to say.

'I think it's my family. I pray it is. I can't be sure. Not after Their Majesties slaughtered all and sundry when they took back the city in '92.'

'I'm so very sorry.' He knew about loss, but not on this scale.

'They threw all the bodies in here. Hearts and bones alike.'

Another reason for the *Mudéjares'* discontent, another atrocity to stoke the flames of rebellion.

The old man continued, 'Our mosques are almost gone, my friends have gone to Fez, my family's gone. The only thing not gone is the cemetery, and it's getting fuller.'

'I lost my wife too. I'm thankful to still have my children. I'll pray for the souls of your family.'

The man gave Isaac a small smile.

'I'm trying to save someone very dear to me. The man I'm looking for can help me.'

'Then Allah be with you. But I can't help you. I haven't seen anyone.' He turned his back and looked down at the gravestone.

For a moment Isaac considered dismounting and offering the man some comfort. But there was no time to show kindness to strangers. Instead he called out, 'If you see a horseman, his name is Alejandro. Please ask him to wait for me.'

The old man raised a hand and Isaac assumed that he understood. He snapped the reins to urge his horse forward on the road towards Sacromonte. If he could spot Cisneros' men he would know how much time he had left to wait for Alejandro.

Isaac galloped on over the dusty track. He passed under a canopy of trees arching over it from both sides, forming a long tunnel. As he emerged from the gloom into the light he wondered whether he should stop. Would Alejandro be at the graveyard now? Just as he was about to turn back he spotted a flash of red in the far distance – a glint of reflected sunlight from a sword or a shield. He pulled on the reins and brought the stallion to a halt. The horse snorted and stamped at the ground, bobbing his head – he was thirsty. He patted the stallion's flanks. He narrowed his eyes; a group of about a dozen. They didn't appear to be riding fast. The lead horseman was holding an ensign. They were too far away for Isaac to make out whether it was the black raven of Cisneros. He wheeled his horse around, creating a cloud of dust in his wake. Alejandro better be waiting at the cemetery. Isaac was no swordsman.

Isabel was resting her head on her mother's shoulder being jiggled rhythmically up and down. Mama was trying to lull her to sleep, it felt so calming. 'Shhh,' Mama said, 'shhh, little one,' and sang, 'Mama loves you, Papa loves you, we both love you very much,' over and over. Snorting and whinnying interrupted the lullaby. Jerking her head up she looked groggily around. She was on a horse, sitting behind someone. She recognised the green gown; it was Aisha who had the reins in her hand. Isabel tried to move her hands, but they were tied together around Aisha's waist.

'Good, you're awake,' Aisha said. 'You fainted, my dear. They tied you up so that you would not fall off.'

Isabel saw their horse was tethered to a soldier riding in front of them. And there were about a dozen other red caped soldiers on horseback surrounding them. She was confused. 'Where are we going?'

'To the Alhambra.'

'That's good.'

Aisha half turned and grimaced at her. Then she remembered. These were Cisneros' men, and they were taking Aisha for interrogation. Then she remembered something else. 'Khaled died?'

Aisha hung her head.

'What did they do with him?'

Aisha pointed at a body slung over the back of a horse.

Isabel said, 'At least we can give him a decent burial.'

'The captain told me they respected Khaled's bravery. That's why they didn't butcher him, because he was a fierce warrior.' Aisha snorted. 'A lot of good it did him.'

'Did Ibrahim escape?'

'I don't know where he went, but I have a good idea why.'

Isabel tried to recall what had happened. Why hadn't Ibrahim fired any arrows and what was the meaning of the look that passed between him and the captain. 'Did he inform on us? He told Cisneros where we were?'

'There's no other explanation for the way he behaved. Coward.' She spat onto the ground. 'Abdul Rahman will have his head.'

'He must have done it to save Omar, his younger brother.'

'I don't care why he did it,' Aisha hissed. 'His first loyalty is to my husband. He took him and his brother off the streets when they were thieving vagabonds. He looked after them.

Ibrahim should have trusted him to free Omar. He just needed to be patient.'

Isabel was so tired. She rested her head against Aisha's back. The gentle rhythm of the horse soon had her drifting off again until she was disturbed by shouting. They were nearing the city and she looked ahead to see the sheer sandstone walls of the Alhambra dominating the horizon.

'A rider, Captain,' Isabel heard one of the soldiers call out.

She peered into the distance and could just make out a cloud of dust at the very edge of her vision. It seemed to be riding away from them.

The captain replied, 'It's one man, what can he do?'

CHAPTER
TWENTY-SIX

ISAAC CROUCHED FORWARD IN THE SADDLE, digging his spurs into the stallions' flanks, urging him forward. His stomach and back ached from the effort - pains he would never have felt in his younger days. At least the physical exertion stopped him from thinking and brought temporary relief to the anxiety flooding through him. Alejandro had to have secured the letter from Ferdinand. He couldn't bear to lose Aisha. How had the old man at the graveyard borne such loss and carried on living?

Isaac reined the horse in as he neared the cemetery walls again. If Alejandro didn't appear soon he would ride to the Alhambra and throw himself on the king's mercy. Get down on his knees if that's what it would take to save Aisha. After Juan's execution, after Maria's death he couldn't lose someone else that he loved. He couldn't face the guilt of being responsible for another death.

As Isaac approached the cemetery the old man was locking

the gate. He looked up and smiled. 'Did you find him?'

'No. Did anyone come?'

The old man shook his head. 'The omens are not good,' he said with a sigh. 'An eclipse portends evil events. Perhaps even the day of judgement.'

The man's pessimism irritated Isaac. But would he think any differently? This man had lost much more than even he had. 'Let's hope not.'

'*Inshallah*, my friend.' He held up a palm and turned away.

As Isaac watched him trudge off toward the city a rider appeared. He flew past the old man, narrowly avoiding colliding with him. It was Alejandro. Isaac felt relief flood through him. Alejandro prepared to dismount but Isaac said, 'No time, they're just behind me. Did you get it?'

'Of course, did you doubt me?' Alejandro said with a broad smile.

They remained mounted and stationed themselves in the middle of the track adjacent to the walls of the graveyard. It was now the middle of the afternoon and Isaac was desperate for water, but neither of them had thought to bring any. His throat was dry and he could taste the dust that had settled there. Only the cawing of crows – or were they ravens? – broke the silence. Neither of them said anything, both staring straight ahead, straining to see the first signs of the convoy. The horses snorted and stamped; they were thirsty too.

Alejandro saw something first – younger eyes, Isaac thought – and pointed. He squinted and saw gleams of sunshine that must be the reflections from armour, shields and swords. He exchanged a glance with Alejandro and was surprised to see worry and fear in his face. What they were about to do was dangerous, but Alejandro usually relished these situations. And the letter from the king guaranteed their safety. Then a distressing thought occurred to him: did Alejandro really have the letter? Surely he wouldn't lie about that? Whether he had it or not it was too late now to do anything but brazen it out.

The gleams of light disappeared as the soldiers entered the shadows of the tree canopy. It was replaced by the steady, rhythmic rumble of hooves that grew gradually louder as the convoy cantered towards them. Isaac shifted in his saddle as he felt his sweat sodden tunic against his back. The soldiers emerged from the tunnel and the cardinal's ensign of a black raven was held aloft, rippling in the breeze. The lead rider held up a fist and the group slowed to a trot until they came to a halt about twenty paces from them. The dozen or so helmeted soldiers all put their hands on the hilts of their swords. Isaac made eye contact with Aisha and she smiled wearily at him. Her hair was unkempt and she looked like she hadn't slept for a long time. But she was still beautiful. He mouthed, 'Isabel', at her. Aisha shrugged her shoulders and Isabel peered out from behind. He smiled at her, trying to reassure her.

The leader removed his helmet and said, 'Out of our way. I'm Captain Leon and we're on Cardinal Cisneros' business.'

Alejandro nudged his horse forward and called out in an authoritative voice, 'I'm Señor Alejandro de Cervantes and we're on His Majesty's business.'

The captain arched a brow. Good, he's surprised, Isaac thought.

'I'm His Majesty's adviser.' Alejandro paused. 'I have his authority to extend his protection to the two ladies you have with you.'

'I know who you are now, señor,' the captain said, bowing his head. 'But,' he jerked a thumb at Aisha and Isabel, 'I have direct orders from the cardinal to take these two ladies to him at the Alhambra. The one you call Aisha is accused of apostasy and fleeing the city. The other is accused of abetting her.'

Alejandro seemed hesitant.

Isaac wondered how good his chances were of grabbing the reins of Aisha's horse and riding off into the mountains to find Abdul Rahman. Not very high, he decided.

Alejandro reached into his jacket pocket and produced a scroll which he held aloft. 'This bears the king's signature,' he called out. 'It guarantees the ladies' protection.' He held the captain's eyes. 'Do you intend to disobey His Majesty?'

The captain remained silent for a moment; his eyes locked on the scroll. Isaac could see that he was weighing his options, fingers twitching near the hilt of his sword. Finally, with a resigned sigh, he raised a hand to his men, signalling them to stand down.

'Does the king command the women's release?'

Isaac hoped Alejandro would not lie about this, it would be worse in the long run.

'No, only that they have his protection against arrest and incarceration.'

'There's nothing to prohibit the cardinal from questioning them?'

Alejandro said, 'No, but the king requires that the ladies are accompanied at all times by myself and Señor Alvarez.'

The captain looked at Isaac for the first time. 'I've heard of you. One of Talavera's lot. The heretic from Seville.' The captain's men laughed.

Isaac remained stony faced. Any response would only inflame the delicately balanced situation.

'Right,' the captain said decisively, 'you can accompany us to the Alhambra and discuss this with the cardinal.'

Alejandro tucked the scroll back into his pocket, and turned his horse towards the city. As the soldiers followed him, Isaac made his way over to Aisha and Isabel. Tiredness was etched into their faces.

'All will be well,' he whispered, 'I have a plan.'

Isabel gave him a weary smile.

Aisha said nothing and fixed her eyes on the road ahead.

He hoped the scroll Alejandro had brandished so confidently did have the king's signature. Isaac couldn't ask him about it for fear of being overheard. And now would not be a good time to accuse him of lying. One thing was for certain though: the captain might not have the confidence to call Alejandro's bluff, but Cisneros certainly did.

CHAPTER
TWENTY-SEVEN

ISAAC WAS SURPRISED BY CISNEROS' CHAMBERS at the Alhambra. He had thought the cardinal's austere character would be reflected in his rooms. But they were as opulent as the rest of the palace. Silk tapestries adorned the walls, rich Persian carpets underfoot, golden crosses, delicate vases – and this was just the antechamber. The cardinal kept the four of them waiting for more than an hour, a richly jewelled golden wall clock striking at every quarter. Aisha and Isabel whispered together on a sofa. Their closeness was a consolation. Alejandro paced, muttering oaths about the cardinal. Finally, a friar appeared at the door to the inner chamber and said, 'His Eminence will see you now.' They made their way past the two guards.

The room was shuttered and lit by flaming torches set in wall sconces. The air was rich with the sickly smell of incense. As Isaac's eyes adjusted to the gloom he found Cisneros sitting in a throne on a dais at the far end. He beckoned them with a bony forefinger. Isaac took the lead with Alejandro, instinctively shielding Aisha and Isabel. A friar stood in attendance on each side of the cardinal, behind each of them was an ensign of the black raven. Cisneros was a man of the cloth and yet he behaved like royalty. His slight frame was swaddled by red and black robes that had the effect of making him look insubstantial. A bulbous nose separated furrowed cheeks. Isaac held the gaze from his deeply set eyes, determined not to be cowed.

Isaac broke the silence. 'I am –'

'I know who you are,' Cisneros said in a deep, menacing tone. 'I know who all of you are.' He looked at each of them in turn. 'Alejandro the liar.'

Isaac put a restraining hand on his friend's arm. He must be referring to Alejandro's tale of the brothel in Salamanca. Surely not the letter from the king?

'Isaac the heretic and,' he tipped his head from side to side, 'probable priest murderer.' His smile was forced. 'Isabel.' He waved her forward, 'the apothecary's apprentice and abettor of fugitives.' He gave her a gimlet stare. 'And finally,' we come to the reason we are all here, Aisha.' She took a step towards him. 'Apostate,' he spat' out.

Isaac glanced at Aisha; her features composed in a neutral expression – unreadable. Is that what goaded Cisneros into erupting?

'You disgust me, all of you,' he roared. He coughed violently. A friar poured red wine from a carafe and handed it to him. Cisneros gulped at it greedily.

Isaac tried to use the silence to speak but the cardinal cut him off. 'What I don't understand is why you men are here? I did not invite you.'

Isaac replied, 'We are here at His Majesty's direction. He has offered Aisha his protection and has forbidden her arrest and incarceration.'

Cisneros arched a brow, 'Has he now?'

Isaac felt his heart pound. If Cisneros asked to see the letter and it proved false that would be the end of them. Alejandro would be guilty of misusing the name of the king, judged a traitor and executed.

'I understand you have a communication from His Majesty.' Cisneros held out a hand.

Alejandro hesitated, then reached into his jacket and produced the scroll. He handed it to a friar who passed it to Cisneros, who unfurled it. All the while the cardinal's eyes remained fixed on Alejandro, a smile playing across his lips. As he studied the parchment the smile disappeared. He threw it to the floor, where a friar hastily retrieved it. Isaac clicked his fingers, and the friar passed the letter to him. He might have need of it soon.

'Very well, let us begin.'

Relief coursed through Isaac; the letter had been genuine. They still had a chance of surviving this. He stepped forward and said, 'I represent Aisha as her lawyer, in the absence of her husband. I'm confused as to what exactly she's charged with?'

'She is a convert to Islam. Deserter of The One True Faith.' He pointed at her. 'Apostate, *renegado*,' Cisneros replied.

'Aisha has done nothing wrong. The Treaty of Granada,

signed and ratified by Their Majesties in 1492, specifically stipulates that converts who become *Mudéjar* will not be forced to return to Christianity.'

'Impressive, Señor Alvarez, you've done your homework. Once a lawyer always a lawyer,' Cisneros said.

Aisha looked relieved and Isabel gave Isaac a broad smile. This might be easier than he'd thought.

'However,' Cisneros paused, 'those same agreements allow *renegados* to be questioned by Christian clerics to determine their sincerity.' He paused. 'I have the authority.'

'That is correct, but only in the presence of a *Mudéjar* cleric. And as I do not see one in attendance ...'

Cisneros snapped his fingers.

A friar exited the door behind the throne and returned leading a tall man wearing a white and blue striped kaftan and a skullcap. He limped forward, looking downcast. The friar pushed him, he fell and cried out. Alejandro helped him to his feet.

'Hamza,' Cisneros said, 'an *alfaqui*, a religious scholar of Islam.' He grinned.

Isaac thought he recognised him. Then he remembered the pitiful call of, "Abu, Abu" as this man was dragged away from his son at the book burnings. He must be in fear of his life to agree to this. Was the limp from the beatings at the hands of Cisneros' thugs?

'Shall we proceed?' the cardinal said. His sarcastic tone signalled that he knew he didn't need permission. He turned his basilisk stare on Aisha. 'Why did you become an apostate?'

'You mean why did I embrace the beauty of Islam?' Aisha replied without hesitation.

Cisneros' features hardened. A slight smile passed over Hamza's lips.

Receiving no response she said, 'For love. Firstly, for my husband and then as I got to know him I could see how his religion had shaped him. It made him the great man he is. I began to love Islam.'

Even though she was talking of her love for another man Isaac felt a surge of warmth at her words. He knew what it was to be passionate about a spouse and a faith.

'What a beautiful story, my dear,' Cisneros said, with insincerity apparent in every syllable. 'Your dear husband.' His tone deepened and he spoke in a deliberate manner. 'The man who tried to blackmail the king by threatening to blockade the city unless I was removed as cardinal.'

Isaac and Aisha shared a surprised look.

'Yes, my spies are everywhere. They know *everything*.' He was relishing the moment. 'Alfaqui, find out what the apostate knows about her adopted religion.'

Hamza fired a rapid series of questions in Arabic at Aisha. Isaac understood enough to know that he was asking her to repeat verses from the Holy Quran and quizzing her on daily rituals. After about ten minutes of this Hamza bowed his head respectfully to Aisha, turned to Cisneros and said, 'She is both knowledgeable and, in my opinion, sincere.'

Cisneros screamed, 'Get out!' and Hamza limped away back through the door behind the throne. Isaac wondered if it would cost Hamza his life to have told the truth.

Before the cardinal could continue Isaac said, 'The Treaty states that a sincere worshipper is permitted to follow their new religion.' He bowed, 'If that will be all Your Eminence, we will take our leave.' He took Aisha's arm and prepared to exit the chamber.

'You will leave when I say so,' Cisneros shouted. 'Aisha, there was a warrant issued for you to report to me, was there not?' He didn't wait for an answer. 'But you ran away to the hills, accompanied by the apothecary's apprentice.'

Isaac said, 'If I may Your Eminence –'

'Shut up, heretic!' Cisneros roared. 'If I had my way I'd burn you at the stake, just like your dear friend Juan.' He set his jaw and snarled, 'Yes, I know all about that too. And I will soon know the truth of the story you and your dear friend,' he glanced at Alejandro, 'cooked up to save your skin in front of the king. I know you killed Father Tomás and soon my spies will have the truth. Then both of you will burn.' He unclenched his jaw and smiled.

Aisha held Isabel's hand.

Alejandro drew himself to his full height and, in a quiet tone, spoke for the first time. 'Your Eminence, we have His Majesty's protection. We have attended as requested and answered all your questions. We are leaving.'

The veins on Cisneros' forehead throbbed and his face turned red. Perhaps he would have a paroxysm and die. Isaac hoped Isabel would not use her newly acquired skills to save him. Before the cardinal could master his rage sufficiently to respond the door behind them opened and a cultured voice said, 'My goodness, this is quite a sight.'

CHAPTER
TWENTY-EIGHT

ISAAC TURNED TO SEE WHO HAD SPOKEN. The Infanta was in the doorway, dressed in a flowing red silk gown. She had an air of elegance and grace about her that evoked the polished marble statues in the gardens of the Real Alcazar.

Cisneros cleared his throat and said, 'Your Highness, what a surprise.' Isaac noted the remarkable change in the tone of his voice.

Alejandro and Isaac bowed deeply, Isabel and Aisha curtseyed.

The princess made her way towards Cisneros. One of the friars offered her a chair but she waved it away. She stood at the base of the dais with her back to the cardinal and said, 'I apologize for interrupting, Your Eminence, but I was on my way to ask your opinion on a verse from Matthew and I couldn't help but overhear your little discussion.' Her self-possession at the fourteen was remarkable. She scanned the group and gave Isabel a broad smile. Her gaze rested on Aisha, and she asked, 'Who is this?'

Cisneros said, 'A *renegado*, Your Highness. A traitor to the faith.'

The princess raised an eyebrow. 'A woman in love hardly seems like a traitor. A woman sincerely following her religion is not a heretic. I seem to remember the Treaty of Granada, which my mother and father signed, being quite clear on the matter.'

Isabel stepped forward, a fierce light in her eyes. 'Your Highness, Aisha is a good woman. She has done nothing wrong. She is only guilty of following her heart.'

The princess regarded Isabel closely. After a moment, she turned to Cisneros. 'I want Aisha released into my care.'

'I'm afraid I cannot do that Your Highness,' Cisneros said.

The Infanta arched an eyebrow. This should be interesting, Isaac thought.

'She may not be guilty under the terms of the Treaty; however, she fled the city to evade my warrant. I insist she is imprisoned for further questioning.'

Alejandro said, 'His Majesty has guaranteed her safety –'

'For the original charge of apostasy, not for evading my warrant.'

'Is this true, señor?' the Infanta asked Alejandro.

He bowed his head and whispered, 'Yes, Your Highness.'

'Guards! Take them both away,' Cisneros barked. The two soldiers who had stood outside on guard entered and flanked Aisha and Isabel.

'Both?' the princess asked.

'Yes, Isabel is an abettor,' Cisneros said.

'My apologies, Your Eminence, but you will not arrest one of my ladies-in-waiting.' She paused. 'I will deal with her.' She gave Isabel a stern look.

Cisneros made to protest, but a warning glance from one of the friars seemed to change his mind and the words died on his lips.

Isaac looked to Isabel for explanation, but she just widened her eyes and shook her head slightly. He glanced at Alejandro who just shrugged. Isaac said, 'I insist on accompanying Aisha to prison. His Majesty guaranteed her safety, I must ensure his wishes are carried out.'

Cisneros narrowed his eyes at Isaac, calculating how to respond. He descended the steps from the throne and stood very close to Aisha. 'I will see you very soon.'

She did not move and held his glare.

Cisneros dipped his head at the princess and departed through the door behind his throne. Isaac thought that he was brave to show her such a minimum of respect. He must be very sure of the strength of his relationship with her mother.

'Isabel, Señor Alejandro, with me,' the princess said as she turned on her heel.

Isaac held Aisha at the elbow and felt her sagging as the guards positioned themselves on either side of them. 'Trust me, it will be fine,' he whispered, even though he wasn't at all confident. Calderon better have made the necessary preparations for her flight to Fez. He would kill him if he hadn't.

'*Inshallah,*' she replied.

'Did you see the look on the old monster's face!' the Infanta squealed with delight.

Isabel watched Alejandro as he listened to the princess and felt a stab of jealousy. Was it just admiration, or was there lust in his eyes as well? The Infanta was just a girl for goodness' sake. She must be mistaken; she shouldn't allow jealousy to get the better of her.

The princess had whisked them away to her chambers, waving away the attentions of her courtiers and ladies-in-waiting. She'd bolted the door to her bedroom and laughed so hard that Isabel was afraid she might injure herself. She was seemingly unaware of the impropriety of allowing strangers – one of them a man – into her private chamber.

'My parents adore you,' the princess said to Isabel as she lay across the bed, her head propped on her hand.

Isabel and Alejandro stood at the foot of the bed, neither of them knowing quite how to behave in this highly unusual situation.

'Well,' she continued, 'Pa certainly does, he remembers the way you dealt with Torquemada. Never had any time for him, glad when he died.' She covered her mouth with her other hand. 'Oops, shouldn't have said that.' She got up and studied herself in a tall golden framed mirror, turning from side to side. 'Ma is not quite so enthusiastic. But that's more about your father, you know, the heresy thing. Pa is not so inflexible.

As long as the coffers stay full.'

'Your Highness,' Alejandro said, 'I wonder if you might excuse me.'

She turned and arched a questioning brow at him.

'I should inform your father of what just occurred.'

'Of course you should. He'll already know. Pa will be ...,' she hesitated. 'Amused but probably angry with me as well.' She returned to studying herself in the mirror.

Alejandro bowed deeply and then whispered to Isabel, 'I'm going to see what's happening with your father. Stay here, you're safe.'

As he unbolted the door a courtier tried to enter but the princess shooed him away with the back of her hand. She sat on the bed and patted the space next to her. Isabel joined her. What on earth was the princess going to do or say next?

'Now that you're one of my ladies-in-waiting you must come to England with me.'

'What?' Isabel couldn't keep the shock out of her voice.

The Infanta gave her a stern look.

'Your Majesty.'

'You know I've been engaged to Prince Arthur, Henry's son, since I was three?'

'Of course, but what has that to do with me? Your Majesty.'

The Infanta frowned. 'Do you know what our ambassador to England says that they'll call me?' She didn't wait for an answer. 'Ca-the-reen,' she said wrinkling her nose as she pronounced each of the syllables.

'I can't put into words how grateful I am for your help, Your Majesty, but I thought my working for you was a just a ruse.'

'It was, but the more I think of it the better it would be. All your knowledge of medicine would be invaluable. The English are such backward heathens, they know nothing about hygiene I'm told.' She took a breath. 'And you wouldn't have to do any real work.'

Isabel's spirits sank. Real work was what she wanted to do, not to be just a royal lackey. She needed to use her knowledge of herbs and medicines to help ordinary people. The people of Andalusia – be they, Muslim, Jew or Catholic – not some savages in a cold, dark country far away about which she knew nothing.

'It will be such fun!' the princess clapped her hands repeatedly.

No, it wouldn't. Being at the beck and call of a princess held little appeal. That old Hebrew verse Papa always quoted when he was in trouble with the king sprang to her mind. Something about being caught in his tongs as he protected you from the fire with one hand whilst setting the flames against you with the other. She always thought Papa a bore when he quoted it. But now she knew exactly what he meant.

Aisha winced as the shorter of the two guards tied her wrists together in front of her. As he looped a long length of rope over the knot, Isaac said, 'You're not doing that.' He gave the guard a menacing stare. He would not allow Aisha to be led through the streets like a donkey.

The guard looked at his companion, who put a hand on the hilt of his sword.

'You may not have any respect for me,' Isaac said, 'but you would do well to remember that this lady has His Majesty's protection.' He produced the letter from the king, making sure they saw the royal seal of Aragon.

The taller guard grunted. They relented, a little, allowing her to conceal her hands inside her gown. A modest capitulation. They set off for the prison, the soldiers flanking Aisha, Isaac following close behind. He had expected them to be on horseback. But Cisneros clearly wanted to make Aisha suffer the maximum indignity. A small-minded man.

They trudged down the steep cobbled street leading from the Alhambra to the fringes of the Albacîn. It was hot and Isaac thought Aisha must be suffering underneath her long gown and mantilla which she had drawn over her face. Mercifully it was only a few minutes further to the prison where it would be cooler. Small mercies.

The groups of angry men he'd first noticed on his ride out of the city – had that been today? – were still in evidence. And if anything they were larger and louder. Cisneros must have been aware of them, as his spies apparently told him everything. So why had he only sent two guards to escort Aisha? What was he plotting, or was he just arrogant?

Isaac heard footsteps and looked back. A group of about half a dozen men were following them. At first they kept their distance but as their numbers swelled they became bolder and got closer. Isaac silently willed the guards to march faster, but they were constrained by Aisha's ability to walk quickly in her gown. He glanced nervously behind; the mob was getting closer. They were calling out in the guttural accent of Granada. Isaac could make out "sister," "pigs," and "help". They must be offering their assistance to rescue her. They were aggrieved and emboldened. Cisneros had miscalculated badly with the book burnings. He did not appreciate the forces he had unleashed. The Holy Quran embodied the literal word of Allah for the *Mudéjar*. Cisneros had committed the ultimate sacrilege in their eyes. Their anger had not cooled, and it was about to spill over.

Aisha said to the soldier on her left, 'Let me speak with them.'

'Not a chance,' he replied.

'I can calm them,' she said.

The soldiers laughed.

They were about to enter a narrow lane overarched by tall houses on each side. The balconies were full of chattering people pointing at Aisha. Word had spread fast. Isaac heard a repeated phrase, but he didn't understand it. The two guards looked at each other, spun around and advanced on the men. Isaac put a hand on the hilt of his rapier and searched for an escape. If the mob overwhelmed the guards perhaps they could take refuge in one of the houses. To do that Aisha needed to be free. He unsheathed his rapier and cut through her bonds. She rubbed at her wrists.

The soldiers brandished their swords and shouted, 'Go

home, get lost.' The men stopped, folded their arms, and stared. The soldiers took a step towards the mob, but they did not retreat. The chanting from the balconies became louder. Isaac heard the same words, over and over accompanied by rhythmic clapping and the sound of metal on metal. He looked up and saw that people were beating the balcony rails with daggers and swords.

Aisha moved closer, and Isaac instinctively put an arm around her. This was not how he'd hoped and dreamt this would happen. Then a selfish thought: at least the mob would know he was on her side.

'What are they chanting?' he asked her.

'One of us.'

The soldiers exchanged nervous glances, turned around, grabbed Aisha by the arms and dragged her forward into the lane. She yelped as she tripped over her gown and fell to the hard cobbles. Isaac helped her up.

'One of us,' was now being bellowed as a war cry. The mob took it up as they ran full pelt at the soldiers.

CHAPTER
TWENTY-NINE

'IT WILL BE MY FOURTEENTH BIRTHDAY IN A FEW DAYS,' the Infanta said. I'll be of an age to finally marry Prince Arthur. We're supposed to set off for England soon. It's so exciting!'

She held Isabel's hands and looked into her eyes but she was only half-listening. She was weighing how to politely decline the 'request' to go to England.

'But Ma wants to delay. I don't know why.' The princess tilted her head. 'Maybe she doesn't want to lose another child.'

That made Isabel think of Gabriel, Juana and Martín. It would be Christmas soon and they were supposed to be travelling from Seville. They couldn't possibly make the journey now. The road was dangerous at any time, let alone when a rebellion was brewing. She said, 'It must be terrible for Her Majesty to lose two children in such a short space of time.'

'And a grandchild,' the Infanta added quietly, her eyes brimming with tears.

The princesses' empathy for her mother made Isabel reconsider her judgement. Maybe she was more than just a selfish, empty-headed brat. And she had shown bravery in standing up to Cisneros. If she couldn't stay in Granada an adventure in England might be appealing. And perhaps she could persuade the Infanta that the children should accompany them? What an opportunity for them. Mama would have approved, she was always encouraging them to take an interest in the world outside Andalucia. But what would Papa do? Before she could indulge in further speculation there was a loud knock at the bedchamber door, and it was immediately flung open.

'Señor Alejandro, how lovely to see you again so soon,' the princess said.

Alejandro bowed deeply. 'Your Highness, we've received distressing news of serious disturbances on the streets of the Albacîn. I must ensure the señorita gets home safely. Immediately.'

The princess looked puzzled. 'Surely, this is the safest place for her. It is a fortress as well as a palace,' she said with a laugh.

Alejandro hesitated before replying, 'I would usually agree with Your Highness, but we've received reports that the señorita's father has been seriously injured and requires her healing skills.'

Isabel studied his face carefully. 'I will need to stop at the Apothecary first to collect some medicines.'

'We must leave, now.'

The Infanta said, 'I will send two of my men with you for protection.'

Alejandro appeared alarmed by this. 'That is exceptionally

kind of Your Highness but might prove dangerous. It would attract unwanted attention as,' he paused, 'the *Mudéjar* are not well disposed towards Their Majesties at the moment.'

'Because of the book burnings,' the Infanta replied.

Alejandro nodded. He took Isabel by an arm and made to leave.

'Very well. Godspeed to both of you. Isabel, I expect you to return on the morrow. We can talk about our plans for England.'

As they hurried out of the palace Alejandro said, 'England?'

'I'll tell you later. Once you've told me the whole truth.'

Alejandro smiled but said nothing.

Isaac held Aisha close as the mob ran at them. The chant of "one of us" had disintegrated into savage screams. The men had a wild look in their eyes and some of them wielded large, curved scimitars. He was no longer sure of their intentions. Was he a target? He felt the drumbeat of Aisha's heart against his chest, or was that his own mingled with hers? She was muttering verses that he recognised from the Holy Quran. He cradled her head protectively with one hand and brandished his rapier with the other. If he was going to die at least it would be with honour. Maria would approve, he hoped. He would soon be able to ask her if the mob despatched him to heaven. If that's where God decreed he deserved to end up. He closed his eyes, asked God's forgiveness, and embraced his destiny.

He felt the rush and smelt the stink of bodies surging at

them and then around them. Then a surprising moment of stillness. He opened his eyes. The pack had passed them by. The soldiers were backing away, desperately holding them at bay with their swinging swords. The balconies were even more crowded. A giant of a man, face red from shouting, shook a meaty fist. The guards were retreating to the end of the lane where it opened out into a plaza. If they got there they could make their escape. Isaac couldn't prevent that; he had to stay and protect Aisha. Perhaps the enormous man had the same thought as the guards approached the area under his balcony. Isaac watched in astonishment as he raised a chunk of stone – where had he got that from? – above his head and threw it over the railing. It plummeted down, landing directly on top of the shorter guard with a sickening thud that induced a gasp from the crowd.

Aisha screamed and held a hand to her mouth. Isaac was too stunned to react. The gasp became a wild cheer as the mob set upon the remaining soldier. It was like a pack of wild dogs savaging a rabbit.

'We need to get away,' Isaac said. 'The king will send reinforcements. It'll be chaos.' He felt a tug at his sleeve. He wheeled around preparing to fight.

'Come with me,' an old man in a red and white striped kaftan said. He exchanged rapid words with Aisha.

'It's safe, Isaac,' she said, 'we can trust him.'

What had he said to convince Aisha so quickly? Then he recognised the hollow cheeks and deeply lined face. What was the grieving man from the cemetery doing here? He beckoned them towards an almost invisible gap between two houses. Isaac hesitated. How could they possibly make it through? It was so narrow they would have to edge along it sideways. Was it a trap? He had no choice but to trust Aisha's judgement. The old man was so emaciated he could almost enter the alley without turning his shoulders. Aisha took a deep breath and followed him, holding out a hand to Isaac. He didn't think he could fit. He regretted the weight he'd put on from indulging in so much of Aisha's food. Isaac considered finding another way, but he couldn't leave her with a stranger. He inhaled, asked God for strength, took her hand, and shuffled into the gap.

For the first few steps the strange exhilaration of holding Aisha's hand distracted him from his fear. Then as the space narrowed even further she let go and Isaac struggled to shove himself sideways. He was stuck. He was panting and his heart rate was increasing. He heard scurrying and scratching. Something ran across his boots. Rats. Aisha yelped somewhere to his right. Sweat trickled down from his brow. Isaac couldn't wipe it away as his arms were trapped by his side. He tasted the saltiness of the sweat on his lips. The sunlight was fading from where they had entered the alley and there was no light from the direction they were headed. Then she took hold of his hand and pulled hard. She'd come back. He inhaled deeply and pushed off from his left foot. It was just enough to free him.

'Almost there,' the old man said.

Isaac's thoughts spiralled. Even if they made it out of here, who was waiting for them? Then a calming voice said, *'I'll be waiting for you.'* It was Maria's voice. He felt a warmth and then a steadiness. Yes, whatever happens, as long as he did the right thing, she *would* be waiting for him. With a shock he realised that Alejandro had been right. He was attracted to Aisha because she reminded him of Maria: her courage, her strength and yes, her beauty. How stupid he had been.

'I told you,' said the old man as they pushed themselves out into the sunlight.

Isaac clasped his hand. 'Thank you.'

'Now you know me,' the old man said with a twinkle in his eye. 'Abdullah.'

'*Salaam*, Abdullah,' Isaac replied.

'*Shukran*, Abdullah,' Aisha said.

'Most welcome,' he replied with a dip of his head. 'Follow me.'

'The quickest way to Abdul Rahman's compound is through the Albacîn,' Alejandro said, 'but it's too dangerous.' They were wending their way through the Alhambra and Isabel had no idea where they were. Alejandro held her by the elbow and urged her forward. They were walking so fast the glistening white marble floors passed in a blur. The scent of *azahar* perfumed the air. She would have liked to take time to stop and smell the lemon and myrtle trees. He told her what they had heard: that Aisha being led through the streets had provoked the mob into violence and that the two soldiers escorting her to prison had been killed.

'And what about Papa?'

'I'm not sure. I've been told he disappeared with Aisha once the soldiers were dead.'

'I knew you were lying. You have a tell.'

'What is it?'

'That would be telling.'

Alejandro gave a mock laugh, and she punched him lightly on the arm.

They arrived at a courtyard where two horses were tethered. 'We'll circle around the Albacîn and cut back towards the compound. I pray that's where we'll find your father and Aisha.'

They mounted and trotted side by side through the Gate of Justice and down the steep, cobbled path.

'Why didn't you leave me in the Alhambra? The Infanta's right, it's the safest place.'

'You knew I was lying about your father being injured?'

'Of course, but don't deflect, answer me.'

'Because your father wants you to leave for Seville and travel on the next ship.'

'To where?'

'Fez.'

'Why Fez?'

'That's where he's arranged for Aisha to go. He thinks it's best if you accompany her. It's the safest choice for you both.'

She registered the sadness in his voice. 'Do you think it's the best choice?' In the silence that followed her mind whirled.

Isabel wanted to hear him say if she left he would go with her.

'I want what's best for you, Isabel. I always have.' He glanced across at her. 'And I always will.'

It wasn't quite the undying declaration of love that she'd hoped for. But now she had two people trying to control her life. Her father and the Infanta. What about what she wanted? Could she continue to be an apothecary if she left Granada? She would ask Ali. He must have contacts in Fez and London.

As they reached the bottom of the hill the sweet scent of orange blossom was replaced by a bitter smell. The same acrid odour she remembered lingering in the streets on the night of the book burnings. As they wheeled their horses round towards the Albacîn they saw plumes of black smoke curling into the sky. The city was on fire.

Alejandro snapped his reins, quickening his horses' pace. She did her best to keep up, but she was not as accomplished a rider. The main lane into the Albacîn was blockaded with a pile of furniture and chunks of stone. Two men stood atop the barricade shouting at them in unintelligible Arabic. When they started hurling stones the message was clear. They cantered away skirting along the fringes of the city.

'We'll head for Puerta de Elvira,' Alejandro called out. 'If we're lucky the mob won't have blocked it yet.'

Her mind reeled with an excitement that overwhelmed her fear. She had confidence in Alejandro, he would keep her safe, he would give his life for hers. But where would she go now that life in Granada seemed at an end? Even before it had really begun. Returning to Seville and a life of domesticity did not appeal. She hadn't felt alive there since Mama died. England with the Infanta? Fez with Aisha? Wherever she went she wanted to be with Alejandro. Of that much she was certain.

CHAPTER
THIRTY

THE PLAZA WAS EMPTY. Everyone must be hiding, Isaac thought, bracing for what might happen next. Abdullah led them in single file around the fringes of the square, sticking to the shadows. The old man was quick for his age.

'Where are you taking us?' Isaac asked.

'Home,' Abdullah said.

'We don't have time for your hospitality,' Isaac said.

'Not mine. Yours.'

'How do you know where our home is?'

'Every *Mudéjar* knows Abdul Rahman. He's a hero.'

That answered Isaac's next question. He was doing this because he'd recognised Aisha.

Abdullah led them through a dizzying maze of backstreets and alleys. Isaac was thankful that none were as narrow as the first. They were accompanied by continual shouting, banging, and crying. They passed groups of residents constructing barricades to block the soldiers who would inevitably arrive. The bitter, pungent smell of smoke hung in the air. This was becoming the full-blown rebellion that Abdul Rahman had wanted, and Isaac had feared.

After what must have been at least an hour they emerged from a lane and Isaac recognised the horseshoe doorway flanked by tall cypress trees. They were home. Nobody was on guard. Aisha banged at the door and spoke quickly in Arabic. A high-pitched voice responded. It must be one of the servant girls, she sounded frightened. But the door remained shut. They couldn't stay out on the street for much longer. Isaac raised a fist and made to thump on the door. Aisha put up a palm to stop him. Her tone became soft and persuasive. It worked, the door opened, and they rushed inside.

A servant girl fell into Aisha's arms and began to wail. Aisha stroked her hair and spoke to her soothingly. It reminded Isaac of the way Maria used to comfort Gabriel when he was small. Aisha waved Isaac and Abdullah over to sit at the dining table under the balcony whilst she consoled the girl. Once she'd calmed down Aisha held the girl's hand and questioned her. Isaac heard Abdul Rahman's name. Seemingly satisfied with the answers Aisha sent the girl off with instructions to bring mint tea.

'They've had no word from my husband,' Aisha said as she sat next to Abdullah. She spoke in quick, staccato Arabic to him. Isaac understood enough to work out that she was explaining where her husband had gone. She obviously trusted Abdullah. And why shouldn't she, he'd just saved their lives. The girl returned with a tray of mint tea and a bowl of almonds.

Whilst Isaac drank tea Aisha and Abdullah spoke quietly.

She appeared to be trying to persuade him of something. Abdullah had his head cocked, listening attentively to her.

Isaac thought about their situation. They were safe for the moment, but for how much longer? The Albacín was in uproar and Their Majesties would send soldiers to quell the rebellion. The compound was secure enough in normal circumstances but wouldn't withstand a battering from the king's army. At least Isabel was safe at the Alhambra with Alejandro and the Infanta. That was something. But he would need to get her out of there if she was to travel to Fez.

Eventually Aisha turned to Isaac and said, 'It's settled. Abdullah will remain with us. We will have need of good men in the days to come.'

The old man dipped his head and smiled. Aisha clapped her hands, the servant girl appeared and led him away. 'He's going to rest,' she said.

Exactly what Isaac would like to do. But that didn't seem likely anytime soon. There was a loud rap at the main door. He shared a worried look with Aisha. Then she smiled, 'It must be him.'

A voice called out, 'For the love of God, open up!'

Aisha's face fell. He gave her a sympathetic look. Isaac knew who it was. As he opened the door Lorenzo Calderon almost fell over the sill in his haste to get inside. He clasped Isaac's hand and said, 'Thank God. It's a nightmare out there.'

Isaac regarded him coolly whilst Calderon got his breath back. How had he found out that Isaac and Aisha had returned to the compound? Before Isaac could ask, the silk merchant said, 'News of your escape spread like wildfire. I was with a *Mudéjar* client a few streets away when a customer burst into his shop and told us the story. I was pretty sure you'd be here.' He smiled at Isaac and clapped him on the back. 'You're a hero, man. How did you get away across the rooftops?'

Isaac was puzzled for a moment but then realised the story must have become distorted as it had been retold. He assured Calderon that the rooftop escape was a wild exaggeration. Though he had once jumped over a rooftop with Alejandro and Ali back in Seville to escape a fire. It seemed a very long time ago.

Isaac introduced him to Aisha and then said, 'Tell me. Is everything in place?'

Calderon said, 'It was, before this happened. But if we act fast and move Aisha quickly it should be fine.'

Aisha put down her glass of mint tea and arched a brow. She stared at Isaac.

'Forgive me, but I've been making plans for yours and Isabel's evacuation.'

She frowned.

'For you to be with your children.'

Before Aisha could respond there was another knock at the door. 'It *must* be him,' she said. As she opened the door her shoulders slumped. In that moment Isaac became absolutely sure that she still loved her husband. She moved aside to let Isabel and Alejandro enter. They looked tired. Isabel's face was drawn with anxiety. She hugged him but said nothing.

Isaac held her at arms' length and asked, 'Why are you here?'

'What a wonderful greeting,' Alejandro said with an ironic smile.

'I'm relieved you're safe but why didn't you stay at the Alhambra?'

Alejandro said, 'I thought you would want her here.'

Isaac glared at him.

'It's alright Papa, I know about your plan to send me to Fez.'

Aisha said with a smile, 'It seems your dear Papa has been making plans for both of us.' She looked at him from under her brow. He couldn't tell whether she was angry or amused. 'Come, my dear, you must be tired.' She linked arms with Isabel, and they went up the stairs to her bedchamber.

The three men took seats around the table and the servant girl brought more mint tea. Calderon held his glass up and said, 'Cheers.'

Isaac and Alejandro clinked glasses with him, exchanging weary looks.

Calderon said, 'I'd rather it was a drop of the hard stuff but we're not likely to get that here. And I doubt Bar Aixa is open for business.' The shouting, banging, and wailing coming from the streets confirmed Calderon's statement. 'What's the news?'

Alejandro described what they had seen on their flight from the Alhambra. Every entrance to the Albacîn was being barricaded. The mood was mean and violent. Isaac knew that all too well after what he and Aisha had experienced. He shared a shortened version and related how the soldier had been crushed. He omitted his own panic at being trapped in the alley.

'As long as the barricades stop Their Majesties' soldiers we'll be safe here,' Isaac said. 'Everyone knows this is Abdul Rahman's compound, they won't attack it.'

Alejandro and Calderon nodded their agreement.

'But,' Isaac continued, 'night is falling and the soldiers will assault at first light.'

'I'm not so sure,' Alejandro said. 'His Majesty will want to avoid a bloodbath. The object of the rebels' anger is Cisneros, not him. It's more likely he'll try to negotiate. Even if he can't get the queen to get rid of the cardinal he'll reduce taxes or offer some religious freedoms.'

'Do you seriously believe they'll trust him?' Calderon asked.

The question was left hanging in the air for a moment.

Isaac said, 'I think you might be right Alejandro. Wiser heads in the community will probably prevail. In a real fight they'll be easily outnumbered. They'll be slaughtered.'

'His Majesty doesn't want that,' Alejandro said. 'He doesn't want to look like a barbarian, he doesn't want to jeopardise the Infanta's marriage to the English prince.'

'Nor lose any taxes,' Calderon added in a sour tone.

They talked through the options as night fell but they hadn't made any firm decisions when Calderon said, 'What about Fez? The women will have to go tonight.'

'Isn't that up to us?' Aisha asked from the shadows. She appeared as she'd left, arm in arm with Isabel.

'You would be safer in Fez,' Isaac said, 'with your children.'

Aisha fixed him with a stare. 'You are *not* my husband.'

He was dumbfounded, stung by the realisation that she

thought he'd been trying to take Abdul Rahman's place. Perhaps he had. He hadn't been able to save Maria, he wanted to save Aisha. His embarrassment turned to anger, and he shouted, 'He would want you out of harms' way. That's all I'm trying to do.'

'I'm not going,' Aisha said.

'Neither am I, Papa,' Isabel said. She broke away from Aisha and sat next to him. 'My place is with you.' She kissed him on the cheek and held his hand.

He felt an overwhelming sense of weariness with everything and everyone. 'I'm going to my bed,' he said. 'We'll see what the morning brings. Goodnight to you all.' He bowed his head towards Aisha. Her expression was enigmatic. Was that a glimmer of regret in her eye, a burgeoning tear? No, he really was just a foolish old man.

THIRTY-ONE

ISAAC'S EXHAUSTION WITH THE WORLD and all in it mercifully carried over into his sleep, which was deep and dreamless. He was awakened by shouting from somewhere out in the courtyard. Hastily putting on a shirt and struggling to button his trousers over his straining waistline – he had to do something about that – he slammed his feet into his boots. He put his hand up to shield his eyes from the bright mid-morning sunlight and searched for the source of the noise. Abdul Rahman was on the balcony calling down to one of the servant girls. He understood enough Arabic to tell it was something to do with food.

Abdul Rahman must have travelled home in the middle of the night to evade capture. He spotted Isaac and roared his name. His expression was unreadable. What had Aisha told him? Isaac's nagging sense of guilt over his feelings for her made him anxious and he braced himself for an angry scene. The spice merchant disappeared into his bedchamber and moments later came lumbering down the stairs, the wooden treads groaning under his weight. He caught Isaac in a bear hug which went on so long he struggled to catch his breath. Was he happy to see him or trying to kill him? Abdul Rahman kissed him on both cheeks, his unkempt beard scratching them. When he was finally released he saw tears welling in Abdul Rahman's eyes as he said, 'I can never thank you enough.'

Caught between sleep and vague guilt Isaac's puzzlement must have crept into his expression.

'For saving my beloved wife!' Abdul Rahman said.

That was a relief. He couldn't face explaining or defending himself, not today. 'You're most welcome. Anyone would have done the same.'

'She's impossible not to love. Don't you agree?' A twinkle played across Abdul Rahman's eyes.

'Anyway, I had help.'

'So I heard,' Abdul Rahman boomed. Glancing up at the bedchambers he lowered his voice. 'You did the right thing, arranging for Aisha to go to Fez. And your friend, Calderon stands ready should minds be changed?'

'Yes. He's promised to do whatever is needed. But he's not a fighter.'

'We can't all be soldiers. Everyone has their particular use.' A look of intense softness played over his face. 'I was touched beyond words that you would send your own daughter to accompany Aisha.' He looked like he might start to really cry.

If he did Isaac would tell the truth: that he loved Aisha, he couldn't bear to see her hurt, he was just being selfish. He couldn't insult Abdul Rahman's conscience any longer.

He couldn't continue to deceive this man who had been so generous to him. 'I acted out of love.'

Abdul Rahman eyed him suspiciously.

Now was the time to confess.

Before he could the spice merchant smiled and said, 'Of course you did.'

Isaac was relieved. Abdul Rahman understood and didn't seem to be angry. He said, 'You love your daughter, and you love my Aisha, like a sister.'

Hearing those words said aloud confirmed for Isaac how he really felt; it was a fraternal love he felt for Aisha muddled up with his deep longing for Maria.

'She's lucky to have you and Ali as brothers.' A broad grin lit up Abdul Rahman's face. It was impossible not to be captivated by it. 'Stubbornness, her only weakness. A trait I think she shares with Isabel?'

'Yes,' Isaac said, and with Maria.

'Anyway, Allah will guide us. And if it's into the next life, so be it.' His voice had risen again. 'Come, come.'

They sat at the dining table under the shade of the balcony.

'It's just us,' Abdul Rahman said, 'everyone else is still asleep, including my brother.'

Isaac wondered how anyone could sleep through the sound of the spice merchant's booming voice.

'Ali is well?' Isaac was anxious for news of his old friend.

'Never better. Tired, though, getting old.' Abdul Rahman delighted in his younger brother's lower energy levels. Though anyone would struggle to keep up with the spice merchant, both physically and verbally. Isaac certainly did.

The servant girls filled the table with roasted meat, couscous dotted with spangles of pomegranate, and grilled vegetables. More like lunch than breakfast. Isaac affected a look of mock surprise.

Abdul Rahman responded, 'Don't judge me. I haven't eaten properly for days.'

Isaac was ravenous too; he'd hardly eaten anything himself the day before. The food was, of course, wonderful. Attending to his waistline would have to wait until tomorrow. They ate with their hands in silence until Abdul Rahman sat back and emitted a long, satisfied sigh. 'What would I do without her?'

Isaac answered the rhetorical question with a smile.

The spice merchant clapped his hands sharply twice and remained silent until the servant girls had cleared the table. 'Now we can talk. Can't be too careful at the moment.' He narrowed his eyes at the departing servants. 'Aisha has given me a full account of what's been happening.'

'What's the situation in the mountains?' Isaac asked.

Abdul Rahman looked mournful. 'The men are starving. Our supply routes have been cut off by Their damn Majesties.' He paused. 'It's what I would have done. I should have planned for it.' A long moment of silence stretched out. 'We don't have enough healthy men to blockade the city. And I have reports on the Albacîn.' He paused. 'It's grim. Chaos.'

He'd never heard such a defeated tone from Abdul Rahman. It took a lot to dissipate his natural optimism. 'Can't you get a hold of the situation now that you're back? The people revere you.'

The spice merchant looked pleased at the compliment but shook his head. 'If I'd been here when it started I might have been able to. But it's gotten out of hand too quickly. The fires are blazing, both real and in my brothers' hearts. There are rival factions, talk of setting up an independent council.'

'What do we do?'

'I've been communicating with Santa Alfaqui. We think we may have a way out. High risk, though.'

Talavera was a man of integrity and peace, admired by many of the *Mudéjar*. Isaac was not certain that would be enough to avoid further bloodshed.

'You may not see it brother, but I can see the doubt on Isaac's face,' Ali said, appearing at the foot of the stairs. Much lighter than his brother Ali could descend without the treads announcing his arrival. Isaac clasped one of the apothecary's hands between both of his and they exchanged broad smiles. Neither of them was the type to give warm embraces but Isaac hoped Ali knew of his affection for him.

A servant girl appeared, and Ali resisted his brother's repeated invitation to eat and asked only for mint tea. They sat down either side of Abdul Rahman, who asked Isaac, 'Why are you unsure of the archbishop's influence?'

Isaac thought for a moment.

Ali sipped the hot tea cautiously, holding the glass between thumb and first finger.

'Because,' Isaac paused, 'there are limits to even what the most tolerant of priests can achieve with your brothers now, after Cisneros' provocations. And if I may ask you a question?'

'Most welcome,' Abdul Rahman said.

'Why aren't you hellbent on revenge for what they did to Aisha?'

A darkness fell over Abdul Rahman's face.

Ali touched his brother's forearm and said, 'It's a fair question.'

'Even though Aisha is more precious to me than anything in the world her honour is not worth the death of hundreds of my brothers. And Cisneros will find any excuse to slaughter all of us.' He paused. 'She is safe now, because of you Isaac, and we must be practical. Isn't that right, brother?'

Ali smiled. 'Wise words, brother.'

'I heard them from a shrewd man, an apothecary I believe,' Abdul Rahman replied with a grin. 'The situation in the Albacîn is not clear cut. The leader of one of the factions is opposed to any peaceful solution. He commands the support of a few noisy families. The longer the standoff goes on the greater their thirst for retribution grows. They'll do something stupid, and the king will have to act.'

Neither Isaac nor Ali said anything. They knew he was right.

Isaac broke the silence. 'So what, exactly, is the plan?'

THIRTY-TWO

AISHA AND ISABEL were already sitting side by side at the table under the balcony as the *muezzin* defiantly announced the dawn call to prayer the next day. Both had shawls tightly drawn around them against the early morning chill.

'Is this really necessary?' Isabel asked as they looked at the scene playing out in front of them. Abdul Rahman, Isaac, and Ali and around twenty of the spice merchant's men were preparing to leave the compound. They were dressed in red robes, some carried spears, some brandished scimitars. Isabel looked for Khaled and then remembered Ibrahim's treachery had cost him his life. He'd been a good man. So much death. The men were busy arranging their weapons, ensuring swords were securely sheathed and that all had their small, round shields.

'It's even more dangerous for my husband now. A faction wants to control the Albacîn and fight for its independence. They want Cisneros' head. They think Abdul Rahman was weak to only ask the king for his removal.'

'Does everyone feel that way?'

'No, but the ones shouting loudest do. I hope Isaac was right about the wiser heads in the community prevailing.'

Abdul Rahman drew everyone into a semi-circle and talked quietly in Arabic. Ali leant in close to Papa, translating for him, though he probably knew enough Arabic to understand most of what was being said.

Aisha said, 'He's telling them that today is the most important day of their lives and they must conduct themselves with dignity. Nobody is to attack first, only defend.'

'What's their plan?'

'They will walk through the Albacîn to the Puerta de Elvira. Abdul Rahman hopes to gather all his supporters along the way. When they arrive Talavera will be waiting on the other side of the barricades. He's persuaded the king to allow him to propose a peaceful resolution. If we lay down our arms he will agree to further discussions about the status of the Mudéjar and guarantee my immunity from any charges that Cisneros proposes.'

'And will Abdul Rahman be satisfied with that?'

'The only alternative is the slaughter of thousands of our brothers and sisters. He hopes that with Talavera, Isaac and Alejandro on his side the king will find a way we can all live in peace.'

'Alejandro is doing what he can to influence Their Majesties. I had a letter from him yesterday.' He had written other things that made her blush to recall. She turned her face away from Aisha until she felt the heat leave her cheeks.

Abdul Rahman's voice grew louder, and his men responded by banging their swords on their shields.

'That doesn't sound very calm,' Isabel said.

Aisha frowned. 'He wants peace, but he has to prepare for an attack, not least from the other faction.' The worry etched into her face made her look older.

Isabel took her hand and squeezed.

Aisha returned the gesture with a weak smile.

'Papa,' Isabel called out as the group made to leave, 'take care.'

He gave a small bow and mouthed, 'Always.' He did not look at Aisha.

Abdul Rahman grinned at his wife and boomed, 'Lunch at the usual time my dear. We're certain to be hungry. Every single one of us!'

The men trooped out and Isabel and Aisha held hands in the silence.

The spice merchant led the way closely flanked by his men. Isaac followed alongside Ali.

'He obviously wants the best fighters watching his rear,' Isaac said with a smile.

Ali did not reply, his expression inscrutable. Usually his friend would respond to his attempts at humour with a wry riposte. But since Ali's return from the mountains he'd changed, he was less willing to share his thoughts. Isaac had never seen him so worried.

As they made their way through the lanes people joined them continuously: men in brightly striped kaftans and veiled women in long gowns. The woody, sweet scent of sandalwood and oud surrounded them. They shouted their support for Abdul Rahman and he called back his thanks. Children skipped alongside asking the men to brandish their scimitars, but they kept their weapons sheathed. For the moment they were obeying Abdul Rahman's instructions. As the crowd grew Isaac and Ali were pushed back from the main group. Isaac decided there was nothing to be done about this. They would catch up when they arrived at the meeting point with Talavera.

The chill of the early morning had dissipated, and Isaac was becoming uncomfortably warm. They seemed to be taking a circuitous route to get to the Puerta Elvira.

'He's not lost is he?' Isaac asked Ali.

Ali snorted. 'Look around you.'

Of course. Abdul Rahman was taking a long route to gather as large a demonstration of his support as possible, a show of his strength.

The crowd came to a sudden halt. Isaac held his hands out to stop himself from colliding with the woman in front. For a long moment there was silence. Then loud cheering broke out which sounded different in tone to Isaac. There was a wild and dark quality to it.

'What's going on?' he asked Ali.

The apothecary shook his head and pushed his way through the crowd, beckoning him to follow. The noise increased and

Isaac realised it was coming from two different groups. One that supported Abdul Rahman and one that didn't. They weren't near enough to the Puerta de Elvira for the rivals to be the kings' supporters. It must be the opposing faction who aimed to prevent the meeting with Talavera.

They reached the pack of Abdul Rahman's men who allowed them to pass. Those with spears were shaking them but the scimitars remain sheathed. Isaac and Ali positioned themselves behind the spice merchant. He was facing a tall, emaciated man wearing a white turban and a white robe cinched around the waist with a thick leather belt. He didn't appear to be armed. But a group of men standing behind him certainly were.

'That's Akbar.' Ali whispered. 'The leader of the rival group.'

Abdul Rahman began talking in a low soothing tone.

'He's explaining the situation to Akbar,' Ali said. 'He's asking him to be patient and allow negotiations with Talavera to proceed.'

Akbar did not respond. He had a fixed, calm expression with just a hint of a sardonic smile. Abdul Rahman said nothing and stared at Akbar, whose supporters filled the void by shouting his name and brandishing their swords.

Then a rumbling chant rippled through the throng behind Isaac. At first it sounded a long way off. The crowd must have grown behind them. 'Abdul Rahman,' was repeated over and over, becoming louder with every chorus until it was a deafening swell of noise that washed over them. He was caught up in it and couldn't help joining in. It drowned out Akbar's supporters. Abdul Rahman raised a fist and the chanting from those nearest stopped. The silence flowed back through the crowd as though the tide was going out until the hush was complete.

Akbar dipped his head and muttered something.

Isaac looked at Ali who said, 'He said "*Inshallah*."'

God willing. The inherent ambiguity would be understood by his followers as meaning that whatever happened was not Akbar's responsibility. It allowed him to save some face after a battle he'd lost before it had even started. Akbar and his supporters melted away and Abdul Rahman strode forward, the crowd surging behind him. Isaac could feel the weight of supporters growing as they wound their way through the Albacîn. The babble of voices ebbed and flowed between 'Allahu Akbar' to 'Abdul Rahman'. There were shouts of 'Death to Cisneros' which were met with loud cheers. He imagined taking flight as a falcon and looking down on the scene: he saw a sinuous snake curling its way along the tight lanes with Abdul Rahman at its head. They arrived at the pile of stone and broken furniture that had been used to barricade the Puerta Elvira. The church bells were ringing for noon prayers.

'Perfect timing,' Abdul Rahman announced. 'Talavera should be on the other side.' He commanded his men to make a passage through the barricade. They shifted aside the rubble until there was just enough space to pass through. Abdul Rahman signalled two of his men and Isaac and Ali to follow him. They edged through the gap and Isaac had a vivid sense of being in that narrow alley again. Thank God it was fleeting.

When they'd shimmied through to the other side there was nobody there to greet them.

'Not Santa Alfaqui as well,' Abdul Rahman muttered. 'Can't anyone be trusted?' He looked to the heavens.

'Patience, brother, patience,' Ali said in a low tone.

Isaac put a hand to his brow to shield his eyes from the sun and looked up the road to the crest of a hill. Had Cisneros got to Talavera and stopped him from coming? There was a murmur from the other side of the knoll. It grew louder and Isaac recognised it as melodic chanting. Ali pointed at something making its way over the hill towards them. Isaac feared it was a phalanx of the king's guards. Then he saw the leader was dressed in white and held a large cross out in front of him. They were soldiers: Christ's soldiers led by Bishop Talavera himself. It was a procession of priests and friars. They were intoning a prayer that Isaac didn't recognise but found moving in its beauty and simplicity.

Abdul Rahman said, 'I didn't doubt him for a second.'

Talavera called a halt about twenty paces from the barricade. He held up a palm and the chanting stopped. He called out, 'We come in peace.'

'On whose authority?' Abdul Rahman boomed back.

'His Majesty's. And The Almighty's.' Talavera paused. 'And I pray, Allah's.'

There were cheers from behind the barricade as Allah's name was invoked. Isaac assumed that this exchange must have been agreed between them beforehand. As a way of reassuring the crowd.

Abdul Rahman took a step forward. Something flew past him and landed at Talavera's feet, causing a cloud of dust to rise as it skimmed past him. Isaac was horrified to see that it was a rock. It must have been thrown from behind the barricades by one of Akbar's supporters. They were trying to sabotage the negotiations. It was followed by several more and then a hail of pebbles thudded into the earth around the priests. Some of Abdul Rahman's less committed followers must be joining in. One rock knocked the crucifix from the bishop's hands. That was too much for the priests and they scattered, screaming and shouting. All except for Talavera, who knelt, picked up the cross, and advanced towards them, slowly and steadily. Alone.

Isaac had never seen such bravery. The bishop was saying something, but Isaac couldn't make it out. The hail of stones subsided. There were the sounds of a struggle from behind the barricade. Abdul Rahman's men were gaining the upper hand. Talavera was now close enough for Isaac to hear his words, 'Yea, though I walk through the valley of the shadow of death I will fear no evil, for thou art with me.' He stopped and held out his hand. Abdul Rahman clasped it between both of his and said, 'Thank you, Santa Alfaqui.'

There were loud cheers from behind them and a steady stream of *Mudéjar* clambered over the barricade. They surrounded Talavera, cheering him, some of them even kissing the hem of his garment. They repeated "alfaqui" over and over and another phrase Isaac was not familiar with. He asked Ali what it meant.

'"The fearless one,"' he replied. 'A simple act of bravery

convinced them of his essential goodness. He showed he wasn't scared of them. They respect that. Cisneros' destruction of our holy books only demonstrated he feared us. He demonised us and we couldn't respect that.'

Abdul Rahman put an arm around Talavera's shoulder and led him into the Albacîn to continue the negotiations.

'It's the nearest thing I've ever seen to a miracle,' Isaac said.

CHAPTER
THIRTY-THREE

ON THE FOLLOWING NIGHT Abdul Rahman and Aisha threw an open house. After the evening prayers the compound was filled with friends and neighbours. Isaac sat on a stool outside the door of his apartment. Observing. He sipped a glass of sweet *nabidh* and marvelled at the scene before him. The air was full of the spicy aroma of *ras-al-hanout* from the food stacked on the tables lining the far wall of the courtyard. The heady scent of sandalwood wafted from incense burners nestling atop poles. Two musicians sat on a platform that had been erected in front of the fountain. A man with long fingernails plucked at the strings of an oud, whilst his companion rhythmically caressed a drum cradled on his lap. They were accompanying a tall woman singing plangently in Arabic. Her deep voice was at once both joyful and mournful.

Abdul Rahman was circulating, gesturing wildly, laughing loudly. Calderon arrived and the spice merchant clapped the silk merchant on the back, no doubt thanking him again for the arrangements he'd made for Aisha's evacuation, which were no longer required. Abdul Rahman was always energetic, but Isaac had never seen him this animated. Aisha was at his side, looking beautiful in a blue gown, mantilla pulled back from her face and draped over her shoulders. She was simultaneously guiding him by the elbow to talk to specific people whilst gesturing to the servant girls who immediately disappeared into the kitchen or attended to the food tables. Husband and wife were in their element.

He saw Isabel break off from her conversation with Ali and make her way through the crowd towards him.

'Papa, why are you by yourself?'

'You know me, I'm not comfortable in these situations. I'm enjoying it in my own way.'

She studied his face. 'You don't think we actually have anything to celebrate, do you?'

'Do you mean does the peace accord mean anything?'

She nodded.

He thought for a moment. 'Tranquility has been restored to the Albacîn. Aisha has been granted full immunity by the king. Cisneros can't do her any harm. Talavera has promised to broker further discussions with Their Majesties over the future of the *Mudéjar*. What more could we want?'

She held his eyes for a long, searching moment. He knew she understood that this was only a temporary respite. Cisneros would not give up the fight to wipe out the *Mudéjar*. He wouldn't stop until he converted or killed them all. And he enjoyed the full support of the queen.

'You're right, Papa. We should enjoy the moment.' She

paused. 'You do know what today is?'

'Of course.'

It was Christmas day and although Isaac had ambiguous feelings about it – as a "christ-killer" how could he commemorate Jesus' birthday? – they had always celebrated it enthusiastically when Maria had been alive.

'Is that why you're sad?' she asked.

'I miss the children.'

'So do I. But they can come now, perhaps to celebrate the new year?'

'Let's talk tomorrow. We'll make plans.' She was distracted, scanning the crowd. 'Be off with you. Alejandro is over there isn't he?'

Even in the dark Isaac could see her blush at the mention of his name. He couldn't understand what was stopping them getting married. When all this was over he would have a serious talk with Alejandro. He had to marry Isabel or give her up once and for all. This on and off relationship was no good, least of all for Isabel's reputation. Maria would not have allowed it. Besides, Isaac wanted a grandson — or maybe a granddaughter — before it was too late.

Isabel kissed his forehead and turned to join the fun. He closed his eyes and let the singer's voice wash over him. Joyful or mournful?

Half-asleep Isaac wrinkled his nose against a bitter scent working its way into his nostrils. Something was alight. In his barely conscious state he wondered if Cisneros was burning books again. Surely not in the middle of the night? A stupid thought. The celebrations had gone on late and perhaps someone had forgotten to extinguish all the incense burners. He turned over and tried to get back to sleep. Then he heard the screams.

He jumped out of bed. No time to change out of his nightshirt. He threw his door open to be engulfed by a wave of heat and noxious fumes. Black smoke was billowing from the main house. The servants were running around the courtyard, some dipping buckets into the fountain and throwing water at the fire. It wasn't doing any good, the flames grew. A pair of girls huddled together. Others were screaming. Abdullah was trying to soothe them. A mischief of black rats scampered out of the house and swarmed across the left-over food on the tables. The servants would catch it from Aisha in the morning. Aisha. Where was she? And Isabel?

Ali came running down the stairs from his bedchamber.

Isaac screamed at him, 'Where is everyone?'

Ali shook his head. He surveyed the situation, and then called Abdullah over and shouted at him in rapid Arabic. Abdullah corralled the servants into a circle and gesticulating wildly he gave them instructions. They formed a human chain leading from the fountain, filled their buckets from it and passed them down the line.

A guttural scream came from above. Isaac looked up, Abdul Rahman was on the balcony wrenching at his hair and beard. '*Harami. Harami,*' he screamed.

Isaac knew the formal translation was, "sinner" but he was sure Abdul Rahman was using it to mean, "bastard." For a moment Isaac was puzzled. Who was he referring to? Surely even Cisneros wouldn't stoop to this. It must be Akbar. He hadn't accepted defeat gracefully after all.

Sloshing buckets of water were rapidly passed from hand to hand, then thrown over the fire billowing out from the base of the house. But the flames kept on growing.

Isaac grabbed Ali by the arm and shouted, 'It's pointless. We must get everybody out.'

Abdul Rahman appeared at their side screaming, 'Where is Aisha? Where is she?'

Ali said, 'Not with you?'

'No,' Abdul Rahman sobbed, 'she slept in the back because of the noise from the party.' Anguish distorted his face. 'With Isabel.'

'Show me,' Isaac shouted.

Abdul Rahman grabbed him by the hand and hauled him forward into the house. He'd never been invited in here. He'd stayed in his apartment and shared meals in the courtyard. Perhaps Abdul Rahman had wanted to keep some boundaries between them? It wasn't the time to ponder that. As they ran through the house all he could make out was a blur of highly polished floors and Persian rugs used as wall hangings. He was finding it difficult to keep up, the spice merchant was moving quickly. A beam creaked and he looked up to see flames licking across the ceiling. It was getting hotter. He pulled the collar of his nightshirt over his mouth to keep out the fumes.

Abdul Rahman came to an abrupt halt and held a hand across his face as they were greeted by a wall of orange and yellow fire. 'This way,' he shouted turning left down a long corridor, then right and right again. Then he disappeared into the smoke. They must be circling around the fire to access the rooms where Aisha and Isabel were. Isaac kept moving forward on that assumption. Then there were high-pitched screams of, 'Help.' He recognised his daughter's voice. He caught sight of Abdul Rahman at the end of the corridor through a haze of smoke, standing completely still. After a moment's hesitation Isaac saw him wrench a rug off the wall, wrap it around his head and shoulders and charge forward through a barrier of flames and batter open a door. He collapsed onto the floor and rolled around to put out the fire engulfing him.

Isaac rushed into the smoke-filled room and helped him up. Isabel was sitting on the bed, coughing, and cradling Aisha's inert body in her arms. Had she passed out from the fumes, was she dead? Isabel was seemingly unable to move, caught between securing her own safety and looking after Aisha. 'We couldn't make it to the door,' she yelled.

Isaac reached out a hand and yanked her up. Aisha's body fell out of her arms and slumped onto the bed.

He pushed her towards the door. 'Run!' he shouted.

'We have to help,' Isabel screamed.

Abdul Rahman was holding his wife, slapping her face, screaming, 'Wake up, wake up, my love.' He looked up at and said, 'Go. Save your daughter.'

Isaac pulled Isabel forward and glanced back over his

shoulder, through the smoke. Abdul Rahman was holding Aisha in his arms and shouting something which he couldn't hear clearly over the roar of the fire. It was, 'Run.' He was sure of it. Then the ceiling in front of the door to the bedchamber collapsed and Abdul Rahman and Aisha disappeared.

BOOK III

Granada
January, 1500

CHAPTER
THIRTY-FOUR

ISAAC NURSED A GLASS OF SHERRY IN A DARK CORNER of Bar Aixa, lost in trying to make sense of what had happened over the past few days. It was the middle of the afternoon on New Years' Day. The bar was quiet after the festivities of the previous night. But the dawn of a new century was not a time of celebration for Isaac. He had attended two funerals in the previous week. Both had taken place at Ibn Malik graveyard. The place where so many *Mudéjar* victims were buried. The place where Isaac had first met Abdullah; an old man who had been grieving for his family but who had shown so much courage in saving his and Aisha's lives. The place where Abdul Rahman was now laid to rest.

The funerals took place within a day of the deaths, as was required by Islamic law. Both were officiated over by Hamza, the alfaqui who Cisneros had bullied into questioning Aisha. Ali had led the prayers. He was distraught but managed admirably. The cemetery and the surrounding streets were packed with mourners. Abdul Rahman would have been delighted. Perhaps what would have pleased the spice merchant most was the attendance of Santa Alfaqui, who arrived by himself and was greeted with a hushed reverence. He stood quietly apart from the burial plot. Isaac joined him, both outsiders at this funeral. They bowed their heads, muttering prayers from their own faiths.

Two people were not at either of the funerals. Isabel and Aisha. It was not customary for women to attend *Mudéjar* burials. But Aisha would have been at her husband's funeral if she had been physically able to. She was at the compound in Isaac's bed, being cared for by Isabel. The main house had been destroyed, but the outbuildings, including Isaac's apartment, had withstood the fire. Ali had found Aisha unconscious on the ground outside the bedchamber at the back of the house, surrounded by shards of glass. Abdul Rahman must have smashed the window and thrown her outside. Before he could join her he was overcome by the smoke. Ali examined her but would not be drawn on whether she would survive. He'd prescribed a sleeping draught to allow her body to rest. A week later she was still drifting in and out of consciousness. Isabel was overseeing her treatment and sharing the apartment with her. Ali reported that her physical wounds were healing but her mind and her spirit needed time to recover.

The fire had caused outrage across the Albacîn. Following the peace accord with Talavera, Abdul Rahman had been at the height of his influence and power. There had been no need for Their Majesties to become involved. The majority of *Mudéjar* who supported Abdul Rahman formed a committee and completed their own investigation within twenty-four hours. Akbar was found guilty and beheaded. That seemed to be the end of the rival faction, according to Ali. The Albacîn became a quieter place.

The second funeral had happened the day after the first and was sparsely attended. Isaac was amongst a handful of people. Abdullah had no relatives left to mourn him and few friends it seemed. And just when he had found another family to be a part of it had been taken away from him. Isaac mourned the loss of Abdul Rahman deeply, but this death felt even harder. The spice merchant had lost his life for a cause, Abdullah had lost his because an act of bravery had led him to the compound. It seemed so unfair, especially after all he had lost. At least Abdullah was now buried alongside his family and reunited with them in the afterlife. *Inshallah.*

Isaac wondered where he would be buried when his time came. As it stood he couldn't take his place in Seville alongside Maria. And if he died outside of his beloved city who would attend his funeral?

'Ali told me I'd find you here,' Alejandro said drawing up a stool. 'How's life at the Apothecary?'

Isaac was staying with Ali, bunking down on the spare bed in the stockroom until he decided what to do. Or until it was decided for him by the king or Cisneros. He'd only seen Alejandro briefly since the fire. They'd agreed it would be better not to be seen together, whilst the dust settled, whilst the flames cooled. Isaac made small talk about the hardness of the bed and hearing Ali snoring in the bedchamber above.

Alejandro signalled to Teresa to bring more drinks. She sashayed across, leant close to Alejandro as she placed two mugs of wine on the table and gave him a wink. Isaac watched Alejandro arch an eyebrow, smile, and then stare admiringly at her rear.

Isaac took a gulp of wine and banged his mug down.

Alejandro shot him an enquiring look.

Good, he had his attention. 'You have to stop this.' He glared at Alejandro. 'You need to grow up,' he hissed.

Alejandro looked bewildered.

He jutted his chin at Teresa. She held his eyes for a moment, then turned away and busied herself wiping down the counter.

Alejandro sighed and wiped a palm over his face. 'It's nothing.' He shrugged. 'Just instinct.'

'This can't go on any longer.' Anger was welling up inside Isaac's chest, threatening to overwhelm him. Normally he could contain it or remove himself from the situation. But not this time. 'You need to stop playing around with Isabel. *My daughter*. Show some respect. To her. For me.'

He had never seen the look that appeared on Alejandro's face: a mixture of shock and sadness. And something else. Recognition? Acceptance?

'Is now the right time to discuss this?' Alejandro said.

'When will it *ever* be?'

Alejandro took a sip of wine.

'Haven't the last few weeks taught you anything? Life is short. Bad things happen. People you love die. Suddenly.' He paused. 'It's so fucking unfair.' He banged the table with a fist.

Teresa glanced over at them. He stared at her until she looked away.

Alejandro said, 'You've been through a lot – '

'We all have but I don't need your sympathy. I need you to decide what you want and,' he leant forward threateningly, 'stop stringing Isabel along. Marry her or forget about her.'

'She's the one who rejected me.'

'You're both as bad as each other. You love each other, anyone can see that.'

A sheepish look crossed Alejandro's face.

'Your continued interest deters other suitors.' He paused. 'And Isabel can't move forward whilst you waste all of our time playing games with barmaids.'

Alejandro bowed his head.

'And,' Isaac's tone softened, 'I want a grandson, before it's too late. Hopefully, he'll have Isabel's looks and intelligence.'

Alejandro looked up and grinned. 'Not a granddaughter?'

Isaac ignored the attempt to distract him. 'You would make a fine father.'

Alejandro reached out, took Isaac's hand, and stood up. 'You have my word, señor, within the month, I will settle this matter.'

'Now, what was it you came to see me about?'

CHAPTER
THIRTY-FIVE

'ANY CHANGE MY, DEAR?' Ali asked Isabel as he entered Isaac's former apartment at dawn.

She looked up from the chair next to Aisha's bed and shook her head. Isabel closed Mama's Book of Hours and put it in the cradle next to the bed. She rubbed at her eyes with the heels of her palms. She'd been seeking consolation from the prayer book, reading it by candlelight through the night. Small enough to cup in her hands but it contained multitudes. But rereading Mama's favourite parts hadn't brought her any solace. Burning Aisha's favourite sandalwood incense day and night hadn't stirred her since Ali had instructed her to discontinue the sleeping draught. Praying to the Lord hadn't seem to do much for either of them.

Ali picked his way through the gloom and opened the shutters. 'That's better. Now let me see.' He stood on the other side of the bed and held Aisha's wrist. Isabel noticed how gaunt he'd become. 'Her pulse is a little quicker,' he said.

'Is that good?' she asked.

Ali tipped his head noncommittally from side to side. He put the back of his hand on her forehead. 'Her fever is subsiding.' He leant close to her. 'Her breathing is more regular.'

'Good signs!'

'Yes. I think we may see some further improvement by the morrow. But we mustn't be too optimistic.'

The delight on Isabel's face turned to a frown.

Ali said, 'Come my dear. Let's walk.'

Isabel glanced at Aisha.

'She'll be fine. We'll stay within earshot. Some fresh air will do you good.'

Isabel took his arm, and they circulated the courtyard. The house had been reduced to a heap of rubble. It had stopped smouldering but an acrid smell lingered. So much for fresher air.

'What will be done with the house?' Isabel asked.

'We'll have to wait for Aisha to regain her health. It's her decision. My brother would have rebuilt it. He's left her more than enough money to do so if she wishes.'

Their voices were the only sounds in the courtyard. The fountain was silent, the water exhausted in a vain attempt to quench the fire. The parrots had disappeared. Isabel missed them, she'd become used to their squawking. Why is it we only appreciate things, people once they've gone?

Isabel asked, 'How are you?'

'Struggling. That's the truth of it.'

'If you're struggling, you're still fighting. It means you haven't given up.'

Ali smiled. 'When did you become so wise?'

'It must be from spending so much time listening to all the wisdom you great men speak,' she said with a grin.

Ali gave her a wistful look.

'You must miss him terribly.'

'It's like my right arm has gone. We were apart for so long when I stayed in Seville. I was stubborn, I should have moved to Granada earlier. We would have had more time together.'

'At least you had some time,' she said. 'And you have some wonderful memories.'

'You're right, I should be grateful for what we had.' He patted her hand. 'There was a matter I wanted to discuss with you.' He paused for a long moment.

Isabel thought she knew what he wanted to say, but why was it so difficult for him?

'I'm thinking of giving up the Apothecary.'

This wasn't what she'd expected.

'When we were in the mountains Abdul Rahman asked me to take over the running of his business in the event of his death.'

'And Aisha?'

Ali was shocked. 'What do you mean? What have you heard?'

His tone was unusually fierce. 'I meant wouldn't Aisha like to run the business?'

Ali looked relieved. What had he thought she meant?

He continued hastily, 'If she wishes to, she's most welcome. But I'm sure it would bore her.' He stopped walking and turned to face her. 'If you would like a half share of the Apothecary, it's yours. You've earned it. I will be a sleeping partner. You will run it the way you see fit.'

She didn't know what to say. She'd hoped one day to be offered the shop, but not so soon. There had been no time to think through the ramifications of Abdul Rahman's death. The future now held so many – too many? – possibilities. Should she travel with the Infanta to England? If she even had a choice in the matter. She would miss the children in Seville but knew in her heart she couldn't return to a life of domestic confinement.

Ali smiled, took her arm and they walked again. 'How is Alejandro?'

'I've only seen him briefly since the night of the fire.' He'd been busy organising the intelligence that his spies provided for him about what was going on the Albacîn.

'And, if I may ask, my dear, what are your plans?'

'I'd very much like to know the answer to that question too.'

'I ask as Alejandro may have a view on you running the Apothecary were you to be married.'

'He might very well "have a view," but until he asks the question he's not entitled to it.' She heard the harshness in her voice. 'My apologies.'

'There is no need, my dear. We know each other well enough to have a frank exchange. And if you're going to run a business you'll need to be robust.'

They walked in silence.

Ali said, 'You'll need a few days to consider my offer.'

'Thank you, Ali.' She'd already decided to accept but she would have to ask Papa's advice first. He wouldn't stand in her way, she was sure of it, but better to let him give his opinion rather than present it as a done deal. She would need to tell Alejandro as well. Perhaps it might encourage him to make his own decision.

'Shall we say a week, my dear?'

She agreed. A lot could happen in a week. As she'd just found out.

CHAPTER
THIRTY-SIX

SEVEN DAYS LATER ISAAC ROSE GROGGILY from his bed at the Apothecary and clutched at a spasm in his lower back. He would have to find somewhere else to stay. Apart from the lack of straw in the mattress and Ali's snoring he'd been kept awake by the anxiety of what was to happen later that day at the Alhambra. He'd been trying to parse what Alejandro had told him. Trying to understand what might be going on in Ferdinand's mind and what that would mean for him. His nerves were getting the better of him, and he could feel a pit forming in his stomach.

His Majesty had summoned him, Talavera and Ali to be present at Cisneros' audience with Their Majesties. The cardinal would present his plans to solve the *Mudéjar* situation. The king wanted the three of them there as he did not want to inflame the situation in the Albacîn. After Akbar's execution the king was unsure of who was best placed to represent the interests of the *Mudéjar*. Word had reached him that Talavera and Isaac had been accepted by the community at Abdul Rahman's funeral. Ali would be his brother's representative. Isaac had spent the last week discussing with Ali what they thought would happen at the audience and how they should play it. They had gone round in circles and eventually given up.

Alejandro said that Ferdinand had to be seen to be trying to be even-handed. Isaac thought it was all a charade. The queen would decide what would happen and Ferdinand would just go along with it. He almost always did unless he thought he would lose money.

Ali came down from his bedchamber and grunted, 'Good morning.'

'We need to hurry.'

They stood at the counter in the shop and silently ate crusts of rye bread and drank mugs of water. How different from the feasts Aisha had prepared. He'd become used to them, had taken them for granted. He should have learnt his lesson by now: nothing lasts, everything changes.

The shop had remained closed since Abdul Rahman's death. Ali would not open it until forty days of mourning had passed. It smelt musty and could do with a good clean. And when it reopened Isabel would be running it. That's what she'd told him the day before. But that decision had changed several times over the past week. Isaac didn't know what to make of her choice. Being an apothecary was a noble calling, but was it suitable for a woman? And she couldn't possibly manage the shop and be married and look after the children. His, and Maria's, grandchildren. Ali had been busy organising

Abdul Rahman's business and overseeing Aisha's recovery. He was spending a lot of time with her.

They finished their meagre meal, and as Ali locked up the cathedral bells tolled for Terce prayers. Cisneros' audience with Their Majesties would begin once the service was over. They had barely enough time to make it to the Alhambra and set off at a fast clip. He couldn't shake the feeling that something was going to go badly wrong. The cardinal's proposal – whatever it might be – would not be well received by the *Mudéjar*, and he worried what the consequences of that could be.

It was a warm morning, so he took off his hat and let the sunlight play over his face. 'How is Aisha?' he asked. He'd been asleep when Ali returned last night, and they never talked of serious matters over breakfast.

'She's slowly regaining her strength every day.' Ali paused. 'Well enough to receive visitors.'

He heard the pointedness to Ali's last comment. He had not seen Aisha since the fire. His heart and his head were a jumble of thoughts and emotions that he couldn't disentangle. Of course he was relieved she'd survived. He felt guilty for running from the fire and leaving her behind, even though he believed Abdul Rahman had told him to. He had seen how strong her love had been for her husband, and how strong his love had been for her. Isaac had allowed himself to believe he could intrude into that. For a while he'd betrayed Abdul Rahman's trust, in his mind and in his heart. Thank goodness he'd come to his senses in time before he'd done anything really stupid. He had Alejandro to thank for that.

'I'll see her this evening,' Isaac said.

'She'll be delighted.'

They walked on in silence through the narrow lanes. There was an unusual hush in the Albacîn; it had been like this since Abdul Rahman's funeral. Even the smells of spice and incense seemed muted. As though the whole neighbourhood was in mourning.

'Isaac, there's something you should know before you see her.'

He glanced across at Ali, who avoided his gaze.

'Tell me.'

'I will, after we've seen Their Majesties. I've been meaning to tell you for a few days but needed to find the right time.' He paused. 'There never seems to be one.'

Exactly what Isaac had said to Alejandro about marrying Isabel. He had an inkling of what Ali wanted to tell him. Isaac would let his old friend pick his moment.

They began the climb to the red citadel.

CHAPTER
THIRTY-SEVEN

THE ALHAMBRA WAS BUSTLING WITH SERVANTS running errands, guards patrolling, and courtiers hurrying to their appointments. Isaac and Ali entered the Hall of Kings and began the long walk towards the dais where Their Majesties were seated on golden thrones. The chamber was almost empty, unlike the last time Isaac had been here, fighting for his life, defending the accusation of murdering Torquemada. The opulence of the hall was even more apparent now it was almost empty. Their Majesties must have decided that they didn't want Cisneros' plans to be made public.

Isaac saw the back of a red cloaked figure addressing the monarchs. He was too far away to hear the exact words, but he could make out the wheedling tone. He hadn't heard Cisneros talk like this before, he was normally so certain, so commanding. Talavera, in his white Dominican robes, and Alejandro were standing to the king's right.

Ferdinand locked angry eyes with Isaac and beckoned him forward. What did the king want from this audience?

Cisneros stopped talking, turned around and stared at Isaac. His deep-set brown eyes burnt with hatred. His mouth turned from the smile he'd been presenting to Their Majesties into a vicious scowl. Isaac held his stare, determined not to display any weakness. As he and Ali parted to pass either side of the cardinal he whispered, 'Not this time, not this time.' What did the wicked bastard have up his sleeve?

Isaac and Ali bowed, and the king waved the back of his palm indicating that they should stand to the left of the queen. What game was Ferdinand playing? He had deliberately stationed four of the cardinal's biggest opponents on either side of the throne and left the cardinal to address all of them, alone. Was he trying to cow Cisneros? Isaac studied the cardinal's face and thought he saw doubt there.

'As I was saying, Your Majesty –'

The king held up a hand to stop Cisneros and turned to the queen. 'Your cardinal has cost us dear. His imprudence has made us lose in a few hours what it took us years to gain.'

So, Ferdinand was trying to get rid of Cisneros. He must have calculated that there was more revenue to be gained from a peaceful, prosperous *Mudéjar* community. Isaac shared a surprised glance with Ali. This could still turn out well. If Isabella shared her husband's view.

Isaac couldn't see the look that the queen gave her husband, but her tone was icy. 'He is our cardinal,' she replied imperiously. 'But,' she glared down at Cisneros, 'my husband is right. Your actions have cost us the trust and the faith of the *Mudéjar*. What have you to say?'

'Your Majesties, I admit that my zeal for our one true faith,' he glanced pointedly at Ali, 'led me to, perhaps, act imprudently.'

The king thumped his armrest. 'No "perhaps" about it,' he snarled. 'Burning religious books! That is not an excess of zeal, that is insanity.'

Cisneros bowed his head. 'On reflection and after much prayer I admit you are right, Your Majesty. The texts should have been banned, not burnt.' His tone was soft and full of regret. It was a clever performance, but Isaac didn't think it would be enough.

The queen was nodding and smiling. 'Your humility has led you to wisdom, cardinal. It does you much credit.'

Cisneros bowed deeply.

The king said, 'I doubt his humility and wisdom will give much consolation to the *Mudéjar*.' He glanced towards Talavera who nodded in agreement.

Cisneros said, 'Although my love of the Lord led me to commit an unfortunate act it is the *Mudéjar* who are guilty.' His voice was rising, becoming more defiant. 'It is they who broke the Treaty of Granada by engaging in armed rebellion.'

'Quite correct,' the queen said.

What was Cisneros up to? Isaac shot an enquiring glance at Alejandro, which he returned with a shake of the head. Whatever it was Isaac was certain the king wouldn't let him get away it.

The cardinal rushed on before His Majesty could intervene. 'However, we are all human, we all make mistakes.' His voice took on a portentous tone as though he were preaching from the pulpit. 'And mercy is paramount. As Psalms tells us, "Blessed is the one whose transgressions are forgiven."' He took a moment to look at each of them, as though inviting them to reflect on his wise words. Then with a flourish of his arm he said, 'The *Mudéjar* should receive a collective pardon.'

There was a moment of stunned silence. Isaac could not quite believe his ears. He'd thought Cisneros was begging for his own forgiveness to secure his position in Granada.

'Absolutely right,' the queen said.

The king glanced at her and then narrowed his eyes at Cisneros.

'Mercy should be extended to the rebels on one condition.' He scanned each of their faces. 'That they convert to Christianity.'

Issac heard Ali's sharp intake of breath. But he had to admire Cisneros. He'd admitted fault, forgiven his enemies but still got what he'd wanted all along. How could anyone deny him?

The queen said. 'That's a very fair solution, husband. Don't you agree?' She said it so quickly that Isaac was sure she and Cisneros had planned this.

The king pressed his teeth into his bottom lip. His knuckles whitened from the tension of gripping the armrests of the throne. He looked over at Talavera, who shrugged. Even he had no answer to the proposal. The bishop wanted the same thing as Cisneros: the conversion of the *Mudéjar* to Catholicism. It was the cardinal's violent methods he opposed. How could he disagree to a pardon and peaceful conversion?

Brilliant, absolutely brilliant, Isaac thought. He could see the rage simmering behind Ferdinand's eyes. His expression shifted from anger to contemplation. He must be actually considering the practicality of the proposal. The *Mudéjar,* though rebellious, were an asset to the kingdom. They had skills and knowledge that were beneficial to the economy. As the king pondered, Cisneros stepped forward, his voice humble and persuasive. He argued that the Church should oversee the conversions ensuring the process was carried out peacefully, without coercion. How cleverly Cisneros used his deep-rooted beliefs to manipulate the situation to his advantage. The cardinal knew that if her were successful, he would become a hero of the Church, his reputation and legacy assured. Sainthood surely awaited him.

The king replied, 'A good idea, cardinal. But what if they refuse to convert?'

Cisneros smiled, his eyes glinting with something akin to triumph. 'Then they must leave Granada, exiled to North Africa, to live among their own people.'

Isaac was shocked. Banishing an entire community was cruel, and he didn't believe the king would agree to it. But he saw hesitation in Ferdinand's eyes; he was seriously considering the proposal.

The queen added hastily, 'This is more than fair. We welcome the *Mudéjar* to our Kingdom if they follow our faith. If they do not wish to do so they may leave.'

Isaac was now convinced that the queen and Cisneros had

planned every move of this. Her Majesty was renowned at chess, and she had played this game beautifully.

The king finally spoke, his decision made. 'I will agree to the pardon and conversion of the *Mudéjar*, but only if it is done peacefully. Cisneros, you will take responsibility for ensuring that. But,' he glanced over at Talavera, 'the bishop will work alongside you to ensure it is.'

Cisneros's eyes darkened at the mention of his rival's name. This was something at least, Talavera would try to ensure the conversions happened peacefully. But Isaac couldn't shake the feeling that it was a hollow victory. He had just witnessed the authority of religion being used as a tool for political gain. Another way for the powerful to exert their control over the powerless.

The king dismissed them with a wave of the back of his hand and beckoned Alejandro to join him. Cisneros conferred with the queen. Talavera joined Isaac and Ali as they walked back down the long corridor out of the Hall of Kings. He leant across and whispered to them, 'Cisneros has achieved even more than Their Majesties. They only conquered the soil; Cisneros has gained the souls of Granada.'

Isaac kept silent. Ali merely grunted. Isaac knew the bishop well enough to realise that he felt a complex mixture of emotions; jealous that it had not been his victory, concerned for the *Mudéjar*, but glad that their souls had been saved. Many of them would not convert and would flee to Fez or fight rather than turn their backs on their religion. What would Ali choose to do? And what about Aisha?

CHAPTER
THIRTY-EIGHT

ISAAC AND AISHA SAT facing out into the courtyard on either side of the doorway to his old apartment. Now hers. It was nearing sunset on the day of Cisneros' audience. The air was cool, the cicadas were singing, and the air was infused by a mixture of lingering fumes from the fire and the sandalwood incense Aisha was burning. They had exchanged pleasantries and he'd told her what had happened at the Alhambra. She'd already known most of it, she had her spies amongst the staff at the palace. They had lapsed into a companionable silence. She pulled her mantilla closely around her and closed her eyes. Her face was lined with exhaustion, and she looked much older than she had a few days ago. She was still frail, and he left her to drift in her thoughts for a while longer.

He had spent the time since the audience discussing the outcome – amongst other things – with Ali, Talavera, and Alejandro. They shared a mixture of bemusement, fear of the future and admiration for Cisneros' cunning. But they couldn't see a clear way forward. Talavera would do his best to ensure the baptisms and conversions were carried out peacefully. But how many would choose to stay? Alejandro promised to play his part, but there was little he could do. Then he'd walked back to the Apothecary with Ali who'd shared with him the news he'd promised to before they had gone to the Alhambra. Isaac had expected it but was still shocked to hear it. The congratulations he gave to Ali sounded hollow to his own ears.

He inhaled deeply and looked at Aisha, who was still lost in thought. The events of the past week had taken a terrible toll on her. He leaned back in his chair and watched as the sun quickly descended behind the high walls of the compound. As darkness fell the melodic cry of the *muezzin* rippled across the courtyard.

'That might be the last time we ever hear that sound in Granada,' Aisha said.

He didn't know how to reply. Sadly, she was right.

'It won't take Cisneros long to shut down the remaining mosques,' she said.

'First the synagogues, now the mosques,' Isaac said.

'Has he told you?'

Isaac smiled. 'Yes.'

'And?'

'Ali explained that it's normal in your community for a brother-in-law to marry his brother's widow. To protect her. To keep the family together.'

'We'll have to wait three months before we can officially marry,' she said, 'but we are engaged already.'

'It's still quick. After Maria died ...' His voice trailed away into the darkness.

'It's different for a man. You have choices.'

'So do you.'

She looked at him sharply. 'If I remain single every lecherous man in Granada who wants a piece of Abdul Rahman's business will prey upon me. He worked too hard for too long, sacrificed so much. This is the best way to protect his legacy.'

He said nothing.

She was right.

He was about to ask her whether she loved Ali when she said, 'My husband was right about you.'

He feared Abdul Rahman had known the truth of his feelings for Aisha and hated him for it.

'You love me.'

His heart jumped.

'Like a sister.' She reached over to grasp his hand. 'I'm very grateful to know you Isaac Camarino Alvarez. You're a good man.'

He was glad it was dark and that she couldn't see him struggling to contain his tears. Isaac squeezed her hand and then let go. He coughed and wiped a hand over his face. 'Where will you go?' he asked.

'We'll stay until we're married. It will take time for Cisneros to complete all the conversions or scare everyone off. Ali has spoken with Santa Alfaqui; he'll protect us for a while. Then we'll decide whether to stay or go to Fez to be with my children.'

'I hope you'll invite me to the wedding.'

'Of course, my dear, you and Isabel will be the guests of honour.'

He would manage the ceremony; to honour Abdul Rahman's memory and for his friendship with Ali. Even though it would hurt.

Aisha continued, 'I'm glad she's taking over the Apothecary. For Ali's sake. He'll have enough to do managing the spice business.' She paused and asked softly, 'What will you do?'

'Honestly, I don't know. I can't return to Seville unless His Majesty relents. Alejandro is going to propose that he ends my banishment, as a way of recognising my help.' The words were out of his mouth before he could stop them.

Aisha didn't let them pass. 'Help with what?'

He was too tired for evasion. 'Passing information about the rebels. About Abdul Rahman's plans.'

Aisha stared at him. It was too dark to be sure of her expression, but he felt her eyes boring into him. Then she threw back her head and laughed. 'Oh, we knew about that.'

'How?'

'It's exactly what Abdul Rahman would have done in the king's position: recruit you as a spy.'

'Why did you allow me to stay in your home?'

'We got the benefit of yours and Alejandro's insight. You had to give us something to get anything.' She paused. 'And I, we, liked having you around. You're quite good company sometimes.'

'You were using me as much as I was using you?'

'You could put it like that. Or you could say that it was a mutually beneficial relationship. And,' she paused, 'you got the better end of the bargain as you ate my food every day.'

She laughed again and this time Isaac joined in. Why not? It was all so absurd.

'Speaking of that rascal, when is Alejandro going to propose to her?' Aisha asked.

When indeed, Isaac thought.

CHAPTER
THIRTY-NINE

AS ISABEL TRUDGED UP THE STEEP HILL to the Alhambra she found herself struggling to breathe. Was it because as the sun set the air seemed to get thicker? Or was it the excitement? The message Alejandro had sent to the Apothecary asking her to meet him in his official chambers had surprised, and then flustered her. She suspected what he intended but she dared not admit it to herself, dare not name it. She'd returned to the compound to bathe and change her clothes. Nearing the Gate of the Pomegranates – feeling hot and sticky – she cursed him for not coming to visit her. He wasn't always as attentive to her needs as he should be. But she was intrigued: he'd never asked her to attend him at the palace before. And the red citadel at night was a magical place.

Isabel flourished the letter bearing Alejandro's seal to the guards. They waved her through to the tree-lined avenue that led deep into the palace grounds. The last time she'd been here was when Alejandro had rushed her out to return to the compound so that she could flee to Fez with Aisha. It had been a thrilling adventure, escaping on horseback with him through the burning Albacîn. It was as if he had been her knight, though she would never admit that to him.

Reaching the main part of the palace she found her way slowly through the labyrinth of corridors and patios towards the Court of Lions where Alejandro had said he would be. She took her time to admire the white marble floors shimmering in the torchlight, luxuriate in the perfume of orange blossom, lemon, and myrtle, and to be soothed by the gentle babble of water. She wanted to absorb every moment of this journey, to savour it. He had waited for her for years; he could wait a little longer.

Isabel stood with her back against a pillar at the entrance to the Court of Lions. She was glad of the coolness of the stone. She peeked round and saw him impatiently pacing around the twelve white marble lions encircling the fountain. Good. She strained to hear what he was muttering, but his voice was too low. His expression was serious, worried even. She smiled to herself, counted to one hundred and then glided onto the patio.

'There you are,' he said, his irritation evident.

She regarded him icily and said nothing. Waiting.

He looked at her closely and smiled. 'You look wonderful.'

Isabel had chosen the powder blue gown she'd had made in Seville but had not had the occasion to wear in Granada. She wore a necklace with a golden filigreed pendant. The inscription in the centre read, 'Hail Mary Full of Grace.' It was Gabriel's salutation to Mary when he revealed to her she would give birth to the Christ Child. Mama had given it to her on her fourteenth birthday. Thank goodness she'd stored some of her things in a trunk in Papa's apartment or else they wouldn't have survived the fire. She could have lived without the gown but losing the pendant would have been too much to bear.

He took her hand and led her up a narrow, winding bare wooden staircase, dimly lit by torches set in wall sconces. Her excitement grew as he unlocked the door at the top of the stairs. What would it open on to? There must be so many mysterious, wonderfully decorated rooms in the palace. She was disappointed to find a high-ceilinged room, plainly decorated, with a desk and two chairs. Had he invited her here for a business meeting? She let go of his hand and folded her arms.

He sat down behind the desk and gestured towards the other chair.

She shook her head.

'This is where I work,' he said.

She looked at the faded wall hangings and the shabby furniture.

'Not impressed?' he asked, a smile playing over his lips.

'I'm sure you have many very important conversations, talk of great things and make interesting plans,' she replied.

He looked at her knowingly, her irony hadn't escaped him. 'Try this.' He walked over to the far wall and drew back a pair of floor to ceiling wooden shutters. She gasped at what he revealed. The door opened onto a large terrace with a view of

Granada beyond it. The city was lit up with hundreds of lights that seemed to mirror the myriad of stars above. She peered over the balcony and let the slight breeze caress her face. She called out, 'Where's the Apothecary?' Then she pointed into the distance and said, 'Is that the compound?' She was so caught up in the beauty before her that she didn't notice Alejandro standing beside her until he spoke.

'Remember when we used to look out over the Guadalquivir from your Papa's house in Seville?'

A shiver ran through her at the mixture of feelings this memory evoked. She stole a sidelong glance at him and found his gaze fixed on hers, searching her eyes as if he would find something hidden there. He brushed a strand of hair behind her ear before allowing his fingers to linger against her cheek. 'So beautiful,' he whispered. Then he broke away abruptly and said, 'I can't do this.'

She said nothing, waiting for him to explain.

He said, 'Someone recently told me, "Life is short. Bad things happen. People you love die."'

'Papa was never the most optimistic of people,' she replied without hesitation.

He looked at her in surprise. 'You know him so well.'

'He's right though. That's why you must be brave and take your chances.' She paused. 'Because they might never come again.'

'What if you're scared? What if you've been hurt before?'

'What's that old phrase?' she said. 'Leap before you look?'

'I think it's look before –.' He cocked his head in

acknowledgement of her knowing grin. He gripped the balcony and looked out into the night.

She stood her ground. It had to be his decision.

In one sudden movement he slapped his palms against the balcony, knelt on one knee before her and took her hand in his. 'This is me leaping,' he said. 'Isabel will you do me the great honour –'

'Yes, you fool, yes.'

He took her in his arms and kissed her. When they finally parted from the embrace, she felt a deep sense of contentment fill every atom of her - nothing else mattered. Finally, she could be with Alejandro. It would be all she had ever dreamt of. She would make sure of it.

CHAPTER
FORTY

One month later ...

'GOOD TO SEE YOU, ISAAC,' Ferdinand drawled. His shirt tails were flapping outside his breeches, and he was barefoot.

Isaac gave a deep bow. About time, he thought. His Majesty had been in Granada for six months and this was the first time they'd met in private. He was looking sprightly, as though he'd lost a little weight. Perhaps the mountain air agreed with him.

'Shall we?' The king said and without waiting for an answer began strolling under the colonnade surrounding the Court of Lions. 'Excuse the informality of my dress, but I find it helps me to concentrate. Being dressed in all that ermine and gold restricts ones' freedom of movement and thought.'

Isaac said nothing. Having never worn ermine or gold, he had no idea how to respond.

It was shortly after sunrise, the patio was empty, only birdsong from the birds swooping in and out of the myrtle bushes to hunt for berries keeping them company.

'I won't detain you. I know you have a busy day ahead of you.'

Isaac dipped his head and fell into step with the king.

'I'll come straight to the point. You did a pretty good job with the rebels. Passed on some useful information. Helped me get a sense of what was going on.'

That's a good start, Isaac thought.

'Difficult hand to play, both sides at once. Made even more difficult when there's romance involved.'

What did he know about his feelings for Aisha? Or was he talking about Alejandro? Better not to ask for clarification.

'You did such a good job that I've got a reward for you.'

I can return to Seville.

'Got another mission for you. Even more important. In England.'

Isaac glanced over at the king who raised an eyebrow. His surprise and anger had revealed itself. Isaac said, 'At Your Majesty's pleasure.'

'Good man,' the king said. 'Our ambassador to England, excellent chap, Rodrigo de Puebla, sent some very good news. The civil wars have been settled. A few executions required of course, can't be helped. What was it he wrote?' He stopped and closed his eyes. '"It has pleased God that all should be thoroughly and duly purged and cleansed." Likes a florid phrase. Anyway, long and short of it is the true blood of Henry VII has been established and the Prince of Wales is now heir to the throne. Understand?'

'Yes, Your Majesty. The Infanta can now travel to England

to marry Prince Arthur.'

'Exactly right. Interesting your daughter and mine getting married at almost the same time,' Ferdinand said, slapping him on the back.

'My congratulations, Your Majesty. But, begging your pardon, what has this got to do with me?'

'I want you to go with her. I don't completely trust the English. They're barbarians. I want you to help Rodrigo. He needs a man who has my complete trust.' He paused. 'You're not hiding your disappointment very well, Isaac, but that's why I trust you. Your true feelings and thoughts are always apparent.'

'Your Majesty,' was all Isaac could muster.

'It will be at least six months before we're ready for her to set sail, maybe a year. Need a lot of time to prepare for a wedding. But I don't have to tell you that do I?'

His laughter sounded forced.

'It will give you time to learn some English. And,' he paused for a long moment, 'I will allow you to make short visits to Seville during that time. In disguise of course. And –'

Here it comes thought Isaac, the dangled reward.

'– if all goes well in England after a year, perhaps two, three at the very most, we can think about your return to Seville.'

'Your Majesty,' Isaac said bowing deeply. What other choice did he have? He could just run Ferdinand through with his rapier and be done with the whole thing. But perhaps not the wisest idea on Isabel's wedding day.

'Give my regards to the happy couple. They're a well-matched pair. You're a lucky man Isaac,' Ferdinand called over his shoulder as he walked away.

Isaac sat in the front pew of the small chapel that was situated in a quiet part of the Alhambra. The king used it for prayer and confession. The Infanta had made all the arrangements for Alejandro and Isabel's wedding. When Isaac had asked Isabel why the princess was being so helpful she was vague. He would ask her again, something about it troubled him.

Maria would have wanted the wedding to be in the cathedral in Seville. He felt her absence today, more than at any other time. She should have been here to fuss over and squabble with Isabel. But she was here in their hearts, as were all the family. Catalina, Rodrigo, and the children had arrived from Seville the previous week. Gabriel was sitting next to Isaac. He couldn't believe that he was almost as tall as him now. His son had greeted him with an awkward handshake and a bow. Isaac wanted to hug him until he couldn't breathe but had refrained. He clearly thought of himself as a young man now, to be respected. Juana and Martîn didn't seem to have changed at all. Irrepressible, chafing at Catalina's care. She was thriving and enlivened by looking after the youngsters. It was not how Isaac felt. They tired him out after only an hour in their company. But the children had spent most of their time with Isabel, exploring the Alhambra. Juana was delighted by the palace, and he'd heard her call it 'magical' over and over.

Talavera was conducting the wedding ceremony in a

reassuring tone. Isaac couldn't concentrate on the words; he was swept away by emotion. Isabel's long brunette hair was braided into an intricate design, and she wore a simple yet elegant powder blue dress. Her warm brown eyes sparkled with happiness. Alejandro stole admiring glances at her throughout the ceremony. Isaac could still remember what that kind of love felt like. As Talavera finished the ceremony, Alejandro kissed Isabel briefly on the lips. It was tender, filled with hope and promise. They all clapped and cheered.

The reception was held in the gardens of the Alhambra. Aisha and Ali joined them, their religious beliefs prohibited them from being in the chapel. Aisha had recovered her health. They looked happy together, and Isaac tried to be happy for them. They had still not made a final decision whether to convert or flee once the mourning period was over and they were married. Ali had confided in him that he wouldn't convert. He didn't want to live the life that Isaac had, keeping his true faith a secret. Isaac told Ali that he understood. He would miss them both.

There were tables filled with food and drink, and music. The same trio of *Mudéjar* musicians who had played at Abdul Rahman and Aisha's open house were there. Isabel insisted on this, and the Infanta had been delighted by this breaking of convention. He thought it was mainly because it would upset her parents, a way of showing her power.

Isabel linked arms with him and led him away into a quieter corner of the garden. Her face was alive with excitement, but there was something worrying her. 'Papa,' she said in a serious tone. 'I need to tell you something. And you mustn't be worried or angry.'

He remained silent. He knew his daughter well enough to allow her free rein when she was in this determined mood.

'You asked me why the Infanta was so eager to arrange everything?'

'I did.'

'Well ... promise you won't be angry?'

He inclined his head noncommittally.

'She wants me to be her personal apothecary. And when she travels to England to be wed, she wants me to go with her. And the king has offered Alejandro a diplomatic position in London.' She was becoming breathless but carried on at pace. 'I know this will upset you and I know it means I can't look after the children anymore. But Catalina and Rodrigo will take care of them. And Gabriel is such a fine young man he doesn't need me anymore. Besides, perhaps he will come to England too. I feel awful leaving you here all alone.' She looked close to tears.

He could not allow that, not on her wedding day. That might be the one thing Maria would not forgive him for. He held both her hands and smiled. 'Let me tell you about a conversation I had with the king this morning ...'

EPILOGUE

Seventeen months earlier ...

The Convent of St. Thomas Aquinas

Ávila, Spain

Daybreak, September 16th, 1498

ISAAC GLANCED UP AT THE SOUND coming from outside Torquemada's bedchamber. The bells were announcing the Lauds service. The convent would soon be stirring. He'd wasted too much time. Again.

He turned back and unsheathed his dagger.

Torquemada's eyes were wide open, and he was grinning. 'I've been expecting you. Why did it take so long?'

Isaac held the dagger out in front of him like a cross.

'I'm not the devil,' Torquemada said and yawned. 'Shall we have a sherry first?'

Isaac thrust the dagger towards his face, struggling to keep his hand steady.

Torquemada didn't flinch. 'Perhaps not.' He paused. 'Best get it over with.' He scratched his chin. 'Would've been good to have shaved.' He shrugged. 'They can do that after I'm dead.' His eyes flickered to the shaking dagger. 'Can I make a confession?'

Isaac lunged and sliced the blade across the bastard's chin. 'Don't toy with me,' he hissed.

Torquemada clutched at the cut and a thin trail of blood oozed through his fingers. 'Forgive me, I know you're serious.' He pulled at a corner of the bedsheet and dabbed at the blood. It was only a superficial cut. 'I'm serious too. Would you listen to my confession? You're the only person I know that might understand what I must confide. And then you may do as you wish.' He closed his eyes, clasped his hands, and muttered a prayer.

The sounds of chanting and nuns calling to one another

filtered through the locked bedchamber door. The sisters would soon work out that something was wrong, probably assuming Torquemada was dead. And, against Isaac's better judgement, he was intrigued. 'Be quick, damn you.'

Torquemada opened his eyes and looked directly at him. 'My family is of *converso* stock.' He smiled. 'I am like you.'

'Liar! You're nothing like me.'

'I swear by Almighty God, may he sentence me to hell for all eternity, if I'm lying.'

Isaac had never paid the vague, whispered rumours that Torquemada's family had originally been Jewish any credence. But he doubted Torquemada would swear a false oath, even under these circumstances. He was too pious, too zealous, too much of a true believer. That he shared Jewish heritage with this demon was too much to bear. It made him even more determined to kill him.

Torquemada said, 'I told you once how much I admired your persistence, your devotion to your faith. That was sincere.' He paused. 'I'm dying anyway. The physician says my time is short. The gout has poisoned every bit of me. Why would I lie?'

Isaac didn't know what to say.

'It's all the same to me, either way is a victory. You would be putting me out of my misery. But, my son – '

Isaac jabbed the dagger at him again. 'I'm not your son,' he snarled.

Torquemada raised his palms in acceptance. 'If you kill me the sin will be all yours. And,' he paused, 'you would give up the chance to spend eternity with Maria.'

'*You* murdered her!'

'I admit I went too far. It was a mistake. I admired her courage at the end. I have prayed to the Lord many times to forgive me. I beg your forgiveness too.' Something in his tone sounded sincere. 'You can kill me, but it won't bring you the satisfaction you desire. Trust me, I know.'

There was movement from outside and a knock at the door. 'Father?'

Isaac jabbed the dagger at Torquemada who put up a hand and called out, 'Sister, I am well. I will ring the bell when I need you.' He waited for her footsteps to recede. 'My mission has always been to save the souls of my flock. Even though you're a heretic you can still avoid hell by recanting.'

'Never,' Isaac said, putting the tip of the dagger to Torquemada's fleshy throat, who lengthened his neck as though welcoming the release. 'You will rot in hell. I do not forgive you, neither will the Lord.' He pushed the dagger a little further and broke the skin. A slow trickle of blood wended its way down Torquemada's jowls. Doubt suddenly assailed him, the same doubt that had stopped him from acting for the past three years. Was avenging Maria's death worth losing the chance to be with her again?

Too much blood. Too many deaths. 'But you're not worth my soul, my place in heaven.' He replaced the dagger in its sheath.

Torquemada swallowed and wiped the blood away with the collar of his nightshirt. 'You won't believe me, but I wish you well, Isaac. We might have done great things together had we been on the same side.'

Isaac looked into Torquemada's eyes and saw a dark vacancy. 'I almost pity you,' he said.

Torquemada's perplexed look was a sort of victory.

I'm coming Maria, I'm coming.

HISTORICAL NOTE

In late medieval Andalusia oppressive policies and attitudes forced many Jews to embrace Christianity. These *conversos* were suspected of continuing to practice Judaism in secret. The religious establishment sought to save the souls of these heretics by persuading them to return to the right path.

The Spanish Inquisition was instituted in 1481 and a royal decree in 1483 expelled the Jews from Spain. Tomás de Torquemada, Queen Isabella's confessor, was appointed, 'Grand Inquisitor of All Spain'. Pope Sixtus agreed to the formation of 'The Holy Office of the Propagation of the Faith' in return for continued Spanish military support to defeat the Ottoman Empire.

The Inquisition used torture to elicit confessions and delivered judgment at public ceremonies known as *autos-da-fe*, 'acts of faith', before they gave their victims over to the secular authorities for punishment. The first *auto-da-fe* was held in 1481, and in total some thirty-thousand men, women, and children, were condemned to death and burnt alive. Their gruesome fate was intended to set an example to others.

After fifteen years as Spain's Grand Inquisitor, Torquemada died at the monastery of St. Thomas Aquinas in Ávila in 1498. His tomb was allegedly ransacked in 1832, his bones stolen and ritually incinerated in the same manner as at an auto-da-fé.[1]

---

1. *Murphy, Cullen (17 January 2012). God's Jury: The Inquisition and the Making of the Modern World. Houghton Mifflin Harcourt. p. 352*

The Spanish Inquisition was not finally abolished until 1834. The Spanish government only formally rescinded the decree expelling the Jews in 1968.

This is a work of fiction. Although the narrative has a historical foundation some dates and events have been conflated or amended to meet the dictates of the story. If the book inspires you to research the period, I found the following texts to be useful starting points:

- Carr, Matthew. Blood & Faith, *The Purging of Muslim Spain 1492 - 1614*, Hurst & Co, 2017. Fletcher, Richard. *Moorish Spain,* Phoenix, 2001

- Green, Toby. *Inquisition: The Reign of Fear*, Pan Books, 2008.

- Karabell, Zachary. *People of the Book*, John Murray, 2007.

- Lowney, Chris. *A Vanished World,* OUP, 2005. 308

- Mount, Toni. *Medical Medicine,* Amberley, 2015. Menocal, Maria Rosa. *Ornament of the World,* Little Brown and Company, 2002

- Rubin, Nancy. *Isabella of Castile,* St Martins, 1991. Ruiz, Teo!lo Z. *Spanish Society 1400-1600,* Routledge, 2001.

- Schama, Simon. *Belonging: The Story of the Jews, 1492 – 1900,* Bodley Head, 2017.

- Thompson, Augustine, O.P. *Dominican Brothers, Conversi, Lay and Cooperator Friars,* New Priory Press, 2017

ACKNOWLEDGMENTS

Thank you to Moises Anselem in Seville for inspiring the *Isaac Alvarez Mysteries*.

Thank you to my Wednesday Evening Critique Group - Sarah Clayton, Gillian Duff, and Katrina Ritters. This book would not have been as good without your insight and support.

Thank you to my son, Adam, who continues to give expert IT advice.

ABOUT THE AUTHOR

Michael Lynes's debut, *Blood Libel*, the first full-length *Isaac Alvarez Mystery*, was first published in 2021. It won a prize at the 2020 Emirates Literature Festival. The second novel in the series, *The Heretic's Daughter*, was first published in 2022. He is from London, but currently lives with his family in the United Arab Emirates.

You can find out more about him and sign up for his newsletter at: www.michaellynes.com